# NO ORDINARY LOVE

SWEETBRIAR COVE: BOOK SIX

MELODY GRACE

MELODY GRACE BOOKS

❀ Created with Vellum

Thank you for reading!
It's always a joy returning to Sweetbriar Cove. After six books, the characters and town feel like old friends, and Eliza Bennett is no exception. Like her namesake in Pride & Prejudice, this smart, headstrong woman is looking for an equal match - and she may just have found it in Cal Prescott. But not without a few complications along the way...

I hope you enjoy reading No Ordinary Love as much as I've enjoyed writing it. So please, enjoy a taste of summer (and lobster), wherever you are.
xo Melody

~

ALSO BY MELODY GRACE:

The Sweetbriar Cove Series:
1. Meant to Be
2. All for You
3. The Only One
4. I'm Yours
5. Holiday Kisses (A Christmas Story)
6. No Ordinary Love
7. Wildest Dreams
8. This Kiss

The Beachwood Bay Series:
1. Untouched
2. Unbroken
3. Untamed Hearts
4. Unafraid
5. Unwrapped
6. Unconditional
7. Unrequited
8. Uninhibited
9. Unstoppable
10. Unexpectedly Yours
11. Unwritten
12. Unmasked
13. Unforgettable

The Oak Harbor Series:
1. Heartbeats
2. Heartbreaker
3. Reckless Hearts

The Dirty Dancing Series

The Promise

Welcome to Sweetbriar Cove: the small town where happily-ever-after is guaranteed.

Book Six
No Ordinary Love

For journalist Eliza Bennett, summers in Sweetbriar Cove were her happiest childhood memories. Now that she's been unceremoniously fired, evicted, and dumped (all in the same week), she hopes the small town will work its magic again and help get her life back on track. She definitely isn't looking for a distraction like the handsome stranger she meets on her way into town... especially when she discovers he might be the man behind her recent misfortunes.

Cal Prescott is in Sweetbriar Cove adjusting to (or escaping from) his new role as head of the family company. He's always prided himself on his cool logic, but reckoning with the outspoken spitfire, Eliza, is making him forget his responsibilities - and why falling in love would be such a bad idea.

The sparks between them are red-hot, and soon, their passion is heating up the summer nights. But can Eliza and Cal find a way through their differences - or will this opposites-attract romance burn out before it even begins?

Find out in the latest swoon-worthy Sweetbriar Cove romance from New York Times bestselling author, Melody Grace!

The Sweetbriar Cove Series:

1. Meant to Be
2. All for You
3. The Only One

# 1

Ever since she was a kid, summers for Eliza Bennett began with the drive out to Sweetbriar Cove.

The moment school was over, they loaded up the car: she and her older sister, Paige, crammed in the back of their dusty family Honda, squeezed between beach toys and books, and a cooler full of homemade tuna-fish sandwiches. Their mom would complain about the traffic, and their dad would commandeer the radio with his old country mixtapes, but as the clogged freeway made way for the sandy two-lane highway, and that first glint of ocean glittered on the horizon, all the stress and arguments faded away.

Summer had arrived.

Even now, at twenty-seven, driving the familiar road alone with the brisk chill of spring still in the air, Eliza could taste it. Melting ice cream, and saltwater taffy; evenings by the firepit, and mornings combing the rock pools for new adventures. She crossed the Sagamore Bridge, the unofficial gateway to Cape Cod, and suddenly felt a well of sadness in her chest so sharp, she had to call Paige.

"Tell me you're nearly here." Her sister sounded harried.

"Another hour away."

Paige groaned. "Mom's driving me crazy. I swear, she's drawn up a list of every single man on the entire Cape, ranked by eligibility. Anyone would think we're in a Jane Austen novel!"

Eliza laughed.

"She's got one for you, too," Paige warned.

"What?"

"I took a peek. How do you feel about Tommy McAllister?"

"Tommy? I used to babysit for him!" Eliza exclaimed. "He would run around with no pants on, mooning everyone on the beach."

"And now he's legal." Paige giggled. "Hey, just be glad you get the toy-boys. I'm practically a spinster. I've got a couple of widowed bachelors on mine."

Eliza sighed. "That woman is impossible. Someone needs to stage an intervention."

"She's just looking out for us." Paige's voice softened. "She's probably just trying to distract herself. It can't be easy, coming back here."

"I know."

Eliza's heart ached again. It was just over a year since their father had passed away; a year of painful firsts that made the loss feel fresh, every time. She'd thrown herself into work and making new friends, moving on as best she could, but this was the first time the whole family was venturing back to the beach house—without him.

"Do you know why she asked us both to be out there?" Eliza asked, focusing on the road.

"You mean besides securing us good marriages?" Paige teased. "No, she hasn't said what the big deal is. She probably wants us both there for moral support. You know she hasn't even packed away his things yet."

"How long can you stay?"

"Just a week." Paige sounded reluctant. "Things are crazy at work right now, we have a big order due." Paige was a designer for a kids' clothing line. "But I figure we can both pop back on weekends if she needs. Will the newspaper give you any more time off?"

"About that . . ." Eliza eyed the backseat in her rearview mirror, currently piled with boxes containing all her worldly possessions. "It turns out, they're giving me all the time I need." She sighed. "They fired me."

"Eliza! What did you do?"

"Nothing!" Eliza protested. "It's this new boss. He laid off half the staff, he's turning the paper into some crappy website." A *revolutionary, forward-facing news vertical,* the memo had said, whatever that meant. "He put us all on probation, to prove we could 'evolve' with the company. And, well . . ." Eliza trailed off with a guilty pause.

"I knew you did something."

Eliza exhaled. "It doesn't matter. I've got plenty of time to help Mom with whatever project she's got going now."

"I'm sorry," Paige said, comforting. "Who knows? Maybe Tommy will sweep you off your feet."

Eliza managed a smile. "I won't hold my breath. Listen, my cellphone's about to cut out. See you soon."

She hung up and took a deep breath, trying to inhale that summertime feeling again. But thanks to a passing truck, all she got was a lungful of exhaust fumes.

This year wasn't going according to plan.

It was all Cal Prescott's fault. Or rather, Calvin Archibald Prescott IV, heir to the Prescott media empire, and her new boss. Not that Eliza had ever met the man. All his new rules had been handed down by memo—dozens of them, addressed to the staff in crisp, impersonal business-talk as he set about dismantling the most prestigious newspaper left in Boston. Probation was bad enough—they'd all been walking on eggshells since news of the takeover hit—but then the not-so-helpful suggestions started arriving too. More fluffy human-interest stories, more celebrity coverage. More advertisements, less investigative journalism. Eliza should have been pleased. Features was her beat, she loved profiling oddball people and writing up local events, but even she chafed at her list of assignments, nothing but ritzy society parties and puff pieces . . . until one of those puff pieces landed her in hot water—and out of a job.

It wasn't fair. How was she supposed to know that the mayor's wife was a Prescott cousin, and the paragraph about her screaming at the kids' nanny wasn't what Cal had in mind for a "behind the scenes" look at her new charity launch?

OK, Eliza had known. And maybe she'd written the story as a way to thumb her nose at the Prescotts. But wasn't journalism supposed to be about the facts—speaking truth to power? It was what her father had always said. He'd been her biggest supporter, from the time she'd decided, aged eight, she was going to be an intrepid reporter, all the way through school newspaper assignments, and those nerve-wracking years just out of college, pitching freelance articles and interviewing all over town. The day the *Boston Herald* had published her first byline, her father had gone out and had it framed. He kept it hanging in his office at the college where he taught, proudly telling anyone who'd listen about his daughter, the journalist.

It was a good thing he wasn't around to see her now.

Eliza swallowed back the pain and focused on the road ahead. She wasn't far now, just another few miles of highway before the turn-off to the house. Already, the light seemed brighter, the midday sun glinting off the ocean through the dense, green trees. Eliza felt her tension ease. Maybe some time on the Cape was what she needed right now. She could regroup, catch up with her friends, and try to figure out what she could do next to get her career back on track.

If Cal Prescott hadn't blacklisted her for good.

The radio switched to an upbeat song, and she was just reaching to turn the volume up and sing away her stress when she saw a car pulled over on the side of the road. The trunk was open, and a man was waving a cellphone in the air, looking frustrated. Eliza was so close to the beach she could almost taste the soft-serve ice cream, but her father had always taught her to help out where she could. *You never know when you'll be the one needing a hand.*

Eliza pulled over. "Having problems?" she called, getting out of the car.

"I've got a flat tire, and I can't get a cell signal." The man turned. He was dressed immaculately in navy pinstripe pants and a crisp white shirt, a jacket slung on the roof of his car. As Eliza came closer, she could see it was an expensive sedan, gleaming and spotless despite the sand on the road.

Rich people problems.

"This is a dead spot," she explained. "There's no signal for a couple more miles. Let me take a look." She bent over and examined the wheel. It was totally deflated, with . . . *Ah.* A rusty nail was embedded near the rim. "Here's your problem," she said, working the nail out of the rubber and holding it up.

She found herself looking straight into the man's eyes. His piercing, midnight-blue eyes.

Eliza blinked. He had a chiseled jaw, and tanned skin, and dark hair that fell in a perfect rumpled wave over his forehead like something out of a fashion shoot. It was movie-star hair,

McDreamy hair, the kind of hair that came from $200 salons that valeted your car and gave you a special scalp massage.

The man took the nail from her and sighed. "Just perfect. Sorry," he added, with a rueful look. "It's been one of those days. Make it one of those months. So, what now?"

"Now?" Eliza arched an eyebrow. "Don't tell me you don't know how to change a flat?"

"Sure I can," the man replied, looking amused. "But it's a little hard without a jack. It looks like my guy forgot to put it back after the detailing."

Make that *really* rich people problems.

"No worries, I've got one," she said reluctantly. "Your spare should be enough to get you to the nearest garage. Save waiting on triple-A all afternoon, at least."

"Thank you." The man's face finally relaxed into a smile that lit up his handsome face and left Eliza breathless.

*Hello.*

She quickly turned on her heel and went to fetch the jack from her trunk—and smooth down her hair. She was wearing jeans and a sweater, picked for comfort on the drive down, but this guy made her feel like she was roaming around in her slouchiest pajamas.

You're doing *him* the favor, she reminded herself.

"And thank you for stopping," the man added, looking grateful when she returned. "I swear, half a dozen cars sped right by. So much for small-town hospitality."

"Don't take it personally," Eliza told him, bending over to fit the jack in place. "It's just the summer people thing."

The man looked confused.

"You know, rich city people buying up houses and stopping by for Fourth of July," Eliza explained, starting to crack the handle. "You surge up the property prices, leave them empty, then come swanning around once a year demanding non-fat almond milk and gluten-free fries."

"Tell me how you really feel, why don't you?" The man grinned, looking amused.

Eliza smiled back. "You're a grown man, I figure you can take it."

He laughed. "You've got me. Well, almost. I haven't bought my place yet, I'm staying with family here, taking a look around. And I had almond milk by accident once, in my coffee. It was sacrilege."

"Amen," Eliza agreed.

"Here, let me." The man suddenly seemed to realize what she was doing. He rolled up his shirtsleeves—revealing tanned, elegant forearms—and took over, expertly jacking the car up and then loosening the wheel nuts with a few turns of the wrench.

Eliza admired the line of his muscles rippling under his shirt. For a preppy summer guy, he was *toned*.

"So, you live around here?" he asked, pausing to wipe his brow.

"No. But my family has been coming here for years," she added quickly. Still, the man gave her a teasing look.

"Hmm. Every summer? Like . . . a summer person?"

She laughed. "It's not like that. My grandpa built our place himself, back in the fifties. He and my grandma retired out here, so we've been coming my whole life."

"An honorary local."

"Pretty much. You should watch out," she added lightly. "You think you'll just stay a week or two, but the place has a way of growing on you."

"It's off to a good start."

The man held her gaze for a long moment, and Eliza's pulse

skipped. She flushed and looked away, but the man didn't seem ruffled at all.

"So, do you have any tips for me, to blend in around here?" he asked, effortlessly moving the spare wheel into place.

"You could lose the suit, for starters."

He glanced up, looking amused.

She flushed. Why did that come out sounding so dirty? "I just meant, people dress pretty casually around here. It's a good place to switch off and leave your stress behind."

"Hence the lack of cellphone signal."

"That's just along this stretch of highway," she reassured him. "It's Cape Cod, not the back of beyond."

"I don't know, maybe a forced detox would be a good thing," he said, with that rueful, tired look again, and out of nowhere, Eliza was struck with the sudden urge to push that stray dark lock off of his forehead . . . and run her fingers through that perfect hair.

*Down, girl.*

This was what happened when she spent her whole life working; she had inappropriate thoughts about the first vaguely attractive man to cross her path. OK, *very* attractive. But still, that was no excuse. He wasn't her type at all, with that knowing smirk, and clean-shaven jaw, driving a car that was probably worth more than her student loan.

And that was really saying something.

Still, that didn't mean she couldn't be friendly. "You should check out Sweetbriar Cove while you're here," she found herself suggesting. "It's a cute town, just a few miles farther. There's a great pub, and the bakery is world-class. The sticky buns aren't to be missed."

"Really?" He gave her that wicked smirk. "What man could resist an invitation like that?"

Eliza blinked. "I didn't mean . . ." she said, flushing again, but luckily, she was saved by the buzz of his cellphone.

He snatched it up and pressed it to his ear. "Philip, can you hear me? How about now?" He moved away, trying to get a clear connection.

Eliza finished up with the wheel and went to stow his tools in the trunk of his car, still feeling flustered. She looked around for a rag to wipe her dirty hands on, but of course, the car was empty and spotless, save a leather overnight bag on the backseat, beside a stack of papers.

Eliza couldn't help but lean in to sneak a look, curious about the man who could rattle her so effortlessly—and look good while doing so.

*Expansion proposal . . . Revenue projections . . . Prescott Foundation Agenda . . .*

Wait, *Prescott*?

Eliza reached in the open window and moved his briefcase aside to get a clearer look at the papers below.

The envelopes were all addressed to Calvin Prescott IV.

She paused in disbelief. Seriously?

The handsome stranger was her boss.

Correction: her *ex*-boss. The reason she'd been fired from her dream job, perp-walked out of the building, and was currently broke, homeless, and unemployed.

*Bastard!*

Eliza quickly stepped away from the car, checking Cal hadn't noticed her snooping. He was still pacing by the roadside, bellowing into his phone to be heard.

Typical. She should have known it the minute she clocked his fancy suit and expensive watch. Men like him thought they could just bulldoze their way through life, never mind who got crushed underfoot. And to think she'd actually helped him!

Well, maybe it was time karma paid a little visit.

Eliza glanced around again, and then paused by the wheel. She reached down and felt her way to the tire valve, then quickly unscrewed the cap and slipped it in her pocket. She could hear the faint hiss of air escaping as she stepped away. It would take a little while to deflate completely, so he had a chance of making it to the next town. Or maybe not, and he'd have a chance to break in those leather shoes of his.

Either way, it would give him plenty of time to take stock of his life.

"I'm heading out," she called over to Cal.

He paused and lowered his phone. "Oh. Well, thanks . . . ?" He waited for her to fill in her name, but Eliza just gave him an innocent smile and got back behind the wheel of her car.

"Welcome to the Cape," she called. "I hope you have an . . . interesting trip!"

# 2

By the time Eliza turned down the bumpy dirt road that led to the beach house, her triumph had faded . . . and an annoying streak of guilt was flickering in its place. Cal Prescott would be fine, she reassured herself. He had probably already called in a private helicopter to airlift him to town, or whatever else it was that billionaire media scions did when they got into a jam.

She put him out of her mind as the house came into view, framed by sand dunes and an overgrown scattering of seagrass. The simple frame was modest compared to some of the mansions that had sprung up along the shore, but Eliza loved every inch of it, from the faded blue shingles to the old swing in the corner of the front porch. She pulled up in front and took a deep breath of the salty ocean air.

It felt like coming home again.

"Lizzie?"

"Hi, Mom." Eliza wasn't even up the front steps before her mom appeared on the porch and smothered her with a hug.

"Look at you!" Linda beamed, giving her a once-over. Her

smile slipped. "Did you cut your hair again, honey? I thought we agreed, you look so much nicer with it pulled back off your face. And did you get that article I sent about the new low-carb diet? Your metabolism isn't what it used to be—"

"It's great to see you too, Mom." Eliza hauled her bag past her into the house. "Paige?"

"In here!"

Eliza followed her voice to the kitchen. Her sister had her blonde hair pulled back in a Mom-approved braid, and she was pouring iced tea. "Five seconds," Eliza hissed. "Five seconds before she started criticizing me. That has to be a record."

Paige winced. "Remember, empathy. Did you tell her about the newspaper yet?"

"What about the newspaper?" Their mom bustled in.

"Nothing, Mom," Eliza said loudly, and gave her sister a warning look. "The place looks great," she changed the subject quickly. "Did you redecorate?"

"Just a little sprucing," Linda replied. She opened the doors out onto the back porch. "It needs so many repairs, your father always said . . . Well, we'll talk about that later."

Eliza placed a hand on her mother's shoulder and gave a gentle squeeze. Paige was right, however sad she was to have all these reminders of their dad around, this must be a hundred times worse for Mom.

Linda turned back with a brisk smile. "You should get settled in, and then maybe do a grocery run to town? There's a list on the fridge."

"Sure, Mom."

"And then you can tell me all about what's been happening at the newspaper."

Eliza backed away. "I'll get my things. But Paige has plenty of news, don't you?"

Paige rapidly shook her head, but it was too late. Linda turned, brightening. "Tell me you gave Doug another chance! I knew you two could work it out."

"No, Mom –" Paige was trying to protest.

Eliza mouthed "sorry" and ducked out, leaving Paige to face the inquisition alone. She brought in the rest of her things and headed for the stairs, but she stopped in the hallway by the door to her father's old office. The door was open, and the room was untouched: mismatched books lining the shelves, and light streaming onto the sun-bleached rug. For a moment, she could almost believe he'd stroll out from by the corner with some old book in his hand and take a seat at his desk, still piled with old newspapers and files.

"Eliza!" Her mom's voice called out again. "Don't leave it too late, or they'll be out of the good bread again. I thought we could have the McAllisters over," she added, appearing in the hall. "Did you know their son, Tommy is back from college? Strapping, too."

Eliza opened her mouth to protest, then closed it again. *Empathy*.

"I'm on my way," she said instead, and gently closed the office door.

She could survive her mother for a little while. At least she could be happy that wherever Cal Prescott was, he was having a worse day than her.

By the time Cal had hiked two miles along the highway to call his buddy Declan to come pick him up, he was hot, sweaty, and had more blisters than he cared to count. So much for small-town hospitality: that woman had been more like a siren —tempting him onto the rocks and leaving him for dead. Well, leaving him for dehydrated, at least. This place should come with a warning. He'd been so distracted by her teasing gaze and lush red lips, he hadn't noticed her sabotaging his tire and leaving him in the dust. It almost made him want to turn around and head straight back to Boston . . .

Where his uncle was waiting, with an army of lawyers and a long list of Cal's responsibilities as head of the Prescott Group.

Maybe not.

He heard Declan coming a moment before a shiny red pickup truck came into view, blasting The White Stripes with the windows down.

"What happened to you?" Declan asked, snorting with laughter.

"Don't ask." Cal shook his head and climbed in. "And since when do you drive a truck?"

"I need the extra space now that I'm hauling supplies for the restaurant all day," Declan answered cheerfully in his Australian drawl. He put the truck in gear and pulled back onto the highway.

"And the beard?"

"It's this country air," Declan grinned. "I'm a new man, mate. And the country women aren't too bad, either," he added with a wink.

Cal chuckled. Declan was a virtuoso chef, but Cal was more used to seeing him prop up the hottest bars in the city than out in nature. They'd met when Declan catered a big event for the Prescotts—and wound up drinking Cal under the table. "Just as long as you haven't lost your edge," Cal said. "How is the restaurant doing?"

"Business is booming. Best investment you ever made."

"Good to hear." Cal nodded approvingly. Most restaurants failed in the first three years, so backing Declan had been a calculated risk, but already reviews were buzzing and there was talk of awards for his food. “Ready to open the next one?”

“Easy there,” Declan laughed. “You’re the businessman, I just want to cook.”

“Sure.” Cal snorted. “Cook, and make the front cover of every culinary magazine around.”

“Can you blame me?” Declan shot back. “Who am I to deprive the world of this face?”

Cal shook his head. Clearly, Declan had found his groove on the Cape . . . and not drawn the wrath of any local temptresses. Cal’s mind went back to that mysterious woman. She clearly had no idea who he was, which was refreshing in itself. Thanks to the gossip columns and a few too many “most eligible bachelor” features, it felt like every woman he met already knew all his vital stats, like a baseball trading card. *Calvin Prescott IV, 31, heir apparent to the Prescott media empire.* His uncle had taught him to wear the family name like a badge of honor, but these days, it was feeling more like a dark cloud. One he was hoping to get out from under with this last-minute trip to the Cape.

“So, what’s your plan out here?” Declan asked, after Cal gave him directions and they turned off the main highway.

“I don’t really have one,” Cal admitted. “Relax, unwind a little.”

Declan snorted. “No, really, mate.”

Cal glanced over. “Am I that much of a workaholic that I can’t take a break?”

“No comment.” Declan grinned. “But if you mean it, you’ve come to the right place. A few beers, some time on the water . . . and of course, the best cuisine in the tristate area, courtesy of yours truly.”

His arrogance would be irritating if Cal didn’t know he could back it up. He glanced out of the window. They were heading through a leafy hollow, with a sign reading *Welcome to Sweetbriar Cove.*

"Sweetbriar . . ." Cal recognized the name. "Someone mentioned this place earlier."

"Cute little town," Declan said. "Even if they do lay on the town spirit pretty thick. I swear, these guys celebrate the mailman coming with a parade."

Cal chuckled. It looked picture-perfect, that was for sure: cute stores arranged around the neat green of a town square, with a clear view all the way down to the harbor. There were banners and ticker-tape advertising a $50^{th}$ Annual Lobsterfest, and he wondered for a moment if he'd see his mystery brunette strolling by.

If he did, he would give her a piece of his mind.

"So, where's this place you're staying?" Declan asked, turning along a narrow country lane. "I would have figured you for a fancy hotel."

"My godmother has a place here," Cal replied. "She's traveling, so she suggested I take some time to get away."

Suggested, or rather, gave him his marching orders. Marion had been his mother's oldest friend, and ever since his parents passed away, she'd taken it on herself to look out for him. *Make sure the Prescotts don't shove that stick too far up your ass,* as she put it—irreverent and brash as always.

"Should be just ahead here . . ." Declan slowed the truck. Suddenly, he hooted with laughter.

"What's so funny?" Cal asked, but then the cottage came into view, and he didn't have to wonder anymore.

It was pink.

Not just a pale, blush pink, but a bright shade of raspberry that stood out like a neon beacon against the leafy yard. And it wasn't just the lurid shingles; there were pink roses spilling over the pink picket fence, pink seashells crushed into a winding path to the front door, and even a row of plastic flamingos welcoming him on the porch. It was Disney-meets-Candy Land. On acid. And it was all his for the month.

"Home sweet home," Declan sniggered. "Good luck bringing any girls back here."

"Believe it or not, that's not at the top of my priority list," Cal said wryly, but even so, he could just imagine the look on the siren's face if she saw this place. She would probably laugh her head off—and then demand a tour.

He got out and grabbed his bags from the back. "Think my car will be OK with the tow people?"

Declan made a vague gesture. "They take their time, but you'll be fine. Call them tomorrow. And stop by for a beer, first one's on me!"

He drove away, stereo blasting, and Cal turned to face the Pink Palace alone. He hunted down the key beneath a seashell on the porch—just the way Marion had left it—and let himself in, bracing for another explosion of pink. To his relief, the palette inside was a little more varied. A yellow sitting room opened up into a bright blue kitchen, and a green bedroom in front, complete with a ceiling-high ocean mural. His phone rang just as he was stepping onto the back porch, and he answered to hear his godmother's mischievous voice.

"So, how are you settling in?"

Cal chuckled. "A little warning would have been nice."

"And rob you of your first impression? I wouldn't be so cruel."

He took a deep breath of salty sea air and admired the view of the ocean. Pink aside, the cottage was well-located and full of creature comforts. And, most important of all, a long way from home.

"Thanks again for letting me stay," he told her, his voice turning sincere. "Let me know when you need to kick me out."

"It's yours for as long as you need," Marion insisted. "I'm just glad you're finally taking a break. I hate to see you working non-stop like this."

"You don't need to worry, I'm fine," Cal protested.

"Really? All the travel, the late nights, and that accident last month . . ."

"It was barely a scrape," Cal said firmly. "I just need a few days to unwind and look over this paperwork, that's all."

"Hmmm." Marion didn't sound convinced. "Well, you have fun. And find out the local gossip for me. Just tell June and Debra I want all the juicy details."

"Will do," Cal promised before hanging up. Immediately, his phone buzzed again—with a flurry of incoming emails, calls, and texts. He'd only spent a couple of hours on the road, but already he knew his voicemail would be full to bursting, with questions and plans, updates from the new acquisitions, and financials that needed approval. His fingers itched to get to work, his brain already ticking over on the endless to-do list he carried in the back of his mind, but he forced himself to take another breath.

The Prescott Group could wait.

He would never admit it, but his godmother was right. Work had always been stressful, but the past few months had passed in a blur of sleepless nights and bad takeout and staring at endless financial forecasts until his head ached. The *Boston Herald* takeover was only the half of it; it seemed like everywhere he looked, there were new fires to put out, and his uncle's stern reminder that these were his decisions now. His name on the letterhead, his signature on every pink slip.

It kept him up at night, every night. Running on empty. And then came the wake-up call, a near miss that showed him just how ragged he was running himself. Another late night in the office, another two a.m. drive home—only this time, the stress and exhaustion had caught up with him, and he'd drifted off to sleep at the wheel. Just a couple of seconds, lights blurring on the freeway, but that heartbeat was enough to send the car slipping into the next lane, straight into the path of a speeding truck. Cal had jolted back to life to find a horn blaring, as he wrenched the wheel for dear life and held on tight until danger had passed and he could safely pull over on the shoulder, his breath coming in wild, desperate gulps.

It had been close. Too close.

So, even though there was still a mountain of work waiting for him, and his uncle calling every day, he'd let Marion talk him into this time away. Just a couple of weeks, that was all he needed, then he could return refreshed and ready to lead.

Cal took another lungful of the cool, salty air and felt his tension ease, just a little. From the hustle of city life, to the calm, wide-open shoreline, it looked like he'd found the perfect vacation spot. No stress, no conflict . . . His blood pressure would finally have a chance to get back to normal.

After all, what kind of drama could he find in a town named Sweetbriar Cove?

# 3

It only took the weekend for Eliza to remember why she kept her family visits few and far between. Her mother was in full force, and by Monday, Eliza had her hair restyled, learned all the things that would give her cancer and/or render her barren, *and* fended off Tommy McAllister (who'd grown into a lanky, beer-guzzling guy with very wandering hands).

"You're getting too old to be so picky," her mother sniffed when Eliza explained that random groping hadn't set her heart aflame. "When I was your age, I was already married, with Paige in diapers and you on the way."

"Maybe I'll never get married," Eliza teased. "I'll just live here alone and have scandalous affairs with the deckhands down at the harbor."

Linda looked faint. "Lizzie! Don't even joke about it. Everyone needs someone to love."

"What I need is a part-time job." Eliza skillfully changed the subject. "I saw a notice down at the restaurant, I'll go see if Declan is still looking for a hostess."

"Declan?" Her mom perked up again. "Is he single?"

"Terminally." Eliza laughed.

She changed into a pair of restaurant-friendly black pants and a white blouse, and went to fetch her bicycle from the dusty garage. Her legs burned pumping the pedals up the hill, but by the time she coasted down the other side to town, she was almost feeling like her old self again. Being in Sweetbriar worked like that, every time. As much as she loved the pace of city life, there was something about the grassy lanes and wide-open skies that always spoke to her, filtering out the hum and static of all that time she spent staring at a computer screen.

And the chocolate croissants didn't hurt either.

Eliza detoured via the bakery on Blackberry Lane and found her friend Summer holding court behind the counter, her hair tied back in a flower-print rag and a streak of flour on her cheek. "Eliza!" Summer cried, brightening. "When did you get in?"

"A couple of days ago, but I was tied up with family stuff." Eliza eyed the counter hungrily. "Any croissants left?"

"I just rolled a fresh batch. Come on, I'll put them in the oven."

Eliza followed Summer into the kitchen, inhaling the delicious scent of butter and sugar. She sighed with happiness. "I missed you."

"You missed my pastries," Summer laughed. "Although, I'm branching out into savory recipes now in honor of the Lobsterfest."

"Don't let Aunt June hear you," Eliza warned. "She's gunning for another blue ribbon for her chowder."

Summer winced. "She says there's no hard feelings, but I still don't think she's forgiven me for stealing her trophy at the eggnog contest over Christmas."

"It'll be butter knives at dawn," Eliza teased.

Summer slid a tray of croissants in the oven and poured Eliza a cup of coffee. "So, what's new with you? Working on anything fun for the newspaper?"

It was Eliza's turn to wince, and she quickly filled in Summer with the developments from the Herald . . . and Cal Prescott and his tires. "You didn't!" Summer spluttered on her drink.

"I did," Eliza admitted, still feeling guilty. "I shouldn't have, but you know I act first and think later. I wonder if he found a ride OK . . ."

"It was just the highway, not the middle of nowhere," Summer reassured her. "I'm sure he's fine. I wish I'd seen his face!"

"His handsome, chiseled face," Eliza said without thinking. Summer arched an eyebrow. "What? Oh, no," she said quickly. "I've had my fill of trust-fund playboys, believe me."

"Shame. Well, we'll have to find you someone . . ." Summer looked thoughtful.

"Why?" Eliza replied lightly. "Because being single is a fate worse than death?"

"No," Summer laughed. "Because you deserve someone amazing to worship and adore you."

"Funny, my mom said the same thing. Kind of." Eliza shrugged. "Anyway, that's the last thing on my mind. I'm unemployed, remember?"

"Good point." Summer tugged the tray from the oven and set it down on the stovetop, steam wafting. "I'd offer you something here, but I'm fully staffed. And I don't think you'd go for the early-morning wake up calls."

"How early?" Eliza asked.

"Four a.m."

"Maybe not," she agreed quickly, and they both laughed.

"How does Grayson deal with your schedule?" she asked curiously, thinking of Summer's intense other half.

"Oh, he's fine with it. Some days, he's the one waking me. Of course, that just means we're both in bed by eight like a pair of old folks," Summer grinned.

"Early nights with your hunk of a boyfriend, you have my sympathies," Eliza teased. "Anyway, I better get going. See you at the pub tonight? We can catch up properly."

"As long as it's an early one!" Summer said, slipping a couple of croissants into a paper bag and delivering it with a flourish. "Good luck."

BACK ON THE ROAD, IT WAS ONLY ANOTHER MILE UNTIL ELIZA reached Sage restaurant, nestling in a leafy hollow. She propped her bicycle out front and ventured inside the old carriage house, the bell above the door ringing out with a gentle *ding!* The place was quiet, closed before lunch, with the tables all set and waiting crisp with white linens and polished silverware. She wandered over to the smooth wooden bar and looked around for signs of life.

"How's my favorite journalist?"

Declan's voice made her leap, and she spun around to find him emerging from the kitchen double doors, sleeves rolled up and a chef's cap set at a jaunty angle.

"Hoping she can become your favorite hostess," Eliza said, greeting him with a hug. "Tell me you're still looking for help."

"That depends, what's your experience like?" he asked, with a teasing twinkle in his eye.

"Handling customers, or handling you?" she shot back.

Declan grinned. "Good point, the job's yours."

Eliza let out a sigh of relief. For all her joking, being between jobs made her feel like walking an anxious, uncertain tightrope. This might not be the journalism career of her dreams, but it would help keep her student loan payments under control, and give her breathing room again until she figured out her next move. "Thank you," she said fervently. "I promise, I'm not useless. I waitressed all through college, and I'm guessing this crowd is easier than Boylston on a Friday night."

"You'd be surprised," Declan said with a smirk. "Come on, I'll show you the ropes."

He took Eliza through the menu and reservation book, and then took her into the back to introduce her to the rest of the kitchen and wait staff.

"Thank God," one of the waitresses greeted her, a pretty auburn-haired woman in her mid-twenties. "We've been short-handed all week. *This* one keeps breaking all their hearts." She gave Declan a look, catching her wild curls up in a bun and shoving a pen through it.

"You should be happy," Declan protested. "Fewer ways to split your tips."

The woman snorted, her blue eyes full of mischief. "You try serving a party of ten while some poor girl weeps in the vichyssoise," she said. "I deserve a raise."

"And I need to get the lamb on." Declan beat a hasty retreat to the kitchen, leaving Eliza with the group alone.

"I'm Jenny," the woman said, breaking into a smile. "I think I've seen you around, you're friends with Mackenzie, right?"

"Yes!" Eliza beamed, and introduced herself. "You know Mac?"

"Since high school," Jenny said. "Cape Cod, born and raised. And not to be over-familiar, but please tell me you're happily married. Or celibate. I don't think I can take another of Declan's restaurant hookups blocking the aisle."

"None of the above," Eliza said, laughing. "But don't worry

about Declan, I'm immune to his charms. His pork belly hash, on the other hand . . ."

Jenny grinned. "I like your priorities. Well, just let me know if you need anything," she said, tying on a crisp waitress apron. "The diners can be, ah, demanding, but at least the tips are good."

"Amen to that."

Eliza stationed herself out front by the front desk, and was all set to go by the time the first few guests arrived for lunch service. "Welcome to Sage," she greeted them smoothly. "Let me show you to your table."

As the dining room filled up, it was clear the kind of people who traveled for miles to sample the artfully plated delicacies and fine wines. There were tasteful pearls, designer watches, and more seersucker than Eliza had seen in one spot since the Fourth of July. The ring of elegant silverware filled the room, blending with the tasteful jazz soundtrack and hum of conversation, and Eliza tried to keep the amusement from her smile as she deftly fielded questions about wine vintages and local farm provenance from slim, brittle blondes who barely nudged their salads. By the time the first seating was over, she was worn out, and paused a moment by the stand to ease an aching foot out of her high-heeled pumps.

"How's dinner looking?" Declan ducked out to check the reservation book.

"Standby seating, only," Eliza replied. "Things must really be going well around here."

"Can't complain," Declan replied easily. "The *Herald* review really kicked things off over here. I'm guessing I have you to thank for that."

"I may have mentioned those short ribs around the office," Eliza laughed. "A few dozen times."

"Just wait until you taste my tenderloin." Declan kissed his fingertips.

"Is that on or off the menu?" Eliza arched an eyebrow, and he laughed.

"Darlin', that's entirely up to you."

"Am I interrupting?"

They both turned, and Eliza's laughter caught on her lips.

It was him—Cal Prescott. He'd traded his suit for a pair of dark-wash jeans and a rumpled button-down, but he was standing right there in front of her, as handsome as she remembered.

Looking at Eliza with clear annoyance in his eyes.

She gulped.

"Cal, mate. Just giving my new hostess a spin." Declan made the introductions. "Eliza, this is a buddy of mine, Cal."

"We've met," he said, in a clipped voice. "It was . . . memorable."

Eliza forced a smile. "Oh look, customers! I'll go see to them." She dashed away before anyone could say a word and busied herself at the door. It turned out to be a tourist who only wanted to use the restroom, but she gave her a guided tour and sat her down with a glass of ice water, hoping that Cal would be on his way.

She was wrong.

"So, you're a waitress," he said, lounging by the bar when she returned.

"No, I'm a person who works as a hostess," Eliza corrected him, feeling her hackles rise. "And I'm sorry, but you've missed lunch."

"No problem. I'll have a glass of wine. Cabernet. The 2012 vintage, if you have it."

He was watching her with that half-smirk on his face, probably expecting her to say something rude, so Eliza took a deep breath. “Coming right up!” she said brightly, and she slipped behind the bar to find him a bottle.

“I finished my journey just fine, in case you were wondering,” Cal continued, still lounging there looking impossibly handsome. “Should I invoice you for the tow truck now, or later?”

Eliza glanced up sharply. “You mean, the tow truck you would have needed even if I’d never stopped to help?”

“Is that what you call it, *help*,” he echoed, still smirking, and for some reason, it made Eliza’s blood start to boil.

“Rutherford, 2012,” she said, setting the glass down in front of him. “Shall I open a tab?”

“Sure,” he said, sliding a black AmEx across the bar. “And you can leave the bottle,” Cal added casually. Eliza glanced at the wine list, and nearly choked when she saw that it cost a week’s rent.

“Sure. It’s all yours,” she managed to say, before Declan came barreling out of the kitchen again, this time holding a fork out.

“Taste,” he ordered her, before feeding her a bite of something meaty, with a citrus tang.

“That’s delicious,” she agreed, and he beamed with pride.

“Not too much lemon?”

“You know it’s perfect,” she said, and he laughed.

“You’re right about that!” He charged back through the doors. When Eliza turned to Cal, that disapproving stare was back.

“So. You know Declan,” he said, making it sound like an accusation.

Eliza gave him another breezy smile. “Yup. We go way back. Isn’t he a sweetheart?”

“That’s one way of putting it.” Cal’s scowl darkened, and she couldn’t resist adding,

"He's so talented. In the kitchen, I mean. There's always a line out the door."

"Sure, if you like that kind of thing," Cal said. "He gets around though. To different restaurants," he added, meeting Eliza's gaze.

She arched an eyebrow. "But he's worth it, don't you think? When a chef is so skilled, it doesn't really matter who else he cooks for."

Cal looked stormy enough to shut the bar down, so Eliza figured her work was done. "I better get back to work," she said sweetly. "Let me know if I can get you anything else."

She waltzed away to straighten up the silverware. Childish? Sure. But Cal had insulted her and implied she was sleeping with Declan while barely pausing for air. Besides, she and Declan were just friends. Despite the harmless flirting, they both knew she had no interest in joining the long, long list of his conquests.

Not that it was any of Cal Prescott's business.

~

CAL'S NEW RELAXED, TAKE-IT-EASY MOOD HAD LASTED LONG enough for him to walk through the doors at the restaurant . . . and find his siren flirting with Declan.

She wasn't his, of course. He didn't know why he thought of her that way. Or even why he thought of her at all. But however he'd pictured running into her again, it wasn't laughing over something Declan had said, with that smart mouth beaming in the kind of smile a man would kill to have inspired.

He should have known she was off limits. The wanton destruction of his property had been his first clue. Still, she didn't seem the type to buy his buddy's lothario routine. She seemed smarter, more discerning than that—

Cal caught himself and gave a rueful laugh. He didn't know what type of woman she was—besides a devious, hot-tempered one. He didn't know anything about her at all. And if his goal was a calm, relaxed mind, he was guessing it should stay that way.

He detoured via the harbor on his way back and took a stroll down to the water, trying to take his time. Three days in, and his brain was already restless, itching to get back to work, and it took everything he had to keep his phone set to silent, ignoring his calls. They could wait.

Except Arthur Prescott. His uncle's name flashed up on the caller display. Cal braced himself and answered.

"Would you like to tell me what you're playing at?"

Cal winced. His uncle was scrupulously polite—the kind of man who valued tradition and manners above all else—so for him to dispense with the pleasantries and cut straight to it, things must have really been bad.

"Taking a vacation," he answered lightly, taking a seat on the bench that overlooked the cove. "You know what they are? A brief spell away from work, often someplace warm."

"Don't be glib, boy," Arthur replied.

Cal took a breath. Somehow, his uncle always made him feel like he was fifteen years old again, in trouble for sneaking a beer from the cellar. "I can take a few days without the company crumbling to the ground," he pointed out, trying to keep his voice even. "The rest of the team is still there, and they know where to find me if something comes up."

"Something always comes up, that's part of being CEO," Arthur replied. "You're there to set an example, show some leadership. If they see the captain has bailed, what's the point of them keeping the damn ship afloat?"

"I haven't bailed." Cal rubbed his forehead. Suddenly, he had a headache coming on. "I'm barely seventy miles away."

"Distance doesn't matter. Now, did you look at those forecasts I sent you? I don't like the numbers coming out of Wichita. We should close the whole branch and be done with it."

"Wait, not so fast." Cal put the call on speaker and scrolled to his emails to find the data his uncle was talking about, earnings from a paper company they'd acquired last year. "It's not that bad. We're breaking even there."

"Which means we're not making any profit."

"Give it some time," Cal urged him. "The company is the main employer in town. If we shut it down, that will devastate them."

"You always did think about people first." Arthur made a sighing sound. "Of course, what do I know? I'm only here to advise you. The decision is really up to you."

"Then I say we don't go cutting any jobs just yet," Cal said, more firmly. "I'll keep an eye on the numbers, and we'll reassess next quarter."

"Very well." His uncle paused. "I know that this is a big responsibility, taking the reins," he said suddenly, "but it's what we've been preparing for. I know your parents would be proud, seeing you continue their legacy."

Cal was shocked. Arthur never mentioned them. Not even—

Of course. The anniversary of his parents' death. It was coming up, next month. Ten years since the car accident that took them from him—and made him the sole heir to the Prescott fortune. Cal usually tried to be far away when the day rolled around, preferably drunk, in some exotic location and in the company of a beautiful woman. But this year, it had crept up on him.

He cleared the lump that was suddenly in his throat. "Thanks," he said quietly. "Look, I should get going."

"Of course." Arthur cleared his throat too, clearly uncomfortable. "Just remember, you have a lot of people depending on you."

As if he could ever forget.

Cal hung up and gazed out at the horizon, the blue curve of the bay dotted with sailboats bobbing on the afternoon tide. He wondered what it would feel like to be on one of those boats, with nowhere to be, nobody depending on him. Freedom. For a moment, he felt a wistful pang so sharp he could taste it, but he shook it off and turned away.

It was crazy to feel jealous of some unknown person on the waves; after all, he could rent a boat like that anytime he liked. Hell, he could buy one, and set sail for the Caribbean if he wanted, spend the rest of his life on a beach somewhere drinking rum and playing cards. Except he had people counting on him. His family, the board, thousands of employees at dozens of businesses all over the country, each of them with families and bills to pay and lives that would be thrown into turmoil if he didn't take his responsibilities seriously and keep the Prescott Group thriving and profitable.

He had a duty, to protect the family legacy, just the way he'd been raised.

And boy, he needed a drink.

# 4

Eliza and Paige walked into town that night the way they had ever since they were teenagers: along the beach, up past the dirt track, and cutting through the back of old Jerry Granger's yard, bramble hedges and all.

"Ouch!" Eliza yelped, as a branch gripped her sleeve. She fought to get free, her flashlight swooping wildly.

"We're too old for this!" Paige protested. "Why didn't we just drive instead?"

"Because it's tradition!" Eliza yanked loose and continued along the worn path. "You and me, sneaking out after curfew to buy cider with fake IDs."

"You know those things never fooled anyone?" Paige laughed. "Mitch knew exactly who we were."

"But we got served, didn't we?" Eliza navigated the stream, her flashlight beam cutting through the dark. "Come on, where's your sense of adventure—" Her foot slipped on a rock, and she stepped down—into cold, rushing water. Splash!

Paige hooted. "Still feeling adventurous now?" she teased,

helping Eliza step back up onto dry land. Eliza shook out her wet foot and winced.

"OK, you win. Next time, we drive."

It wasn't far to the town square, where the old pub sat on the corner, lit up and spilling warmth and laughter into the chilly spring night. Eliza pushed through the doors and made a beeline for the bar, where Riley was pouring drinks, and his girlfriend Brooke was perched with an explosion of wedding magazines spread around her.

"Are you . . . dripping?" Riley asked, peering over the bar.

"Don't ask!" Eliza groaned. "We took a wrong turn."

Brooke jumped down. "I have some spare clothes stashed upstairs," she offered. "Want to change and dry off?"

"No, I'm fine. This half of me is dry." Eliza grinned. "And this half of me just needs some French fries." She batted her eyelashes at Riley. "Extra large, with a couple of burgers on the side."

"Coming right up."

Brooke plucked down a bottle of wine and three glasses as Paige joined them. "It's so great to finally meet you." Brooke greeted Eliza's sister with a hug. She dropped her voice and gave a wink. "I'm a big fan of your work."

"What?" Paige frowned.

"The lingerie," Brooke explained. "Aphrodite Designs?"

Paige flushed bright red. "You told her?" She elbowed Eliza in the ribs. "I said that was a secret."

"I'm sorry," Eliza protested. "And also, oww."

As well as designing kids clothing for a company up in Boston, her sister also had a line of gorgeous, hand-made lingerie that she sold in a few high-end boutiques—anonymously, of course. Eliza didn't understand why it was such a big secret, but Paige insisted that nobody could know.

"Eliza was only bragging about you," Brooke told Paige,

reassuring. "Your designs are so beautiful. Do you do trousseaus, or any bridal lines? I could add your portfolio to my resource list, maybe help set up some trunk shows."

Paige was looking uncomfortable, so Eliza jumped in. "How are the weddings going? Any famous bookings at the hotel?"

"I'd tell you, but then I'd have to kill you," Brooke replied, deadpan. Then she grinned. "No stars this month, just some very demanding French brides. They want everything imported, I don't know why they didn't just stay in Paris!"

Eliza laughed. "Good luck with that."

They took their drinks—and a heaping basket of fries—and settled in at a table by the fire. Soon, Summer arrived, along with their other friend, a visibly-pregnant Poppy. "Look at you," Eliza exclaimed, carefully embracing her. "You get bigger every time I see you."

"When are you due?" Paige asked.

"Not for another twelve weeks!" Poppy grabbed a handful of fries. "I swear, I feel like a whale already. Plus, she's kicking now, every night like clockwork."

Eliza gasped excitedly. "It's a girl?"

"I think so," Poppy replied, beaming. "But Cooper's painting the nursery yellow, just in case. He wants to be prepared for everything. Which is why there are five hundred parenting books on the nightstand, and I can't hold a conversation about anything except infant nutrition." She sighed and reached for some more fries. "Don't tell him I'm eating these, he's got me drinking all kinds of gross health smoothies."

"Aww, that's sweet," Summer said, nudging her. "He's excited."

"He's terrified," Poppy said cheerfully. "Whereas I'm still in denial. It'll be easy, right? Just like getting a new kitten."

They exchanged looks. "Sure!" Brooke exclaimed brightly.

"Piece of cake," Summer agreed.

Eliza sat back and let the chatter of news and gossip flow around her. Her friendships in Sweetbriar Cove had been the best part of a painful year, and it was comforting to be with everyone again. They talked about Poppy's new book, and Mackenzie's big art show in New York, and all the gossip Eliza had missed since the holidays.

". . . Rumor has it, Bert's been seeing a nice woman down in Truro. And they're closing the *Cape Cod Caller*," Poppy added.

"No!" Eliza exclaimed. "The newspaper was always my favorite weekend read." Not so much a paper as a quirky local gossip sheet, the *Caller* was the first place to find local news and eclectic guest-written columns. "We're only up to part five of Wilber's ten-part guide on how to prune your roses for fall."

"He upped and moved to Florida," Poppy said. "I think he was the only one keeping that place afloat."

"Shame." Eliza sighed. "Where am I going to find what happens after the cuttings now?"

The pub door opened, letting in a blast of chilly night air. She glanced over and froze, a French fry halfway to her lips.

Paige followed her gaze. "Friend of yours?" she asked.

"Not exactly."

It was Cal Prescott, his hair rumpled, sauntering to the bar. He stripped off his navy peacoat and looked around the room, and Eliza glanced away, hoping he wouldn't notice her. Still, she couldn't resist sneaking another glance.

He was staring straight at her. Cal's lips curved in a smile.

*"Hello."*

A voice behind her made Eliza turn. The rest of her group were all checking him out. "Guys," she hissed. "Don't be so obvious."

"Why not?" Poppy replied with a smirk. "We're all respectable married women. Well, as good as."

"Except you two." Brooke nudged Paige. "What do you think?"

Paige flushed and shook her head quickly. As long as Eliza could remember, her sister had been painfully shy about guys.

"He's definitely not your type," Eliza told her.

"And how would you—" Summer stopped, her eyes widening. "Is he . . . ?"

"I said, *shh,*" Eliza shushed her again. "And yes. That's Cal."

"Wait, I'm lost," Brooke piped up. "Who's Cal?"

"Eliza's new nemesis," Summer answered.

"I'll let you tell my shameful story." Eliza left them to gossip and made her way to the bar. She needed another drink, and it had nothing to do with the fact that Cal was leaning there, talking up a storm with Riley.

". . . down to Aruba, last spring," he was saying. "What kind of vessel do you have?"

"Just a sailboat," Riley replied. "Fifty foot."

"Nice." Cal nodded. "Those things are classic."

Of course he sailed. He probably came out of the womb in deck shoes—with a lacrosse stick in the other hand.

"Did you say something?" Cal looked over to her.

"Nope." Eliza ignored him. "Another bottle of wine," she smiled at Riley. "When you get the chance."

"You girls are getting into it, huh?" He found her one from the shelf and reached for the corkscrew. "I'm glad you're back in town," he said, his voice dropping. "There's actually something I wanted to talk to you about, if you have time this week."

"Mysterious," Eliza replied, intrigued. "Any hints?"

"You'll see," Riley winked.

"OK, just give me a call." Eliza paused and glanced back over to the fireplace, where the rest of the girls were still chatting up a storm. "And would I be right in thinking this *something* is meant to be a surprise for Brooke?"

"Yes, ma'am," Riley said, his smile spreading. "So if you could be discreet . . ."

"My lips, sealed." Eliza mimed locking her mouth shut and throwing away the key.

"Thanks for the recommendation," Cal's voice came from beside her, down the bar. He raised his beer to her and smiled. "You're right, this is a great spot."

He was trying to be friendly, but Eliza was already regretting telling him her favorite local haunts. Was he going to pop up all over town now, with that rumpled hair, and those smiling blue eyes, and the way his soft cashmere sweater was pushed up over those tanned, muscular forearms—?

Eliza shook her head.

"Any more tips?" Cal asked. "Declan's food is great, but if there's anyplace else to grab a bite—"

"Nothing up to your standards," Eliza interrupted him. "The fancy restaurants are all out in Provincetown. Perhaps you should look for your place up there," she added sweetly. "You'd probably feel more at home on Millionaire's Row."

Cal didn't expect everyone to like him. He'd had his share of rivalries over the years, and a couple of painful breakups, too. But he couldn't remember the last time anyone had looked at him with the kind of laser-focused disdain he saw in Eliza's dark-eyed gaze.

He watched her walk back to the group of women in the corner, and he whistled under his breath. "Is she always like this?" he joked, turning back to Riley.

But the bartender wasn't laughing. "No," he said, giving Cal a measured look. "Eliza's solid. In fact, I don't think I've heard her say a bad word about anyone. So, whatever you've done, it can't be good."

Riley moved off to serve another customer, his earlier friendliness gone. Cal was thrown. If his siren wasn't slaying men left and right with that sharp tongue of hers, it meant she was just mad at him alone. But for the life of him, Cal couldn't think of a reason. If anything, he should be the one holding a grudge, after the *eventful* way they'd met.

He followed her across the bar. "Can we talk for a moment?" he asked, arriving at Eliza's table.

Her friends stopped their conversation and turned to look at him with naked curiosity. "In private?" he added, flashing them all what he hoped was his most charming smile. "It won't take a moment."

Eliza looked him up and down, but eventually, she shrugged. "Sure."

Cal led her down a back hallway that he found led to a small patio area, empty in the cool night air. He stepped outside, feeling strangely off balance. "Did I do something to offend you?" he asked, deciding to cut right to the chase. "I feel like we got off on the wrong foot, but I have no idea why."

Eliza sighed. "I'm Eliza," she said icily. "Eliza Bennett."

Was that supposed to mean something? "Still drawing a blank here," he said, lost.

"I used to work at the *Herald*," Eliza said, narrowing her eyes. "Until you fired me. Apparently, one of my features hit a little too close to home."

Oh.

Suddenly, it all became clear. "Aunt Mindy," Cal said, with a sigh of recognition. "You were the one who wrote that article."

"Bingo."

Cal exhaled. Family dinners had definitely been . . . *interesting* after that hit piece landed. "I'm sorry," he said apologetically. "If it makes any difference, firing you wasn't my call. I thought the article was funny. Sharp, but funny."

"Maybe you could tell that to my old editor," Eliza replied, her eyes still flashing angrily. "So I can have my job back."

Cal paused. "I don't know about that. We're planning layoffs, and . . ."

"And it would make life a lot more complicated for you," Eliza finished for him. He couldn't disagree. Uncle Arthur would throw a fit, and how could he justify hiring someone back, only to go and fire another dozen people right away? "Typical."

Her comment was murmured, almost under her breath as she turned away, but it needled under Cal's skin.

"You think you you've got me all figured out," Cal said, annoyed.

"What's there to know?" Eliza gave a casual shrug. "Prep school, Ivy League . . . now you're running daddy's company. I've met a dozen guys like you, and I'll probably meet a dozen more. Have fun looking for your summer house."

She turned on her heel.

"Now wait a minute." Cal moved to block her path. "Anyone ever told you that first impressions can be deceiving?"

"And did anyone ever tell you that the simplest explanation is usually right?" Eliza shot back.

"If that's true, then you're a sneaky, destructive vandal," Cal said, his lips quirking in a smile.

"Maybe I am," Eliza replied. "But nothing you could do would surprise me."

"No?" Cal looked at her for a moment. "I'm going to enjoy proving you wrong."

Eliza snorted with laughter, taking a step back towards the door. But before Cal knew what was happening, he caught her hand and pulled her into him.

"What—"

Eliza's question died on his lips, smothered by a kiss.

A hot, wild kiss that sent Cal's heart racing, zero to sixty in a heartbeat.

Her mouth was hot, and sweet, and surprisingly soft for someone who seemed all sharp edges and icy comments. But there was nothing icy about the Eliza in his arms. She swayed against him, warm, and he kissed her deeper, teasing his tongue against her open lips and drinking in the taste of her.

He could have kissed her for hours, he was right there on the edge, but he remembered himself just in time.

He stepped back.

"Surprised yet?" he asked, enjoying the heavy-lidded look of shock on her face. And before she could have the last word, he turned and walked away.

What had he done?

Cal shook his head, retrieving his coat from inside and heading out the front door. It had been a wild impulse, against all his better judgment.

And, more importantly, when could he do it again?

# 5

Eliza couldn't sleep. She tossed and turned all night, replaying the most surprising kiss of her life. It wasn't just the fact Cal had kissed her like that—out of nowhere—that made her feel like her world had tilted dangerously off its axis. No, it was her reaction that shook her to the core.

She'd liked it.

The feel of his lips, urgent against hers; the soft pull of his hands around her waist. And his tongue . . .

Oh, the things that man could do with his tongue.

She flushed, her cheeks hot in the dark. This was Cal Prescott! He'd ended her career with a stroke of the pen—without even bothering to learn her name. She should be vowing to never think of him again, not slipping into a hazy, lustful daydream about the feel of his body, solid and taut against her—

*Enough*!

Eliza leapt out of bed. The sun was barely peeking over the horizon, but she couldn't lie around a moment longer, not with thoughts of Cal so tantalizingly close. She pulled on a sweater and padded silently downstairs so she didn't wake the others. Her father's office was still in a state of cluttered chaos, so she grabbed a couple of garbage bags and some empty boxes, and set about filing, clearing, and trying to sort the last twenty years of his oddball research into some kind of order.

There was a method to the scatterbrained mess, she discovered. Old periodicals may have teetered in perilous stacks, but they were arranged by date and subject. Drawers of hand-scribbled notes divided neatly into boxes, and even the books gathering dust on every spare inch of carpet followed some kind of pattern: biographies by the window, thick history tomes jumbled by the desk, fiction piled within reach of his favorite armchair for an afternoon break.

Halfway through the stacks of old newspapers on the desk, Eliza found a book of clippings. Her old articles from the *Herald*, neatly snipped from the pages and filed away in a special blue scrapbook, everything from the smallest review of a downtown food cart to her bigger, in-depth articles, all pressed into the pages, a father's pride right there to see in black and white.

She sat down on the squeaky old desk chair with a thump.

God, she missed him.

She knew that they'd been lucky, if you could call it that at all. His diagnosis had come too late to help, but early enough to treasure the last months together. Eliza had spent every weekend at home with him, and they'd taken trips, and talked late into the night, but it hadn't been enough.

It would never be enough.

Looking back, Eliza could barely even remember the months after the funeral. She'd muddled through, throwing herself into work to keep from thinking about the raw, bleeding ache in her chest, and coming out to the Cape as often as she could to distract herself with her friends' romantic shenanigans. Now, the pain had faded, a little, to this empty ache she felt while looking around the room, and feeling her father there, like he'd never left at all.

Eliza leafed further. Books, and papers, and random torn recipes. He had a whole stack of the *Cape Caller*, too, with articles marked for reference: gardening tips, coupons, the high tide report. He'd had a top-of-the-line laptop, and all the latest apps on his phone, too, but he'd always preferred the printed word. He'd passed that on to Eliza: the years she'd spent curled up in that corner by the window, reading her thrift-store Nancy Drews while he'd graded assignments, one of his favorite Don McLean records playing on low.

A knock startled her. Eliza looked up and found Paige in the doorway.

"Do you want some tea?" her sister asked gently. "I was just making a pot."

Eliza checked, it was almost ten a.m. She'd been in a dream world almost half the morning. "I'd love some, thanks."

Paige drifted closer, looking around. "Find anything good?"

Eliza held up an old photograph she'd found, showing the four of them on the beach: Paige proudly showing off her sandcastles, while Eliza clutched a book.

"Cute. You should have it framed for Mom." Paige smiled wistfully.

"Good idea," Eliza said. "See any books you want? I thought I'd take that box to donate."

Paige took a look, but didn't delve any deeper. "Unless he had a secret stash of romance novels, I'm guessing it's not my speed."

Eliza smiled. "I don't know, Faulkner can get pretty racy."

She followed her sister out—and saw her bags were packed by the door. "You're leaving already?"

"I'm sorry, we have a big design brief due at work."

"Call in sick, hang out, relax," Eliza urged her, thinking of the next week alone—without a buffer between her and their mom.

"Save you from being alone with Mom, you mean?" Paige grinned, reading her mind as usual.

"A fringe benefit," Eliza admitted.

Paige gave her a hug. "Be strong, it's just for a few days. And I need to get the last of my stuff from Doug's apartment."

They both winced.

"How are you holding up?" Eliza asked carefully. Paige had been typically tight-lipped about her breakup, but they'd been together for so long, it can't have been easy.

But to her surprise, Paige gave a casual shrug. "Fine. Good. He's just being annoying setting a time to come pick everything up."

"Do you need me to come?" Eliza asked. "Play backup."

Paige gave her a look. "You really will go to any lengths not to be stranded here with Mom, won't you?"

"Busted." Eliza laughed. She had been thinking more about avoiding Cal, but she wasn't about to go into the details of her own love life when Paige was still so fresh from her breakup. "OK, OK, I'll survive. Who knows, by the time you're back, she might have fixed me up with my dream man. And he might even be over twenty!"

Eliza helped Paige load up her car and waved her off, then fetched a few loads of boxes from the office to donate. She reached for the stack of old newspapers, bound for the recycling center, but she couldn't face just trashing them, not after what Poppy had said about the *Caller* going under.

Eliza paused. It seemed a shame to just let it fade away. She couldn't bring her job, or her father, back, but maybe the printed word had a few more rounds in it yet.

The printed address on the back of the *Caller* led Eliza into town and across the neat square to the Sweetbriar Town Hall, where the town secretary, Franny, was happy to gossip about the newspaper's fate.

"His daughter in Florida just had a baby, and he decided he wanted to be closer to them. Plus, the warmer winters. You know Wilber's arthritis always acted up in the cold," Franny said, digging into the box of her favorite sweet and salty popcorn that Eliza had remembered to bring. "I asked around for someone to take over, but couldn't find any taker's. There's only a shoe-string budget," she explained. "Enough to cover the print costs and delivery, but not much after that."

"Can I take a look?" Eliza asked. "I'm . . . between jobs right now and could use a project. I hate to see it just fold like this."

"Knock yourself out." Franny opened a desk drawer and withdrew a clanking old keyring. "Top floor, in the back. The lock always sticks, so just give it a good shove."

Eliza followed the directions to a cozy office in the attic with tiny porthole windows looking out across the town square. She was braced for more clutter, but to her relief, the room was spotless, in perfect order. Old Wilber had run a tight ship: a creaking old desktop computer held page layouts and subscribers' details, and a bank of filing cabinets stored paper copies of old issues and features, everything including—

"Aha," Eliza exclaimed aloud. "Future articles."

She pulled out the file and settled in. It looked simple enough—a regular rotation of local columns and news, peppered with features on upcoming events. It wouldn't take her long to assemble the first issues and get it out to print, and as for the future . . . Her brain ticked over, already planning upcoming articles, interviews, maybe even some classified ads . . .

Eliza stopped herself before she got carried away. She'd come over to check it out on a whim, but did she really want to take on the responsibility of the whole newspaper? Her time on the Cape was supposed to be a temporary break. A chance to lick her wounds and apply for a new job back in the city—at a *real* newspaper, not one that ran *LOCAL MAN SAVES PUPPY* on the front page in fifteen-point print.

But looking around the little office, with those quirky headlines framed in a proud line on the wall, Eliza felt a surge of loyalty. The *Caller* was worth saving. So what if the biggest scoop they'd ever run was a blistering exposé of the plot to rig the biggest-pumpkin contest at the Fall Festival?

They could all use a little more good news in their lives.

She headed back downstairs to Franny's office, where the older woman was juggling two different phones. "OK if I hold onto the keys?" Eliza whispered. Franny gave her the thumbs up, busy.

"You can't have him arrested just because he planted lilies. I know you're allergic, but . . ."

Eliza left her to it. She already felt better than she had in weeks. Maybe she would only steer the *Caller* for a few issues, long enough to find someone to take it on full-time, but it was something. Between this and her hostess job at the restaurant, she would be plenty busy—with no time at all to dwell on her mistakes.

However good that mistake was at kissing.

She drove across the square and down a side lane, to where Grayson's used bookstore sat, half-hidden behind overgrown bushes of hydrangea. "You need to get those trimmed!" she exclaimed, staggering in with a box of her father's old books balanced in her arms. "I feel like I'm Prince

Charming, trying to fight my way through the Enchanted Forest."

Grayson chuckled and hoisted the box from her arms. "It's my plot to keep time-wasters away," he said in his English accent, setting it down on the counter. "If you don't make it through, you don't want it badly enough."

"You just don't want anyone interrupting you," Eliza teased, nodding to Grayson's cup of coffee and battered John Grisham novel.

"Bingo." Grayson looked through some of the books she'd brought. "Shipbuilding?" he said, surprised.

"I'm cleaning out my dad's old office," Eliza explained. "I figured they deserved a good home."

"Bert's been looking for some maritime history," Grayson said. "He'll be glad to take them."

"Then my work is done." Eliza brushed her dusty hands off on her cut-off denim shorts. She paused, looking around the warm, sunny room. "But now that we have all these empty shelves . . ."

"It would be a crime not to fill them," Grayson finished, giving her a knowing smile. "Aunt June just dropped off a ton of crime books. Laura Lippman and Tana French, they're in the back."

"Thanks!"

Eliza happily lost herself in the stacks, each small, rabbit-warren room opening up to another. With the sun filtering in through the windows, falling golden on the wooden floors, this had always been one of her favorite places in Sweetbriar Cove, and as a kid, she'd probably blown her whole allowance here on secondhand Christopher Pike novels, and scandalous V. C. Andrews. Now, she filled her arms again, pulling down interesting titles, and some thick sagas her mom might like—

"We've got to stop meeting like this."

Eliza looked up and froze. Cal was lounging in the overstuffed chair in the corner, one ankle propped over his knee, and the dusty sunlight falling so perfectly over his relaxed frame that for a minute, he looked like an old painting come to life. He had a book in his lap, and five more stacked beside the chair, and he gave her a warm smile. "Great minds," he said, nodding to the pile of books in her arms. "What have you got?"

"I'm on a thriller kick," Eliza answered. She felt her cheeks flush and her skin prickle with awareness. Her eyes went to his lips, remembering the way they'd felt against hers; the strong press of his body, and—

*No. Nope.*

*Not going there.*

She cleared her throat. "Right now, I have a thing for books about murderous women getting revenge on the men who wronged them."

Cal looked surprised, then laughed. "Should I take that as a hint?"

"Take it any way you like," Eliza said. She couldn't help noticing that he looked more relaxed than she'd ever seen him, lounging there in a rumpled shirt and jeans.

Not that she *wanted* to notice things like that.

"Listen." Cal paused, and got to his feet. "About last night . . ."

Eliza gulped. His eyes met hers, and for a moment, she felt that surge of heat return, the inexplicable craving to toss her books aside and pick up exactly where they'd left off—

"I apologize," Cal finished, looking awkward as he stood there across the small room. "I don't know what I was thinking, kissing you like that. It was madness."

"Madness," she echoed, bobbing her head firmly in agreement even as her body told a different story. "Temporary insanity."

"Exactly." Cal exhaled in clear relief. "I don't know what came over me. But I can assure you, it won't happen again."

Eliza clutched her books. Of course, he was right. She'd decided the same thing.

So why did she feel something like disappointment, just a small pang in her chest?

"Great," she said brightly. "We don't need to feel weird about it. It happened. Just one of those things. Now we can be friends."

Cal arched a curious eyebrow.

"Well, not *friends*," Eliza added, flustered. "Not after you fired me and started dismantling the newspaper I love. But, you know, civil."

Cal's lips quirked in a smile. "That's very generous."

"You're making fun of me."

"No, not at all. I'm relieved; if I see you around, you won't give me the cut direct." Cal grinned wider. "People might talk."

Eliza glared. "How do you know about Regency etiquette?"

"I know a lot of things." Cal smirked. He strolled closer, and for a terrible, wonderful moment, Eliza wondered if all the talk about madness and manners was a ruse, and he was going to kiss her again. Then he plucked a book from her stack. "*Lady Killers*?" he read the title. "You should carry a warning."

She snatched it back. "Says the man who fires so many people, he can't even have the decency to remember their names."

A flicker of hurt crossed Cal's features, and Eliza wished she could take it back. Then his face set again: stubborn and proud.

"I remember," he drawled. "At least, the important ones."

And then he sauntered past her out of the room. Eliza sank back against the wall with a groan. That man was infuriating!

One minute, she wanted to kiss him, the next, slap that knowing smirk right off his lips.

*His hot, sensual lips . . .*

Eliza gripped her books tighter. She knew exactly where thinking like that would lead her, and it was off limits.

Cal Prescott knew their encounter last night was a mistake, and this was one thing, at least, they could agree on.

It could never happen again.

# 6

So far, Cal's mission to relax was going great—except for one big problem. Well, Eliza wasn't exactly large, but her presence loomed: five-foot-seven of pure, dark-eyed tension that seemed to follow him all over town. First the pub, then the bookstore, and now, the memory of her kiss lingering in the back of his mind, making his imagination tangle up in knots when all he wanted was to unwind.

He spent the next few days trying to steer clear: exploring the nearby towns, driving out to distant beaches, and spending the evenings relaxing in the (relative) comforts of the Pink Palace, but by the time a fourth person recommended the life-changing sticky buns at the local bakery, he decided enough was enough. He wasn't the kind of man to hide away from trouble—and definitely not when there were tasty baked goods on the line—so early on Friday he drove over, and found a line already snaking outside the door in the morning sun.

"These must be some sticky buns," he remarked, and the guy ahead of him chuckled.

Cal paused. "Jake Sullivan?" he asked, recognizing the broad frame of the former football pro. "Cal Prescott," he introduced himself. "We met a few years back. You were kind enough to volunteer as a bachelor in one of my Foundation's charity auctions."

Jake's forehead smoothed in recognition. "Cal! How are you?" He shook his hand. "God, I remember that event. Some woman bid ten grand on me, just to get revenge on her ex. He supported the Jaguars," Jake explained, and Cal laughed.

"Sounds like a bargain."

"She said so," Jake agreed. "So, what brings you to town?"

"Just a vacation," Cal replied. The line inched forwards, but nobody seemed in any rush. "I'm surprised to see you here. I would have figured you for New York or LA, one of those big sportscaster jobs."

"I grew up here," Jake replied. "And my girlfriend is local, so I figured it was time to put down some roots."

"Makes sense," Cal nodded. "Do you still keep up with the team?"

"Every game day." Jake smiled. "I'm an armchair coach now."

Cal laughed, and they talked sports until they finally reached the counter. "What's good?" Cal asked, surveying the display case.

Jake snorted. "I can tell this is your first visit. Just try one of everything, you can't go wrong."

Cal didn't go quite so crazy, but he still walked out with enough pastries to feed an army. "Good start," Jake said approvingly from his spot at a table. "Are you coming by the festival tonight?"

"The lobster thing?" Cal asked, remembering the banners.

"It's kicking off tonight, down at the harbor," Jake said. "Drinks, a band, all the seafood you can eat. You should come by, meet the gang."

"OK," Cal replied slowly, thinking immediately of Eliza. Was she part of "the gang" too? And if so, would she even want him there? "Maybe."

"Just follow the noise," Jake said with a grin. "You can't miss it."

JAKE WASN'T WRONG. THE SUN WAS JUST SINKING OVER THE horizon when Cal heard the music start, drifting from just down the coast. It sounded like a party, so he grabbed his keys and walked the long way down, along winding back roads that were hazy in the dusk light. He couldn't remember the last time he'd walked so much; he never had the time. He had a driver on standby to ferry him around to city meetings, so he wouldn't lose a single moment he could spend on calls or paperwork en route. Here, there were hardly any vehicles on the road, just miles of hedgerows and the glint of the ocean through the trees as he stretched his legs and meandered down towards the harbor, enjoying the evening breeze and the lazy call of gulls circling above the bay.

The party was in full swing when he arrived: a few hundred people gathered on the pier already, with picnic tables, food vendors, and a band set up on a low stage, the speakers blasting. Cal wasn't even searching the crowd, but his eyes found Eliza all the same, spinning in a circle on the makeshift dancefloor. She was wearing jeans and a red shirt, her hair pulled back and her whole face lighting up as she laughed at something her girlfriends said.

He couldn't look away.

"You look like you need a beer," Declan's voice boomed beside him, and Cal turned, glad for a distraction. His friend was even scruffier tonight, with a drink in one hand and some kind of fried snack in the other. Cal looked around for the inevitable gorgeous sidekick, but he couldn't see one around. "Flying solo?" He arched an eyebrow, surprised.

"Not for long." Declan grinned. "Just surveying my options, you know how it is."

"No, but I know how *you* are." Cal chuckled and followed Declan over to the beer booth. "I'm surprised you aren't cooking tonight. Didn't you say you made the best lobster roll on the East Coast?"

"Both coasts, mate," Declan corrected him. "But I'm off the clock tonight. These aren't bad," he said, grabbing one from a nearby table and devouring it in a single bite. And coming from a chef, that was high praise, so Cal paid for a couple too, to wash down with a red cup of something on draft.

"Cal." Jake emerged from the crowd, waving. He seemed in good spirits, even thought he was wearing a novelty hat with a bouncing toy lobster attached to it. "You made it."

"Interesting hat, mate," Declan drawled, but Jake just smiled.

"I know. I lost a bet with Riley. But I'll have my revenge come the Fourth of July. I've got a star-spangled onesie with his name on it."

Declan snorted. "That I've got to see."

"So, you two know each other?" Cal asked, and the two men laughed.

"You could say that," Declan said. "He thought I was macking on his girl, nearly threw down in my restaurant last year."

Cal laughed. "Why am I not surprised?"

"In my defense, Mackenzie's a gorgeous woman." Declan put his hands up. "But I guess I wasn't her type."

"You mean, she has taste?" Jake said, teasing.

"Easy there," Declan warned him, and then was distracted by a passing group of coeds. "*Hello.*"

Cal shook his head and gave his friend a good-natured shove. "They're too young for you. What are you going to talk about, the new Justin Bieber record?"

"Who said anything about talking?" Declan gave a wink, and then sauntered off to catch up with them.

"He'll learn," Jake said, sipping his beer.

"Don't be so sure," Cal replied. "He'll be eighty, still the biggest player at the retirement home."

Jake chuckled. "You'd be surprised. I wasn't exactly Mr. Monogamy until I got together with Mackenzie. Sometimes you're just waiting for the right woman, even if you don't realize it yet."

Cal couldn't stop himself from searching out Eliza again. The dancefloor had cleared between songs, but he caught that flash of red over at one of the big communal picnic tables. She was sitting with a paper bib around her neck, hair pulled back, digging into her food with total gusto.

She was a study in contrasts. He couldn't think of anyone who broadcast their emotions so clearly. When she was relaxed like this, happiness seemed to radiate, but the minute the tide turned . . . God help whoever was on the end of that clear, determined stare. It was no wonder she'd been causing waves at the newspaper, long before the Prescott Group had taken the reins. "She's a trouble-maker," the editor had said, almost helplessly, when that scathing article of hers went live. Eliza clearly didn't care that every newsroom was like a royal court—where favors and allegiances sometimes mattered more than pure talent. And in the end, it had been her undoing. It wasn't lost on Cal that nobody had come to her defense, or even put up a fight to keep her job at all.

She looked up suddenly, and saw him watching, so he raised his hand in a wave and made his way over. He shouldn't feel so off balance around her, he told himself sternly. After all, they'd reached a détente, of sorts. The sooner he got used to seeing her around—without the wayward jolt of tension—the sooner he could have that stress-free trip he'd planned.

*Civil,* that's what she'd said. And he was a Prescott, raised with impeccable manners. He could manage some small talk without either of them pushing the other off the pier.

Right?

~

ELIZA WAS IN A GREAT MOOD. MAYBE IT WAS THE PARTY, OR Aunt June's killer punch, or the bowl of melted butter sitting in front of her, but she wasn't about to let Cal Prescott throw her off her game. Even if the worn cotton of his shirt hugged every inch of his torso, the sky-blue shade bringing out the ocean in his eyes . . . "Is that, gasp, a T-shirt?" she teased, when he reached her. "What happened, the butler forgot to press your dress shirt?"

Cal smiled. "I was told this thing gets messy."

"Well then," Eliza said, shifting to free up space on the bench beside her. "How about you sit down and get your hands dirty?" Somehow, it sounded suggestive out loud, so she thrust a paper bib at him quickly. "You're going to want one of these."

Cal tied it around his neck, and she was almost relieved to see him cover up those distracting muscles.

*Almost.*

"You're really going for that lobster, huh?" Cal asked, surveying her with a smidge of amusement.

"Is there any other way?" Eliza cracked open a claw and happily scooped out the tender lobster meat inside. She sucked butter from her fingertips and gave him a grin. "I mean, you're welcome to try it with a knife and fork . . ."

Cal gave a chuckle. "I think I can remember how." He

reached for a claw and expertly levered it open, leaving a perfect nugget of meat within. "My dad would take us out on the boat when I was a kid. Sometimes we'd pull them straight out of the water whole, and have the chef do a big broil for dinner."

*Boat. Chef.* Eliza bit back a smart retort. So, his childhood had been very different to hers, but that wasn't his fault. She'd been more than lucky herself, running around the beaches of the Cape every summer, her feet wet in the tide pools. "That sounds nice," she said instead, and almost laughed at the surprise on Cal's face.

"It was." He frowned, shooting her an uneasy look. She grinned wider and dunked another piece of lobster meat in butter. Maybe being nice had its benefits, after all. Kill them with kindness, and all that jazz.

"I had to fight Hank for the last brownies," Brooke announced, arriving with a plate and a triumphant smile.

"His *special* brownies?" Eliza asked, eying the gooey treats. Brooke paused.

"What do you mean?"

Cal took a corner and tasted it. "Yeah, you're going to want to keep from operating heavy machinery," he said, breaking into a grin.

Brooke hooted with laughter. "No wonder the college kids are all hanging around him like flies."

"You'll learn." Eliza patted her shoulder. "Once, my mom ate some at the Halloween Hayride by mistake. I found her listening to James Brown at two in the morning, eating Cheetos straight from the bag."

Brooke grinned. "Who knew your mom was such a rebel?"

"That's just the start of it." Eliza took a sip of beer. "I found a whole bunch of photos of her and my dad, dressed up like hippies at some music festival when they were in college. They knew how to party."

Not that her mom would ever admit it now, of course. Eliza's dad was the only one who could tease her into giggling fits, or suddenly whirl her around the kitchen in a spontaneous slow dance. Without him around, Eliza hadn't seen Linda laugh in weeks. Maybe even longer.

She shook off the sad thought. Mom needed time, like they all did. Tonight, she'd gone to Franny's for tea and bridge, so at least she wasn't sitting home alone.

When she looked up, Eliza found Cal watching her, his blue eyes thoughtful. For a moment, it felt like he was looking right through her, and could see all the emotion she'd been struggling to keep pressed down, hidden out of sight.

Eliza shivered.

"I love this song!" she declared suddenly, bouncing to her feet. "Come on, Brooke, let's dance."

She took off back to the dance floor without waiting to see if her friend followed. The band was playing something loud and fast, and she lost herself in the throng of friendly bodies, dancing from one familiar face to the next. She didn't want to think tonight, she just wanted to have a good time, and so the next hours spun by in a whirl of dancing, and local gossip, and several more cups of that deliciously lethal punch, until by midnight, she was thoroughly worn out.

"Time to call it a night!" Poppy said, as the last song faded away. She yawned and smiled at Eliza. "I can't believe I stayed out so late."

"You're a trooper." Cooper kissed her forehead. "Can you make it to the car, or do you want me to bring it around?"

Poppy paused. "Is it terrible if I want the ride?"

Eliza laughed as Cooper went to fetch his truck. "Perks of the pregnancy, huh?" she teased.

Poppy snorted. "You mean, along with my swollen ankles and insatiable need to pee?"

"Good point," Eliza agreed. She waited with Poppy until they headed out, and then was smothered in a hug from Brooke.

"See you tomorrow?" Brooke asked. "Come over for dinner, we can have a real girls' night."

"I have a shift at the restaurant until ten," Eliza said. "But I can swing by after, with dessert?"

"Done." Brooke beamed. "There's lots to discuss." She gave a meaningful look at where Cal was chatting with the guys, and then winked, waltzing away before Eliza could say a word.

Eliza collected her jacket—and some cookies for the road—and headed for the steps down to the beach, but the pier was slick with spilled drinks, and she lost her footing.

"Whoa." Cal caught her arm just as she almost took a tumble. "That punch should have come with a warning."

"It does," Eliza replied. "Didn't you see the designated driver signs up by the lot?"

Cal gave her a mock-stern look. "Do I need to take your keys?"

"I'm walking." It was still warm out, so Eliza stuffed her sweater into her shoulder bag. The party was shutting down now, with people packing up vans and dismantling the booths.

Cal looked around. "Which way? I'll walk with you."

"It's OK," Eliza said. "It's only a mile back across the beach. I've walked it a hundred times."

"It's dark," Cal said stubbornly. "You don't know what's out there."

"Sure, I do," Eliza laughed. "Debra will be walking her dogs, and Randall will probably be out, checking the tide pools for his ecological studies."

"I insist."

Eliza paused. It was perfectly safe for her to walk home alone. The dangerous part was standing right in front of her: looking too tempting for her own good. But what was she supposed to say, *No, thanks, I might lose all self-control and jump your delicious bones*? She could only imagine Cal's response to that, so she just gave a nod. "Sure, why not?"

Cal fell into step beside her, and she led the way, following the winding path back from the harbor down through the reedy marshes and onto the pale sand that curled around the bay.

"Tonight was fun," Cal remarked, strolling with his hands in his pockets. "There's a real sense of community here."

"For better or worse," Eliza cracked. She caught his quizzical look. "Small-town life can be . . . interesting," she explained. "I love being a part of something here, knowing and caring about my neighbors, but the flip side of that is when people know a little too much."

"Right, the gossip mill," Cal agreed. "I had three different people quiz me on my plans and romantic status tonight. I think they were disappointed the rumors about me aren't true. Sadly, I'm not eloping with the movie star Lila Moore."

Eliza laughed. She peeled off her sneakers and wriggled her bare toes in the sand. "Is that what it feels like for you all the time?" she asked, curious, swinging her shoes by their laces. "Having gossip columns track who you're dating, or what event you attend?"

Cal gave an awkward-looking shrug. "I guess. I try not to pay attention to any of it, which is easier said than done. It's easier now—I try not to give them anything to talk about, but after my parents died . . . the press was everywhere."

His words hit her like a thunderbolt. Eliza stopped walking. "I'm sorry," she exclaimed, feeling terrible. "I didn't know. I mean, I must have heard it," she added. "But I didn't remember."

"That's OK." Cal gave her a rueful smile. "Sometimes I forget, too. And then . . . Well, it was a long time ago. Coming up on ten years."

There was silence, just the lulling crash of the waves, steady on the shore. "Does it get easier?" Eliza asked quietly.

Cal paused.

"My dad passed last year," Eliza confided. "And in some ways, it feels like forever. But then I forget, and think, 'Oh, I need to tell him this,' or start sending him an article, and it hits me all over again—" She stopped, the telltale sting already choking her throat.

Cal touched her arm gently. "I'm sorry," he said. "And no, it doesn't get *easier*. But it hurts less, if that makes any sense. You get used to the space they left behind."

Their eyes met in the moonlight, and suddenly, Eliza could see it there: the same pang of emptiness, hidden just beneath the surface. A brief mirror of her own hidden grief.

It was just a moment, but Eliza was shaken. It felt like the first time she'd really seen him. *Cal.* Not just the guy on the other side of a corporate memo, in the immaculate preppy slacks, needling her with smart—and infuriating—comments. No, there was a man behind that charming, handsome surface she'd never glimpsed before. Somebody with private heartache and struggles, just like her.

Cal started walking again, down towards the tide line, and she followed, the sand turning damp beneath her bare feet. He pulled off his dock shoes, too, and waded in the shallows. He looked deep in thought, and Eliza scolded herself for ruining the easy mood. "I'm sorry," she blurted. "I didn't mean to bring anything up . . ."

"It's OK." Cal gave her a smile, a real one, something quieter than the charming grin he flashed around so easily. "Like I said, you get used to it."

"It was a car accident, wasn't it?" she ventured. He nodded.

"You?"

"Cancer."

Their words were light, but Eliza knew now that they were members of the same club.

"You don't understand, until it happens to you," Cal said, echoing her thoughts. "I had a roommate back at boarding school, his mom had just passed. I thought I understood what he was going through, but I didn't have a clue."

"I guess we all learn it, in the end," Eliza said with a sigh.

Cal nodded, then he gave a wry chuckle. "Wow. Look at us. Talk about a buzzkill." He splashed her suddenly, kicking up the shallow water and raining a shower of cold water down on Eliza.

She shrieked, and splashed back, until the two of them were half-drenched. "Mercy!" she finally called.

"OK, OK." Cal stopped, just as a wave crashed around him, the water spraying up to his shoulders. Eliza was in the shallows and jumped back just in time. She looked at him and laughed.

"Karma!"

Cal was soaked through, the fabric of his shirt drenched and clinging to his torso.

*His taut, muscular torso.*

For a moment, their eyes caught again, and Eliza could swear her heart was pounding loud enough to hear. They were completely alone in the moonlight, nothing but ocean and sand.

And the connection that seemed to pulse, bright and wild between them.

Eliza's breath stilled. It was only a couple of steps to him.

She could close the distance so easily: slip her hands around his taut waist, breathe in the scent of him, salty in the water, tilt her face up to meet his lips. She could picture it now. She could *feel* him already—

Then Cal gave a rueful grin. "That'll teach me," he said, shaking out his hair like a wet dog.

The moment was broken. Eliza quickly skipped back to dry sand, her skin flushed and her pulse racing. "I'm just up here," she said, relieved to recognize the outline of her family beach house, shadowed in the dark. Cal walked with her up to the dunes, and through the rickety old gate that divided the beach from their grassy backyard. The lights were off, and her mom was probably asleep by now.

"Thanks," she said, pausing by the back porch. "For walking me."

"And the bracing shower?" Cal asked, his lips quirking in a grin.

"You can talk." Eliza giggled. "You look half-drowned."

His hair was wet, sticking out at wild angles, and before she could stop herself, she reached up and smoothed it down.

Cal tensed.

Eliza snatched her hand back as if she'd been burned, but she was still standing close to him. Too close. Their eyes met in the dark, and she felt it all over again: that inexplicable pull, drawing her closer.

Cal's gaze dropped to her lips, and Eliza caught her breath, lightheaded and—

The lights went on.

"Lizzie?" her mom's voice yelled. "Is that you?"

Eliza barely had time to take a half-step away from Cal before the back door swung open, and then Linda was standing there in her floral dressing gown, with rollers in her hair. "Would you stop— Oh!" she exclaimed, seeing Cal there. Her face changed. "I didn't know you had company."

She shot a look at Eliza, but luckily, Cal's perfect manners kicked into action.

"I'm so sorry if we woke you," he said smoothly, stepping forward. He offered his hand, and one of those perfect smiles. "Cal Prescott, a pleasure to meet you."

"Charmed." Linda's frown melted into a girlish grin. She paused. "Did you say *Prescott . . .* ?"

"Cal was just walking me home," Eliza interrupted, ducking around him to the door. "Thanks!" she said brightly. "I'll see you around."

*"Save yourself,"* she mouthed to him over her mom's shoulder. Cal's eyes widened.

"Oh, but don't let me interrupt," her mom chirped. "Come in, have some coffee!"

Cal cleared his throat. "I better get back," he said. "Again, it was lovely to meet you, Mrs. Bennett."

"Bye!" Eliza dragged her mom back inside and practically slammed the door in his face.

"What's gotten into you?" Linda complained. "I just wanted to meet your friend."

"He's not my friend," Eliza corrected her automatically. But was that even true anymore, after tonight?

Either way, she didn't want to face her mom's inquisition, so she faked a yawn and headed for the stairs. "I'm beat."

"But look at you, you're wet through."

"Good night!" She bolted up to her room and closed the door behind her. Thankfully, Linda didn't follow.

Eliza flopped onto the bed.

*What was she doing?*

Somehow, "civil" had blurred to "friendly," which had teetered precariously close to "tearing off all his clothes and frolicking like nymphs in the surf." This was Cal Prescott she was getting worked up over! The man behind her unceremonious firing, poster boy for Old Money, whose self-satisfied retorts burrowed under her skin and left her smarting for days . . .

*Whose kiss was still branded on her memory, hot as the moment he'd pulled her into his arms.*

Eliza groaned and rolled over, burying her face in the pillows.

It was going to be another long, restless night.

# 7

When Eliza rolled out of bed the next morning and wandered downstairs, she was greeted with a worrying sight: her mom, dressed and bustling, with a bright smile on her face.

"You're up!" Linda greeted her cheerfully. "Coffee? The pancakes are almost ready. I thought I'd make strawberry, I know they're your favorite. I got the berries at the market first thing. Ooh, and I picked up the newspaper for you, too."

"Thanks . . ." Eliza yawned, still sleepy, and her mom patted her head.

"Those late nights will get you. You sit down." Linda steered her to the back porch, where their salt-bleached old table was already laid with a cotton cloth, plates, and silverware. "I'll bring everything out."

Eliza took a seat, suspicious now. Sure enough, there was a plate of bacon, a fresh newspaper at her place, and even a tiny vase with fresh-clipped roses adorning the table.

Something was definitely going on.

She nibbled a piece of bacon, thinking hard. She'd been so

busy with shifts at the restaurant and the *Caller,* she'd barely seen her mom, and aside from last night—

Eliza stopped. Of course.

She stifled a groan, just as Linda bustled out with a heaped stack of pancakes. "Here you go," she said, depositing them in front of Eliza with a doting smile. "You dig in. You must have worked up an appetite, staying out so late. I didn't know you were seeing Cal Prescott," she added smoothly, not even pausing for breath. "How long has that been going on?"

"Nothing's going on," Eliza vowed, but her mom pulled up a chair and looked at her excitedly all the same.

"The Prescotts!" she exclaimed. "I didn't even know they had property here in town."

"They don't," Eliza answered, her mouth full of pancakes and maple syrup. "I think he's looking for somewhere."

"There's nothing he would want around here." Linda frowned. "Except the Ashcroft farm, but that's not ocean-front. No, he'd want to be by the water. Maybe that new development up near Truro? I heard they're asking over three million, but of course, he can afford that. And it's a nice family home, he'll be looking to put down roots."

"I really wouldn't know." Eliza grabbed more bacon.

"I checked, and he's definitely single," Linda gossiped. "He hasn't dated anyone seriously since that Fortescue girl, the socialite. It's the perfect time for him to get serious."

Eliza kept eating. She should have guessed her mom would take that brief glimpse of Cal and run with it. She'd probably spent all night on google, and all morning at the market gossiping with her friends.

"Is he staying long?" Linda continued her stream of questions. "It's just our luck that you're in town for a while. See, I told you, sweetheart, everything happens for a reason. Eliza? Eliza!"

Her head snapped up. "Hmm?"

"Cal. Do you have another date planned?"

"Mom—"

"I know, I know." Linda quickly held her hands up. "You don't call it dating anymore. You just 'hang out.' But Cal Prescott!" She beamed, so full of excitement, Eliza didn't have the heart to break it to her that Cal was most definitely not her future-son-in-law.

"I'm not sure what our plans are, Mom," she said vaguely. "You know he's so busy with work."

Linda's face fell, and Eliza took pity on her. "But if I see him again, I'll wear my hair back from my face, the way you like."

"That's my girl." Linda reached over and tucked a strand behind Eliza's ears. "And maybe the blue sweater next time? Red is so obvious, and he'll be looking for a woman with real class."

The kind of woman who didn't let the air out of his tires, or call him a spoiled, privileged brat? Eliza guessed that counted her out of the running.

"Blue," she repeated. "Got it."

She looked around for something to change the subject, and noticed the peeling paint on the porch swing, faded from years of salt air and spray. "We should fix that old thing up," she suggested brightly. "Maybe give the whole porch a fresh coat of paint. Dad was always saying it could use a spruce."

Linda looked around, and her expression turned lost. "The whole place is falling apart," she sighed dramatically, even though it looked fine to Eliza. "The roof has needed mending for years. And the boiler . . ."

"So, we'll make a list," Eliza interrupted. "It could be a fun project for us. Now that I'm down here, I'll have the time to help."

Linda put down her coffee mug. "Actually, sweetie, I

wanted to talk to you about something . . ." She paused, but Eliza knew what was coming: more concerned questions about her future, or lack thereof.

"It's OK, Mom," she said quickly. "I have a plan. The shifts at the restaurant will keep me busy, and I have the *Caller* now, too. I'll find another job eventually. This is just a hiccup."

"It's not that . . ." Her mom paused again, looking conflicted.

Eliza reached across and squeezed her hand. "I know it can't be easy, being back here without Dad. He was the one who took care of this stuff. But I'm here now," she reassured her. "We can manage together. This place has been in the family for generations. I'm not going to let it fall apart on our watch." She got to her feet. "I can tackle the porch swing today, and then we'll figure out everything else, OK?"

Linda nodded, looking reluctant. "I suppose it can't hurt. But you won't pick a gaudy color, will you?"

"You mean, like Marion Hayes?" Eliza teased. Her mom clutched her chest.

"Don't even joke! You can see the pink halfway into town. I don't know what she was thinking."

"That it's fun?" Eliza reached for another pancake, but her mom whisked the plate away. "I haven't finished!"

"Carbs, sweetie. You need to stay in shape!"

ELIZA SPENT THE MORNING SCRUBBING AND SANDING DOWN THE swing, then drove into town to pick out some—muted, tasteful—paint. The original can she'd found in the storage cupboard was sealed shut with age, but Hank at the hardware store was able to match the pretty blue color, and find her some brushes and rollers, too.

"Your roof could use patching," he warned, ringing her up.

"Ask Cooper, I'm sure some of his guys would take care of that."

"I'm not sure it's in the budget right now," Eliza said, pulling some crumpled bills from her pocket to pay the bill. "But thanks for the tip!"

She should have gone straight home again, but she couldn't resist taking a detour to the *Caller* offices, tucked high above the square. It had only been a few days, but already the cozy attic felt like her retreat, and her next issue was almost ready to roll. Thanks to Wilber's excellent filing system, she had the articles edited and set, and had been writing up the Lobsterfest events and reaching out to old columnists to see if they would keep up their contracts. Luckily, all of them were thrilled to hear the *Caller* was getting another shot. "I was so sad when Wilber moved," gushed Luann, their expert Miss Manners columnist. "I'm only halfway through my guide to thank-you notes."

It wasn't exactly headline news. Eliza felt a brief pang just imagining the madcap bustle of the newsroom back in Boston. Right about now, they would be racing to prep the weekend edition, and glued to the AP wire for late-breaking stories. Sometimes, those sessions lasted late into the night: someone ordering in pizza, the interns fetching coffee, and everyone running on adrenaline and caffeine, racing the clock to get it all done in time. Other staffers griped about the hours, but Eliza never found anyplace better to be than right there, in the middle of the action. Come morning, they would stumble over to the diner down the street for greasy breakfast rolls, exhausted but elated at a job well done, before grabbing a few hours of sleep and heading back to the office to do it all over again.

It was stressful and maddening, and exciting, and crazy, and Eliza had loved every minute.

And now, it was all gone.

She looked around the sunny attic, so quiet and still. She'd been trying to stay positive and busy ever since that humiliating perp-walk to the lobby, clutching her carton of notebooks and coffee mugs, but the failure of her firing still stung, aching in her chest.

Her old colleagues would probably laugh to see her now. They were all still there, racing on without her, while she was sitting here, deciding which photo of Mrs. Anderson's prize-winning roses to run on Page 1.

Cal Prescott had a lot to answer for.

Eliza scowled. Never mind their brief moments of bonding, he was still the one behind her sudden change in fortune. She should remember that the next time she was struck with the inexplicable urge to kiss him.

Not that it would ever happen again.

~

CAL NEEDED TO KISS ELIZA AGAIN.

It was inexplicable. Irrational. And completely out of the question. But the urge was there all the same. He tried reading three different books, listening to a podcast, and even taking himself on a three-mile run along the windy shore, but still, his brain was drawn back to one thing. The moment on the beach with Eliza where he'd almost reached for her again.

That split second, staring into her eyes when it felt like she saw him. *Knew* him. The empty places his parents' deaths had left, and his determination to make them proud all the same. That unspoken drive, he could see it in her, too—along with so much more . . .

It didn't make any sense. Eliza had made it clear how she felt about him, and he agreed: they had nothing in common, except how irritating they found the other. Hell, they'd only just thawed enough to get along in public, so why had he come so close to ruining the détente?

Maybe it was just timing. Moonlit ocean, a warm breeze, light reflecting in her teasing eyes . . . It was the textbook definition of romance, Cal decided. Of course he'd been swept up in the moment, he'd barely stood a chance. He should just be relieved her mother had interrupted them when she did—before he'd pressed her up against the porch railings and done something they both would have definitely regretted.

But damn, that's one regret he would have enjoyed.

Cal arrived back from his run, sweating hard, but as he turned off the road to the Pink Palace, he found a car pulled over out front, and an older woman just walking back from the house.

"Hello?" he called, approaching. "Can I help you?"

"You must be Calvin." The woman was in her sixties, perhaps, with dyed red hair and a vivid silk scarf swathed around her neck. "I'm June Somerville. I'm a friend of your godmother's."

"Not the famous Aunt June?" Cal asked, shaking her hand.

She laughed. "It depends who's asking."

"I think I sampled some of your punch the other night," Cal said.

"Oh dear." June's mouth twitched, her eyes full of laughter. "Did you do anything you regret?"

"No," Cal replied. *Unfortunately*. "Would you like to come in?" he asked, remembering his manners. "I'm sorry I'm a mess, but is there something I can help you with?"

June clucked appreciatively. "Of course, Poppy said you were a polite young man. Some of the younger ones these days, all they do is grunt."

"I try my best with complete sentences," Cal said, amused.

"I just dropped by to give you my card." June plucked another from her purse and held it out. He glanced at the lettering. *June Somerville – Sweetbriar Realty* it said in swirling script. And was that . . . ? Yes. A seashell pattern around the edges.

"I heard on the grapevine you might be looking for a place out here," June continued. "I know I'm not one of those slick high-end firms, but I can promise you I know everything that happens around here. *Everything*. That means a head start on all the best property. For example, Julie DiMarco up in Truro just got herself a divorce lawyer," she said, leaning in conspiratorially. "They have three thousand square feet, with room to build. Gorgeous views. I could make some calls, get you in to see it this weekend?"

"I . . . hadn't considered it yet," Cal said. But it was true, he had been thinking about buying something. An investment, perhaps, or even a vacation place. "How about you put together some options?" he suggested.

June lit up. "What are you thinking? Wait, don't tell me. I have a knack for this." She studied him thoughtfully, and—was Cal just imagining it, or did her eyes linger extra-long on his sweaty body? "You want a bachelor pad, all the bells and whistles. Something impressive, for the ladies. Or . . . a family home? Hmmm." June cocked her head. "You haven't decided just yet."

Cal blinked.

"Well, never mind, we can look at everything," June said, whipping out an old-school Filofax. "How's Tuesday?"

"I . . . sure, why not?" Cal realized he didn't have anything scheduled.

"Perfect." June leaned in and kissed him on both cheeks, then rubbed her lipstick away. "You and I are going to have a fabulous time. I'll even bring a flask of my punch."

Cal laughed. "That's how you get your contracts signed, is it?"

"Damn right it is." June bustled back to her car. "I'll call you!" she yelled through the open window, before revving the engine and driving away.

Cal watched her leave and chuckled. She was a character, alright. But what the hell: it didn't hurt to look. And he could already see himself returning here to Sweetbriar. Just, perhaps, to somewhere a little less pink.

He headed inside and took a shower, but soon enough, he found his thoughts drifting back to Eliza. Was she sticking around in town? She must have been living in Boston, working at the newspaper, but clearly, she had roots here, too—

*No*. He stopped himself before he could get off course again. He had no choice left: it was time to bring out the big guns, especially if he was going to get Eliza out of his mind. He quickly dressed and went to his briefcase, pulling out his laptop and the thick file of reports from the Prescott Foundation, then he settled in with a beer on the porch and started reading.

The Foundation was his favorite part of the job, even if his uncle did think it was a colossal waste of time. "Show up, sign the checks, and then offload it to somebody else," he would say, but Cal refused. Running a successful company was his duty, but there were some things even more important than those profit margins. The Foundation had been set up in his parents' name after they died; it raised money for charity, funded research, and brought awareness to vital causes. It was the part of the job that let him sleep at night, knowing the Prescott name was doing some good in the world.

Today, he reviewed the account reports and some of the applications for funding. His mother had been active raising money for children's cancer research, so he'd tried to focus the

Foundation's resources there: clinical trials, scholarships, and helping to cover expenses for patients at the hospital in Boston. When he'd taken the reins, the family trustee had warned him they couldn't say yes to everyone, but reading the heart-breaking letters from parents and doctors, Cal had soon realized his own family's resources were only just the beginning. So, he cajoled them all into black-tie fundraisers, and $5,000-a-plate charity events, where Boston's social elite could mingle and write fat checks and smile for the cameras.

So far, it was working out. Every time, they raised more than the last one, and this year, the numbers were on track to be their best yet. They had a big charity gala coming up that he hoped would bring in some real funds. Cal worked all day—coordinating with the event planners, calling his finance team, and checking in with the hospital board, too—and this time, at last, the hours flew by, until he surfaced in the afternoon with a rumbling stomach and a craving for Declan's killer roast beef sandwiches.

He was in the car and halfway to the restaurant before he realized Eliza was probably working a shift. Cal paused at the stoplight, torn. He wanted to go see her . . . which meant he definitely shouldn't.

He turned towards town instead. He would pick up some groceries, and fend for himself. Plus, he never did get a chance to buy those books he'd been browsing at the bookstore. But as Cal turned into the Sweetbriar square, he knew he was kidding himself. Choosing *not* to go somewhere because of her was pretty much the same thing as rushing over to see her. Just with fewer arguments.

*And far less kissing.*

He climbed out of the car and crossed the street to the market. Maybe he should take Declan up on his offer to hit the town—and meet some of the bevvy of gorgeous women his friend had programmed into his speed dial. Distraction, that was the ticket. But when he turned the corner around the cereal aisle and almost bumped into someone coming from the other direction, he knew it was useless.

"You." Eliza looked up at him, her cheeks flushed. She was clutching a pack of toilet paper and some chips.

"Me." Cal looked at her, feeling strangely cheerful. It was a sign. Either that, or someone out there was laughing at him, but it made no difference.

There was no escaping her. So why even try?

"How is your hangover?" he asked, remembering her almost-spill.

Eliza's mouth dropped open in protest. "I wasn't drunk! I was enjoying myself. You should try it sometime," she added, narrowing her eyes defensively. "Unless that's not good manners."

"I'll have to consult the handbook, but I think it's allowed," Cal replied, silently scolding himself for saying the wrong thing—yet again. Somehow, every time he tried to be charming, it just made her more annoyed. "How about you give me a lesson tonight?"

"What?" Eliza asked.

"Would you like to have dinner?" he elaborated, and he was rewarded with a stunned look.

"With *you*?"

"That would be the point, yes." Cal cleared his throat. "Unless they've changed the rules on dating in the past week."

Eliza blinked at him. "But why?"

"Didn't you hear the part about it being a date?" Cal was beginning to feel like he'd made a bad, bad decision. Potentially the worst decision in his entire life. Sure, he hadn't been expecting her to swoon by the paper goods display, but was dinner really such an awful invitation? "You, me, an entrée or two," he continued, trying to sound nonchalant. "Who knows, maybe we'll even go crazy and get dessert?"

Cal flashed her a smile. Eliza stared back, her cheeks flushing pinker. She was wearing cut-offs with a ratty old sweater, her hair pulled up in a messy braid, but she looked just as dazzling as ever. He could make reservations at the fanciest restaurant on the Cape and give them both an excuse to dress up for the night. Would she like Italian, or prefer French? Cal wondered. Either way, he could already picture it: a bottle of wine, some candlelight, and the whip-smart conversation he knew would be on the menu—

"I don't think that would be a good idea," she said finally, and his heart sank. "I have plans. And besides, we're not . . . I mean, I don't . . ." Eliza trailed off, looking uneasy, and Cal was suddenly reminded of his first week at prep school, when he'd stood in gym class for what seemed like forever, waiting for someone to pick him for a team.

"Of course," he said, forcing a smile. "Forget I said anything."

"I just mean . . . we'd probably end up throwing things before our food even arrived," Eliza said with a wry smile. "And I don't know about you, but a public disorder citation isn't exactly going to help my CV."

"Right." He cleared his throat again. "Well, I'm sure I'll see you around."

He turned and walked briskly away, before he could embarrass himself even more. Clearly, Eliza hadn't been replaying their kiss together like an old movie on the big screen. It was time he gave Declan that call and put Eliza Bennett out of his mind for good.

# 8

"What did you do that for?" Brooke scolded her, when Eliza recounted the run-in with Cal. It was late, and she'd driven over to Brooke's place after her shift at the restaurant to split a bottle of wine—and some of the left-over bourguignon from that night's special.

"What do you mean?" Eliza spooned the broth out of its Tupperware container and added some crusty French bread she'd snagged from the stale pile.

"Cal!" Brooke exclaimed, pouring the wine. "You turned him down!"

"Yes," Eliza said slowly. "Because I just explained all the reasons why he's the most infuriating, arrogant man around."

"Who you have long, lustful daydreams about," Brooke added. She tasted the stew and made a blissful noise.

"Right?" Eliza agreed. "It's a good thing I'm running around all the time on my shift, otherwise I'd be putting on so much leftovers weight."

"Worth it," Brooke declared. "Can you bring the wine glasses down?"

"As long as you promise not to bug me about Cal."

Brooke grinned and kissed her on the cheek. "Now what kind of friend would I be to make a promise like that?"

She took their plates and danced outside before Eliza could protest. Eliza grabbed their glasses and joined her down in the small courtyard, where a little bistro table was set up among the tangle of potted plants and fruit trees. "I should ask your landlord to write a column," she mused, looking around at the magical little space. "I need a new gardening expert."

"I just hired a landscape design guy at the hotel," Brooke suggested, tearing off a hunk of bread. "He's young, and hot—in a kind of rugged, wind-beaten way. Maybe I'll set you up if this thing with Cal doesn't work out."

"There is no thing!" Eliza protested. But this wasn't her mom, and Brooke knew her too well to be fooled by the denials. Eliza gulped some wine. "OK, maybe there could be a thing," she admitted. "But why even bother, when it's doomed to fail? I mean, I can't spend five minutes with the guy without starting a fight. He just brings out the worst in me."

"Or, he's getting under your skin because he's the first guy you've really liked in a long time," Brooke pointed out.

"I've liked guys!" Eliza said. "I dated that veterinarian, and that guy who traded bitcoin on the internet."

"You texted begging for a fake emergency call," Brooke corrected her. "And Clive, or whatever his name was? You went on like, three dates, and the best you could manage was that he was 'nice enough.' "

"He was."

" 'Nice enough' is when you settle for leftovers because you're hungry and forgot to plan lunch. It's not a recipe for soul-shaking love until death do you part," Brooke pointed out, smiling.

"If that's the standard I'm holding my dates to, then I'm going to stay single a *long* time." Eliza laughed.

"Unless you take a chance on someone who actually makes you feel something," Brooke said meaningfully.

"Sure, like annoyed, irritated, aggravated . . ."

Brooke laughed. "I get it, Ms. Thesaurus. But I saw you and Cal together at the party last night. You guys have it."

"Impetigo?"

"No," Brooke laughed. "Sparks."

"Sparks cause fires. Fires burn things down." Eliza refilled her wineglass. She didn't know why Brooke was being so insistent about this. Surely everyone could see what a spectacularly bad match she and Cal would be? "I know his type. Believe me, I dated his type—back in college, before I knew better."

"Sometimes people surprise you." Brooke gave a little smile. "I had Riley written off as an irredeemable playboy. But . . ."

"He's different."

"I didn't know that at the time." Brooke shrugged. "But I got to know him, and I saw there was another side to him, too."

Eliza paused. She'd glimpsed more to Cal the other night, hadn't she? Walking on the beach, talking like old friends. Connecting.

"So, what's the hot new trend for spring weddings?" she asked, changing the subject. "Still setting Instagram on fire?"

"I get the hint." Brooke grinned. "And it's vertical florals, not that you really care."

"Vertical what now?" Eliza asked, confused.

"Flower walls," Brooke explained. "Turns out, brides go crazy for a photo backdrop. Throw in some neon signs, and they're posting all over social media."

"To Instagram." Eliza raised her glass in a toast. "Cheers."

It was midnight before Eliza climbed back behind the wheel—with a tupperware container of wedding cake samples—and headed for home. It was a cool night, but she rolled the windows down and let the wind whip around her, needing to clear her head.

Was Brooke right, was she pushing Cal away because she felt so off balance around him? The bickering, the banter . . . He was arrogant and infuriating, sure, but she couldn't deny the heat between them, too.

The smoldering, tear-your-clothes-off heat that flared to life whenever they spent any time together at all.

Her solution to that particular problem was vowing to stay away, but what if it was a sign to move in closer instead, and actually explore why this man seemed to drive her so crazy?

Eliza sighed, idly tapping the wheel as her headlights cut through the dark. Her romantic history the past few years hadn't been the best. She went on plenty of dates, but somehow, nothing ever sparked. They guys were nice enough, and with her journalist experience, she always found a way to keep a conversation going, but after they parted ways—with an awkward hug, or a sloppy kiss—the guys always seemed to fade into the background. She couldn't understand it. When it came to her job, she had passion to spare, but Random Tinder Date #17? Not so much.

*Sparked.* There that word was again. She rolled it over in her mind. A flicker of electricity that hinted at so much more.

She wanted sparks, didn't she? Wild passion, something real and raw. But was it worth burning her whole world down? She couldn't spend five minutes with Cal without wanting to scream—and not even in an "oh, yes, more!" kind of way.

He got to her. Itching beneath the surface, always needing to get the last word. She couldn't remember getting riled up by a man like this in . . . forever. It made her wonder what it would be like with him, turning their fights into something more, well, *naked*.

Eliza's mind drifted, back to that kiss. The rush. The heat. The nerve of him! It was arrogant, and way over the line . . .

And the hottest ten seconds of her life, so far.

She was so wrapped up in remembering the feel of his body, crushed against her, that she almost missed the turn from the highway. She pulled down the road just in time, bumping over the sandy potholes until she reached the beach house. Eliza shut off the engine and sat there a moment in the dark.

No matter how hard she tried to deny it, she wanted more. Much more. But no kiss could really have been that epic; she was building it up in her mind. And trying *not* to want Cal only made her think about him more.

So, maybe she'd been coming at this all wrong. Avoiding Cal only made it worse; perhaps the only way to get out of this, was through it. Exposure therapy, that was a thing, right? An hour or two in his presence, and she'd know for sure what a terrible match they would be. And a few more kisses . . . Well, the novelty would wear off, and he would become just as forgettable as all the other guys.

For the sake of her sanity, she was going to have to date the man.

Eliza pulled out her cellphone. She knew she had Cal's number somewhere, and sure enough, it was buried in the email signature of one of those bland "Welcome to the Prescott Group" messages they'd sent after the takeover, along with some corporate waffle about accessibility and open-door management.

She took a deep breath and dialed.

"Hello?"

Eliza almost dropped the phone. It was late, and she'd been

expecting his voicemail, but Cal's voice came clear down the line. Sleepy and deep, just the sound made her stomach flip over—and her brain catch up long enough to wonder what she was doing.

"Is anyone there?" Cal asked again, and Eliza coughed.

"It's me. Eliza. Sorry, it's late. I shouldn't have called."

"No, that's OK." Cal's voice was cautious. "Is everything alright?"

"Fine!" Eliza gulped. "I was just . . . Yes," she said abruptly. "Let's have dinner."

"Oh."

There was a long pause, and Eliza slowly hit her head against the steering wheel. What was she *doing*?

"When were you thinking?" Cal finally spoke.

"I'm off from the restaurant tomorrow."

*Thud. Thud.*

"What's that noise?" Cal asked, and Eliza stopped hitting her head.

"Hmm? I don't hear a noise. So, dinner?"

"Sure, why not?" Cal said. "I'll pick you up at seven?"

"See you then!" She hung up before she could take it back.

At least she had a plan now, she reassured herself as she climbed out of the car and circled around to the porch. Dinner, conversation, a little light make-out action. With any luck, Cal would be his arrogant, infuriating self, and any lingering sparks between them would be well and truly extinguished before they even got to dessert.

And then maybe, just maybe, she'd be able to get a good night's sleep without picturing that handsome face . . . and that body . . . and his wicked, wicked mouth . . .

She couldn't wait.

"You're wearing that? On your big date?"

Eliza had just finished dressing the next evening when Paige appeared in her doorway, lugging an overnight bag. "You're back!" Eliza threw her arms around her sister in a hug. "Thank you, thank you! Please, go run interference with Mom. Take her to get ice cream or something."

"Are you kidding?" Paige smirked. "She's camped out in the chair by the window, wearing her best pearls. She's not leaving until she gets to deliver you into those eligible Prescott arms."

Eliza groaned. "Oh God. I should call, have him meet me in town."

"And break her poor, widowed heart?"

"Don't!" Eliza shoved her playfully. "I should never have told her about dinner. She's been bugging me all day about outfits and my hair."

"And clearly, you didn't listen to a word." Paige surveyed her, looking quizzical. "This is a date, right?"

"Technically." Eliza straightened her T-shirt and buttoned up her cut-off shorts. "But we're just grabbing dinner."

"Yeah, nope." Paige dumped her bag and went to Eliza's closet. "I'm all for being comfortable, but those are barely one step up from pajamas. Wear this." She thrust a navy dress at her. Eliza thrust it back.

"That's for job interviews!"

"Fine, then the black." Paige picked another. "You can't go wrong in a little black dress."

Eliza shook her head. "I wore that to the funeral."

Paige paused. "And you kept it?" She tossed it to the floor. "I burned mine."

"You didn't."

"OK, I donated it," Paige admitted. "Same thing. But I'm serious, why do you look like you just rolled in from a day at the beach? Don't you like this guy?"

"Not really." Eliza turned to the mirror and ran her fingers through her hair. She should really have washed it, but somehow, even that felt like making too much effort. She pushed it back behind her ears instead, and she slicked on some lip balm. When she turned back, Paige looked even more confused.

"Look, this is just a casual thing," Eliza reassured her. "It's the Cape! Nobody does fancy here. We'll be eating fried oysters at a road-side shack."

"Your shirt has a stain on it."

"Fine, clean shirt!" Eliza grabbed a peasant-style blouse and quickly changed. "Happy now?"

Paige sighed. "Just tell me you're wearing decent underwear."

Eliza checked. "They have Mickey Mouse on them?"

Paige threw up her hands. "Have I taught you nothing?"

"Sorry." Eliza kissed her cheek. "But all that silk and lace would be a waste. Believe me, these are staying buttoned tonight!"

The doorbell sounded, and Paige grinned. "Showtime."

Eliza thundered down the stairs and stopped dead at the bottom. Cal was standing in the hallway, holding a bouquet of fresh-cut daisies. He was clean-shaven, sharply dressed, and *delicious.*

"Hi." He stepped forward and kissed her lightly on the cheek. She caught a whiff of aftershave, something cool and fresh that went right to her head, before he stepped back.

Eliza tried to collect herself. Just because he was on her doorstep, looking like something out of an expensive photo shoot, it didn't mean she had to swoon at his feet.

"You brought me flowers? Um, thanks."

"They're not for you," Cal replied. "They're for *you,*" he said, turning to her mother. Linda's eyes just about bugged out of her head.

"Oh, they're lovely! Aren't you sweet? I'll go put them in water." She bustled off to the kitchen.

"Suck-up," Eliza whispered.

Cal grinned. "Ready to go?"

"Sure, I'll just grab my sweater."

For a moment, Eliza was tempted to race back up the stairs and put on a different outfit. A pretty dress, like Paige had urged. Hell, even a coat of mascara. Cal looked thigh-clenchingly good, in a white button-down, open at his neck, and tailored navy pants. She'd never had a thing for guys in suits before, but he looked so casually commanding, she suddenly got the appeal.

She stopped herself. This wasn't a *real* date. She was scratching the itch, that's all.

Eliza retrieved her bag and followed him to the door. "Are you going already?" Her mom appeared in the hallway again, looking disappointed.

"I'm sorry, we have reservations." Cal remained every inch the gentleman.

"Of course, silly me. Have fun," her mom called, beaming, as Eliza hustled him out the door. "Don't stay out too late!"

They stepped outside, and Eliza kept moving fast. "Never linger," she told him, practically dragging him to the car. "She'll have the baby photos out before you know it."

He chuckled. "I could always call and move the table later . . ."

"Please, God, no." Eliza reached for the passenger handle, but Cal got there first. He opened the door for her. "Thanks," Eliza said, thrown, and got inside.

Cal circled around, and then took a seat behind the wheel. She watched as he rolled his shirt-sleeves up and expertly started the engine, turning on the radio and adjusting the mirror with assured movements before backing out of the drive.

The man even *drove* sexy.

"So how was your day?" Cal asked as they pulled onto the highway. Eliza tried to get comfortable, but the leather seats and plush interior felt strange compared to her decades-old convertible.

"It was OK." She sat back and awkwardly crossed her bare legs. "We don't have to do all of this."

"All of what?" Cal glanced over.

"This. Small talk. Appropriate date conversation."

He seemed amused. "So what do you suggest we do instead?"

Eliza had plenty of ideas, but she wasn't about to say them out loud. "I don't know, just relax?"

"Because you look especially relaxed." Cal's lips quirked in amusement again.

"I'm fine," Eliza lied, and she re-crossed her legs. "Completely comfortable."

Cal exhaled in a long breath. "Look, I know we don't always see eye to eye—"

"Understatement."

"But tonight will probably go more smoothly if you stop taking everything I say as an insult."

"I don't!" Eliza protested.

Cal gave her a look. "Or a challenge."

Eliza opened her mouth, and then closed it again. He had a point. "I'm not *trying* to be difficult," she said. "But you have to admit, we don't exactly have the best track record."

"Which part?" Cal smiled. "The petty vandalism, the arguments, or the kiss?"

"The kissing was just fine," Eliza muttered before she could stop herself. "It's everything else you do that drives me crazy."

"That kiss didn't drive you crazy?" Cal stopped at a light, and when she glanced up, he was looking straight at her, his blue eyes full of intensity. "I'll have to do better next time."

Eliza's stomach turned a slow pirouette.

*Wow.*

Cal turned back to the road and drove on, apparently oblivious to the heat suddenly rolling through Eliza's body, circling lower. She felt flushed and off balance, her brain scrambling to find something witty to say next. But for the first time in her life, she was coming up blank.

Thankfully, they were approaching Provincetown now, the streets dotted with cute stores and restaurants. Cal made another turn, and then pulled over. Eliza caught sight of the sign through the window. Beachwood.

Her heart sank.

It was the fanciest restaurant for miles. Hell, it was one of the fanciest places in the state. Even now, a valet was rushing to open her door for her. "Welcome to Beachwood."

"Thanks." Eliza gulped. She really should have taken Paige's advice. Oh, why did she have to be stubborn about her outfit, and think she was proving some kind of point? "Cal?" she leaned in, as they approached the main door. "I, um, don't think I'm dressed for this. I thought we'd be going somewhere more casual."

Cal seemed to take in her outfit for the first time. He paused. "You look beautiful."

Eliza rolled her eyes. "Liar."

He grinned. "It doesn't matter what you're wearing. They won't turn us away."

It must have been nice to have that kind of confidence, but as they stepped inside, Eliza could see Cal was right. The hostess greeted him by name and asked after his uncle; the maître d' whisked them to the best table in the house, and every few steps, it seemed like another diner was bobbing up to shake his hand and catch up on old times.

Eliza had never felt so out of place in her life. She snuck a glance around the room and despaired. The women were all in stylish outfits, designer dresses and tasteful jewelry. Meanwhile, she was wearing fraying denim and sneakers. Sneakers! She could just feel their eyes on her, sizing her up, and even though she didn't want their approval, somehow, their sidelong glances hurt all the same. By the time they settled at their table—candlelit, naturally, with a vase of delicate roses—she felt about two feet tall.

"Can I show you a wine list?" the sommelier asked politely, and she practically grabbed it out of his hands.

"Yes. Please."

She was definitely going to need a drink.

# 9

This was a terrible idea.

Cal sat across the table from Eliza, avoiding her gaze, and wondered where it had all gone so wrong. He'd thought it would be simple: the flowers, the lavish restaurant, the best wine on the menu with the candlelight glowing.

The recipe for a romantic night. Everything a perfect date should be.

But now they were sitting there like two perfect strangers, and for the life of him, he couldn't think of something to say. His jokes all fell flat. His charming lines landed with a thud. And now Eliza was scanning the menu with a grim look on her face, as if she'd rather be settling in at the dentist than enjoying a Michelin-starred meal.

"Do you see anything you like?" he ventured.

Eliza's gaze snapped up. "It all looks fine."

"Good."

Cal cleared his throat. What had happened? The other night, walking home from the party, the conversation had flowed so easily, but now Eliza's guard was back up, screaming *keep out!* in five-foot neon letters.

"Are you ready to order?" The server appeared at his elbow. Cal let out a breath of relief.

"Yes, please. Eliza?"

"I don't know . . ." She hesitated.

"The scallops are good here," Cal suggested. "And the filet. Not that I'm telling you what to order," he added, wary.

"Fine."

There it was again. *Fine*. He didn't want fine! Cal felt like yelling. He wanted to impress her, seduce her, sweep her off her feet and make her beg for more.

"The scallops, then," he said to the waiter with a sigh. "And the steak."

The waiter nodded and whisked their menus away.

Silence.

Eliza gulped her wine. She looked tense, and completely out of place among all the chic cocktail dresses the other women were wearing. Cal had meant what he'd said—she looked beautiful, no matter how casual her clothing—but he could tell she wasn't happy about it. He should have mentioned where they were going ahead of time, or taken her someone more down-to-earth. What had he been thinking?

*That you wanted to impress her with last-minute reservations at the best place in town.*

Strike two. Or was that three? He had a feeling it wasn't a good idea to count.

"So, how are things at the restaurant?" Cal asked.

"It's a job." Eliza shrugged. "Not the one I loved, but we probably shouldn't talk about that." She gave him a pointed look, and he remembered why, exactly, she had a vendetta against him in the first place.

Right.

"Good point." Cal tried to smile. "OK, so what's off limits?" he asked, hoping to lighten the mood. "No talk about the newspaper. Or car maintenance."

"Or family," Eliza added. "And sports."

"You're not a Red Sox fan?"

"Nope."

"Then I guess that leaves us with politics and religion," he joked.

There was a pause.

"Or not," Cal said, relieved when their appetizers were delivered. They ate silently while he wracked his brain for a way to shift the mood. He hadn't bombed like this in . . . well, he'd never bombed like this. Women loved him! Or, at the very least, they didn't act like being alone with him was a cruel and unusual punishment.

"Things good with Declan at the restaurant?" he blurted.

"You already asked that." Eliza regarded him with a frown.

Cal coughed. "Right."

She picked at her food.

"Do you like it?" he asked. "Because we could order something else—"

"No, it's fine." Eliza popped a scallop in her mouth and swallowed. "Tangy."

"Good."

The seconds seemed to tick past, infinitely slow. Their plates were cleared and replaced with entrées, and they managed some small talk about a movie they'd both seen, but it was all start and stop and awkward pauses, none of the whip-smart conversation he'd been anticipating. Cal longed to hit some kind of reset button and start fresh, make her laugh in that brash, exuberant way she had before, instead of saying the wrong thing, over and over again.

"Cal, babe? It is you!" They were suddenly interrupted by

an exclamation, and Cal looked up to find a tall blonde woman bearing down on them, tottering on impossibly high heels.

"Sukie, hi." Cal got to his feet and politely greeted her with a kiss on the cheek.

"How *are* you?" Sukie demanded, straightening his collar. "We missed you in Cabo, Kiki said you were stuck at work, poor baby. You know what they say, all work and no play . . ." She gave a flirtatious smile.

Cal stepped back, uncomfortable. "This is Eliza," he said, nodding to her. "Sukie and I knew each other in school."

"Understatement!" Sukie laughed. "The boys would sneak on the grounds every weekend. *Quelle* scandal. It's been too long," she said, turning her back to Eliza. "But I'll see you at the gala, of course."

"I wouldn't miss it," Cal agreed. "I am the host, after all."

Sukie laughed. "Oh, you. Well, I better get back to Frederick. You know how jelly he gets." She air-kissed him and wafted away.

"Friend of yours?" Eliza arched an eyebrow as Cal took his seat again.

"Her parents are friends with my uncle," he explained. "So we cross paths a lot. Sorry."

"About what?"

Cal paused. "You know, she can be . . . friendly."

"I didn't notice." Eliza sat perfectly straight, regarding him over her wineglass with a cool, thoughtful gaze. "Or am I supposed to be *jelly*?"

Cal stifled another sigh. "Did you want dessert?" he asked, noticing the waiter loitering nearby.

"No, thanks." Eliza's expression turned rueful. "I don't think we should prolong the agony, do you?"

"What? I'm having a great time," Cal lied.

She laughed. "There you go with your perfect manners. I

could toss my wine in your face, and you'd thank me for a delightful evening."

Cal chuckled. "That's probably pushing it. But politeness is underestimated. It doesn't cost anything to be nice."

"Says the man with a million-dollar trust fund." Eliza stopped. "Sorry, that wasn't fair." She shook her head. "See, the sooner we get out of here, the less chance of saying something I regret."

Cal couldn't argue with that. He paid the check and escorted Eliza back out to the car. "Thank you for dinner," she said when they were settled in their seats. "I would have offered to go Dutch, but something tells me I would have been eating ramen for a month."

"No problem," Cal said, starting the engine. "It was my pleasure."

Eliza made another sound, like a stifled laugh. Cal chuckled out loud. "OK, so maybe not," he said. "But we gave it a shot, didn't we?"

"A terrible, awkward, excruciatingly bad shot."

"Hey!" Cal protested, but when he looked over, Eliza was giving him a look.

"Come on," she said. "That was the most awkward date in the history of dating. We could barely think of two things to say!"

"That's because it was all off limits," Cal argued.

"So you wanted to talk about your takeover at the newspaper, or the things I wrote about your aunt?"

Cal paused. "Good point."

"Face it, *this* was just a bad idea from the start." Eliza sounded remarkably cheerful. "We tried, we failed. No harm, no foul."

"I thought you didn't like sports."

"No, I don't like the Red Sox," Eliza corrected him. "Which

you'd know if we'd managed to string some basic conversation together."

"We seem to be doing OK now," Cal said, smiling.

"That's because the end's in sight," Eliza replied, relaxing back in her seat. "My favorite part of a date is always right before I leave, because I know I'll be home soon in my sweat-pants watching Netflix."

Cal laughed. "That says a lot about the guys you've been dating."

"I know." Eliza sighed. "That's why I said yes to dinner tonight. I figured maybe, since we have this spark . . . But, I was right all along. We don't click."

It felt like they were clicking just fine now, but Cal was more interested in the other thing she'd just said.

"We have a spark?" He looked over, triumphant.

Eliza flushed, then gave a careless shrug. "You know we do. You're the one who asked me out, remember?"

"Vividly. I haven't been rejected like that in years."

"Aww, poor baby. I'm sure Sukie would soothe your wounded pride, if you'd only ask."

"Jelly?" he teased, and Eliza groaned aloud.

"Never say that word again!"

"Deal," he agreed, and they laughed. Then an uneasy expression flickered across Eliza's face. "Are you OK?" he asked.

"Uh huh," she said, frowning. "Just, not feeling great . . . Are we far from home?"

"A few miles," Cal replied.

"OK." Eliza swallowed. He slid the windows down a little.

"There's some water there in the center armrest, if you need."

"Thanks." She unscrewed the cap and took a sip. "I don't usually get carsick, but . . ."

"It's not far," he reassured her. "You'll be in your sweatpants in no time."

Eliza nodded, but he noticed she was gripping the water bottle hard enough to turn her knuckles white. A couple more miles sped past, and then her voice piped up, tremulous. "Cal? I really don't feel good."

He looked over. Her face had gone pale, and she looked queasy, one hand over her stomach. "My place is right up here," he said, wrenching the wheel just in time to make the turn.

Eliza just made a whimpering noise.

He drove fast and pulled up outside the Pink Palace with a screech. Eliza must have been in a bad way, because she didn't seem to notice the house, she just scrambled out of the car and hurried up the front path beside him. He unlocked and flipped on the lights.

"The bathroom's just down there," he said, pointing. "Do you need anything—"

She was already bolting for it, and closing the door with a slam. He heard a retching sound and winced.

Just when he thought the date was getting better. They really should win a prize.

He went to the kitchen and found some seltzer water, and then went to tap gently on the door. "Eliza? I'll leave some water out here. And there should be a fresh toothbrush in the drawer, if you need."

"Mneugh."

Her reply was halfway between a groan and a gurgle. Poor thing.

Then Cal's stomach rumbled.

He paused. It rumbled again, and then he felt a nauseous swell, lurching in the back of his throat.

Uh-oh. Just when he thought the night couldn't get any worse.

He turned and ran for the master bathroom.

~

Eliza wanted to die. Or maybe she was already dead. She couldn't tell. She'd been lying on the bathroom floor for hours, lifting her head only long enough to vomit into the toilet and pray for deliverance. Her skin was clammy, her mouth felt like a used gym sock, and she was so tired she could cry. But of course, she wasn't about to sleep anytime soon, not with the constant vomiting and all.

"Go on a date," she muttered aloud. "Give him a chance. What harm could it do?"

She rolled over and groaned. The tile floor was cool against her cheek, at least. From her vantage point, she could see it was actually a cute room, with blue walls and little fluffy clouds painted on the ceiling—which she'd been staring at all night, wishing she could float away.

There were worse places to spend the rest of her life.

She hadn't heard a peep from Cal for hours. Thank God his perfect manners included steering clear of her humiliation. Maybe that was a chapter in the Preppy Handbook: *A real gentleman never intrudes on a bout of food poisoning.*

Eliza cringed. Oh, what must he think of her now? First, she ruined the date with her bad clothes and spiky comments and awkwardness, and now she was camped out at his place, holding onto the toilet for dear life.

"Eliza?" There was a knock on the door. "Are you still alive in there?"

"No." Eliza closed her eyes. "The door's open. You can come laugh if you want."

"No laughing here." The door opened, and Eliza braced herself for Cal's look of handsome, smooth pity.

She opened her eyes.

"Oh. You too?"

"Me too." Cal slumped to the floor by the sink.

"You look terrible." Eliza couldn't believe it. There were dark shadows under his eyes, and his normally tanned skin had a clammy, pallid tone. He was wearing sweatpants and a baggy T-shirt that was stained with God knows what on the hem.

"You've been better, too." He pushed a bottle of water over to her. "Here. Drink."

"Can't move." Eliza very carefully shook her head. "But thanks."

"For what? Giving you food poisoning?" Cal tipped his head back against the wall and groaned. "It was the scallops, I bet."

"Don't!" Eliza felt her stomach lurch again. She sat up, grabbing the toilet rim. A breath. "False alarm," she sighed, and she slumped back down.

Cal gave a hollow laugh. "So much for wining and dining and sweeping you off your feet."

"That was the plan? Well, technically, you did get me on my back." Eliza shifted her weight and winced. After hours on the hard tile floor, her neck was killing her—but not enough to make her risk doing something drastic, like sitting upright. "Can I just move a mattress in here? I don't think I'm ever getting up again."

Cal paused, then slowly lurched to his feet. "Don't move."

"Ha," Eliza gave a hollow snort. "There's no risk of that."

She lay there, listening to his slow footsteps outside. It felt like the worst of the nausea had passed, at least for now. Now she just felt like a hollowed-out husk of a person. She didn't even want to imagine what she looked like, but if Cal was any indication, it wasn't pretty.

Those damn sparks had a lot to answer for.

The door swung open again. Cal dropped a couple of pillows down beside her, and threw a duvet down, too. "If you can't make it to the bedroom, the bedroom comes to you."

"You're a genius," Eliza said gratefully. She tugged one under her head and sighed. "That's better."

Cal sank back to the floor, his legs overlapping hers in the small space as he got comfortable. "I've never vomited so much in my life. There was the time we got caught in choppy waters during a buddy's bachelor party in Monaco, but this is worse."

"I once got the stomach flu, on a road trip to California," Eliza offered. "I spent two days in a motel dying quietly. But that seems like a vacation right now."

Cal chuckled, then stopped. "Oww, that hurts."

Eliza smiled. Now that they weren't sitting across the table in a fancy restaurant, trying to be polite, they were actually getting along. Go figure. She lay there a while, her eyes shut, trying to find the words. "Why is it so much easier like this?" she finally asked. "You and me, I mean."

Cal sighed. "I don't know."

She opened her eyes and turned her head to look at him. "I'm sorry I was such a bitch, back at the restaurant. I didn't mean to be. I just . . ." She trailed off. "Being in a place like that, it gets my hackles up. And those people . . ."

"I'm one of those people," Cal said, without any judgment in his eyes.

"I know! That's the problem." Eliza stared at the ceiling. "When I was younger, my dad had a teaching gig at this fancy prep school. We could have never afforded the tuition, but between his staff discount, and scholarships, I got to go. And it was . . . awful. Nobody let me forget for a second that I didn't belong there. And no matter how hard I worked, how much I tried to prove myself, it didn't make a difference. I was still just this outsider. So I figured if I couldn't join them, I'd beat them instead. They hated that," she remembered. "I took all their prizes, and the valedictorian spot, but . . . it was a battle. Every day, I was going to war. Same thing in college, with all those trust-fund kids getting all the good internships because daddy made a call. And now . . ." She sighed. "I know, I should be grown up, but it's like I can't see khakis without going into defense mode."

"Note to self, burn my khakis." Cal's voice was light. She looked at him again.

"This is my long-winded way of saying 'sorry.' "

"Then apology accepted," Cal said. He paused. "And if it helps, I know what you mean, about not belonging."

Eliza wondered how someone like him—handsome, confident, wealthy—could have ever felt like an outsider, but then he continued.

"After my parents died, it felt like I didn't have anywhere to call home anymore. I was just finishing college," he said, toying with the label on the water bottle, "so it wasn't as if I were some little orphan boy, but still, I felt . . . adrift. I spent the holidays with family, they always made sure I had a place to go, but . . . They weren't *mine*, the way Mom and Dad had been. I'd watch my cousin, Tish, and her parents together, and I would resent them." Cal gave a hollow laugh. "Even after everything they were doing for me, I was still jealous that they had each other, and I didn't have anyone. At least, it felt that way for a long time."

Eliza watched him grapple with the old memories. Then he gave a faint smile. "So, I hope I'm not like those assholes from school."

"You're not. I mean, look." She gestured weakly. "I screwed up our date in the most spectacular way, and you're still being nice and taking care of me."

Cal shook his head. "I've done my share of screwing this up, too. I mean, I get it: I didn't think about what it meant to have you fired. You were a name on a piece of paper to me, but that was your job, your life. And tonight . . ." He sighed.

"It's three a.m., so technically, it was last night," she joked.

He gave a strangled laugh. "I just assumed Beachwood was the move. You know, wine, candlelight . . ."

"Excruciating food poisoning."

"It gets the ladies swooning every time," he quipped. "But I know, I should have put more thought into it, instead of just rolling out the same old routine. You're different."

"Gee, thanks," Eliza said.

Cal met her eyes. "That's a good thing."

"So, those are your moves?" Eliza asked, flushing.

"Yes, ma'am." He smiled, a lazy, heart-stopping smile, and despite feeling like a rag doll, Eliza still felt that jolt of chemistry, hot in her blood.

"So what would have come next?" Eliza asked slowly, holding his gaze. "If I hadn't needed to rush straight for the nearest bathroom."

"Well, it's a beautiful night. We could have taken a walk on the beach . . ." Cal said.

"That sounds nice."

"And then, maybe I would have challenged you to go skinny-dipping."

"Why, Mr. Prescott." Eliza acted at fanning herself. "On the first date?"

He laughed. "I think we're past that, don't you?"

"Well, we are now. I usually don't become this comfortable in a man's bathroom until the fifth date, at least." Eliza managed a smile.

"Then I guess I still have moves, after all." Cal grinned, and she laughed.

"Easy there. I don't think it counts if we spend the night together moaning in pain."

"It's been a while since the last attack. I think the worst might be over." Cal looked around, and then tapped on the side of the wooden cabinet.

"Dear God, please." Eliza yawned. "I'm too tired to vomit anymore."

"Poor baby." Cal's tone was still light, but the words gave her a strange warm feeling in her chest all the same.

She snuggled lower, and tugged the duvet to cover her up. "Just so you know, this turned into a pretty great date."

"And just so you know," Cal said, his voice sleepy. "If I hadn't been vomiting for five hours straight, I would be kissing you goodnight right now."

Cal reached his hand across the bathroom floor, and nudged Eliza's fingers. She laced them through his, and she squeezed.

"And I would be kissing you back."

# 10

Eliza woke on a mattress of clouds, enveloped in the softest blanket in the world. Or maybe it just felt that way compared to the bathroom floor. She lifted her head and squinted at the unfamiliar surroundings. She was in the guest bedroom, she figured: a neat, pink room illuminated by sunlight burning the edges of the closed drapes.

How did she get here?

Cal must have moved her after she passed out. Eliza's heart caught, and she snuck a look under the covers, but she was still dressed in those ratty shorts and her sweaty, wrinkled top from last night. Was that better or worse than the alternative? Eliza wasn't sure, but she was relieved at least to find a glass of water and some Advil on the nightstand.

She slowly sat up and waited for her stomach to lurch. Nothing.

*Hallelujah*!

Eliza got up and cautiously pushed the door ajar. She could hear music and the sound of somebody moving around, so she padded barefoot down the hallway, adjusting to the bright daylight.

"Hey."

Eliza paused. Cal was in the kitchen, looking more handsome than any man who'd spent the night vomiting had a right to be. His hair was damp from the shower, and he was bare-chested, wearing a loose pair of sweatpants, with a coffee mug in one hand and a spatula in the other.

Her heart shivered. Just a half-beat, a flicker in her chest, but she felt it, everywhere.

*She knew him now.*

"Hi." Eliza gulped. "Feeling better?"

"Finally." Cal smiled at her, warm and easy, and it was enough to make her forget she was a walking disaster in last night's clothes.

For five whole seconds.

"What time is it?" Eliza looked around. The back door was open, and the sun was high in the sky.

"Almost one."

"In the afternoon?" she yelped.

Cal chuckled. "I figured I'd let you sleep. Something tells me you're not a morning person." He strolled closer and offered her a mug. "Coffee?"

"Yes, please." Eliza took a gulp, her brain still foggy.

"Are you up to eating?" Cal asked. "I made some bacon and eggs—" Eliza shuddered. "Or there's toast," he finished. "Dry toast."

"That's probably safer." Eliza clutched her mug, watching him move effortlessly around the small space. "How are you so bright and shiny?"

"I bounce back fast." Cal flashed a grin. "And I have an iron constitution. Most of the time."

He stuck a couple of slices bread in the toaster, refilled

their coffee cups, and assembled two plates, nudging Eliza out to the back porch. She took a long, steadying breath of sea air and finally felt more stable.

"Wait," she said, looking around properly for the first time. "You live in the Pink Palace? I love this house! My mom tried to start a campaign to get Marion to repaint it, but she just laughed in her face."

Cal rejoined her, wearing a loose T-shirt this time. "That sounds like Marion. She's my godmother," he explained. "So I'm using it as a home base. I'm supposed to be looking at properties later, with June Somerville. You know her?"

"Yup." Eliza laughed. "Watch out for her. She has a thing for younger guys."

Cal blinked. "Thanks for the warning."

Eliza nibbled her toast. She was ravenous, but she wasn't about to risk another night on the bathroom floor. She snuck a look at Cal, suddenly feeling self-conscious. Last night, their defenses had been down, but now, in the harsh light of day, she wondered what was going on in his head.

"So, last night was . . . interesting." Cal gave her a mischievous grin across the table.

Eliza relaxed. "Unforgettable, you could say," she agreed.

"I'll pretend that's because of my charm and good company," Cal said, smirking. "And not the—"

"Part that we will never speak of again," Eliza finished for him.

"Deal." He toasted his coffee cup to hers. "Do you have much planned for the day?"

Eliza shook her head. "I have the day off from the restaurant, so I was going to help out with some things at the house. And sleep," she added, stifling a yawn. "All the sleep."

Cal paused, glancing away for a moment. "If you wanted, we could—"

He was interrupted by woman's voice. "Cal? Are you here?"

Cal looked surprised. "We're in the back!" he called, and a moment later, a polished blonde woman rounded the side of the house, toting a leather overnight bag.

"Didn't you hear me? I've been knocking forever. And traffic was a nightmare coming down."

Eliza's heart sank as Cal got to his feet, greeting the woman with a hug. Her mind raced with the possibilities: Girlfriend? Casual hookup? He hadn't mentioned a sister . . .

"Did they ticket you for speeding again?" he was teasing her.

"That was one time!" the woman protested, socking him in the arm. "And he never actually wrote the ticket, we went for dinner instead. What is this place?" She pulled down her sunglasses and peered around. "You can practically see it from space."

Her eyes alighted on Eliza, and she arched one perfectly-sculpted brow. "Oh, you have company."

Eliza gave an awkward wave. "Hi."

Cal smiled. "Tish, meet Eliza. Eliza, this is my cousin, Letitia."

*Cousin.* Eliza felt a wave of relief—which was quickly followed by a bigger wave of embarrassment. Tish was wearing designer jeans and a casual white button-down, but everything about them screamed money and style, while Eliza was still in last night's clothes.

Her sweaty, wrinkled, possibly vomit-stained clothes.

"Wait, didn't Dad tell you I was coming?" Tish turned back to Cal. She saw the blank look on his face and sighed. "So, you don't desperately need my help preparing for the board meeting next week?"

Cal made a face. "I didn't even know there was a meeting scheduled."

"It was in the email sent out Monday. Please tell me you're at least checking emails," she added, her voice turning plaintive. "I know you're doing this whole 'vacation' thing"—Tish said it like a dirty word—"but the Prescott Group doesn't stop working when you do."

This was definitely family business. Eliza got to her feet. "I should go," she said, putting down her coffee.

"No, don't." Cal turned back to her. "This won't take long."

"Really, it's fine. My mom will probably have called the police by now," Eliza added brightly. "And I really need to take a shower."

Cal grinned. "OK, I'm not going to argue with that one."

"Gee, thanks." Their eyes caught, and Eliza felt her skin prickle again. Why did it feel so *intimate*, just looking at this man in broad daylight? She looked away. "Are my things . . . ?"

"By the door. I'll drive you." Cal moved to join her, but Eliza shook her head.

"I can see myself out! It's just a short walk. Tish, great to meet you," she babbled. "Cal . . . I'll, umm, see you around."

Eliza turned on her heel and fled into the house, grabbing her things and rushing out the door before they both could take in the true extent of her grossness.

Or smell it.

Cal watched Eliza bolt out of the house and wondered if he should go after her. Any other girl, he would insist on driving her home, but Eliza was so stubborn, he didn't want to put his foot down and overrule her—and risk ruining the fragile détente they'd miraculously created.

The scallops had been good for something.

"She seems . . . nice."

He turned back to Tish, who was watching him with an amused look.

"Very, down to earth," she continued. "*Au naturel.*"

"Nice try." Cal sat back down and finished wolfing his breakfast. "You'd look under the weather too, if you'd spent half the night up with food poisoning."

Tish burst out in a peal of laughter. "She didn't?"

"We both did."

Tish joined him at the table, looking around with naked curiosity. "Well, at least you're finding some kind of distraction out here. That's what you wanted, right? A break from reality."

"Eliza's not just a distraction." Cal was surprised how forceful his response came out, but it was true. And after last night . . . he wasn't sure what Eliza was, but it was a hell of a lot more than just a passing temptation.

Tish arched her eyebrows, but didn't press. "Dad *is* worried about you," she continued. "And so am I. I get it, you pushed yourself too hard with the takeover and all the layoffs, but you can't hide out here forever."

"Why not?" Cal said, half-joking, but Tish frowned.

"Because you're CEO of the company, and you have thousands of people looking to you for leadership. Honestly, Cal, anyone would think you didn't want to be the one in charge."

"Well, when you make it sound like such a party . . ." Cal said dryly.

Tish rolled her eyes, but she was smiling all the same. They'd grown up together, playing during family vacations, and then later, sneaking out to parties together as teens. After his parents had passed, they'd become closer. Well, as close as it was possibly to get to Tish, who kept her feelings under lock and key. She focused all her energy on the company instead: business school, then internships and board meetings, running the PR department with an iron fist. Cal often thought she would make a better CEO than him, and Tish probably agreed, but the Prescott tradition meant he would sit in his father's seat, the best *man* for the job.

"So, what are you waiting for?" Tish opened her bag and pulled out her slim laptop and a bundle of files. "There were some numbers in the last quarterly we should talk about, and have you seen the figures out of Tulsa?"

Yup, she was all business.

THEY WORKED ALL AFTERNOON, UNTIL CAL PUT HIS FOOT DOWN. "You didn't come all this way to stare at a computer screen," he insisted, dragging her into town for some ice cream. "Besides, didn't you tell me that productivity declines after three hours?"

"Technically, we should be working in twenty-minute bursts," Tish corrected him. "That's when studies show peak attention is maximized."

"She'll have two scoops," Cal told the guy at the window. "And extra sprinkles."

Tish made a noise of protest, but she happily took the cone in the end. Cal claimed his rocky road, and they started strolling across the square and down towards the harbor road. "It's very . . . charming." Tish sounded suspicious, taking in the children playing on the green, and the group of older women doing yoga in the shade of the oak trees. "Not your usual scene."

"I don't have a scene." Cal licked his ice cream, but Tish hooted.

"Tell that to the concierge in Aspen. Or St. Barts. Or—"

"OK, I get it," he cut her off. "And maybe I felt like a change. A slower pace, less drama."

"You do have a skill for finding the drama. Or rather,

finding the girls who love it." Tish gave him a sidelong look. "So, about this Elizabeth . . ."

"Eliza," Cal corrected her. "And what about her?"

"Is she a local?"

"Would it matter if she was?" he challenged, feeling strangely protective.

"No." Tish looked thoughtful. "But it would make long-distance harder. I mean, with the hours you work, and the travel . . ."

"We've been on one date," Cal objected. "Maybe don't get carried away planning our future just yet."

"Of course, what am I thinking?" Tish grinned. "You don't do real relationships. I'll be surprised if you make it to next week."

Cal frowned. "I'm not that bad."

"Really?" Tish licked her cone. "You haven't dated anyone seriously since . . . Charlotte Fortescue, wasn't it? And that was three years ago."

Cal paused. He'd been so busy with the company, he hadn't had time to really get involved with anyone, but still, he didn't realize it was that long since he'd been on more than a handful of dates with the same woman.

"What happened to Charlotte, anyway?" Tish continued. "I liked her."

"So did I," Cal said, remembering their six-month relationship. "But she also liked my friend James, and the dive coach, and her tennis instructor . . ."

"Probably for the best." Tish made a face. "You guys wouldn't have lasted."

He turned, surprised. "Why not? Uncle Arthur and your mom were always telling me she'd make the perfect addition to the Prescott family."

"Perfectly boring." Tish curled her lip. "I mean, she was pretty, I guess. And polished, and from a good family . . ."

Cal laughed at her expression. "Is that such a bad thing?"

"Oh right, I forgot, your idea of a great date is someone who just bats her eyelashes and agrees with everything you say."

"Hey!" Cal protested. He thought of Eliza, with her stubbornly sarcastic comments, refusing to fall for his usual charm. She definitely wasn't agreeable. Which is why he couldn't get her out of his head.

She was different. Infuriatingly, intriguingly different from any woman he'd known.

"So maybe my past dates have had a few things in common," Cal admitted, thinking back over the list of beautiful socialites he'd been involved with over the past few years. High on elegance and drama, low on in-depth conversation.

Tish snorted. "Understatement of the year."

"But aren't you always telling me that whoever we choose as a partner, we're bringing them into the family?" Cal must have heard the lecture a hundred times, from everyone from his grandmother down to distant cousins. A Prescott bride will have responsibilities, just like he had. They would need to be at ease with the social scene, act as hostess for business functions and charity events alike, and always, *always* respect the traditions of the family.

Cal hadn't taken their advice too seriously, but it had always been in the back of his mind. Besides, the circles he moved in, he couldn't help but meet likely candidates: cultured, sophisticated women from the right families who would fit perfectly into the Prescott world . . .

If he hadn't kept getting bored after just a few dates.

Maybe that was why Eliza was such a breath of fresh air. She didn't care about his family or status. If anything, they counted against him. For once, he was trying to prove he was more than just the Prescott name.

And he liked it.

"All I'm saying is a real partner isn't just someone who can host a tea party," Tish said. "What about this Eliza? Is she another of your future socialites?"

Cal snorted, trying to imagine Eliza in pearls serving tea and cucumber sandwiches. "Definitely not. She's a journalist," he added. "She's the one who wrote that profile of Aunt Julie."

Tish almost spit out her ice cream. "Are you serious? Oh my God, my dad wanted to sue. And you're dating her?"

Cal smiled. "I couldn't help it."

"Well . . ." Tish gave him another look, but this one was almost impressed. "Good luck, I guess."

Cal didn't reply, but he couldn't resist pulling out his phone. *Feeling better?* he texted to Eliza.

A moment later, a reply came. *Finally. I've never been so glad to take a shower.*

Cal was slammed with a vision of her, naked under the spray.

How did breathing work again?

"You OK?" Tish's voice came from beside him. "You look . . . tense."

That was one way of putting it.

"I'm fine," Cal said quickly, and tapped out a response on his phone. *Want company next time?*

A bubble of speech appeared on his screen, then disappeared again. He wondered what Eliza was typing—and deleting.

Did she have a spark of adrenaline in her veins, like him? Was she trying to compose just the right flirtatious message?

Finally, her message popped up.

*No comment.*

Cal couldn't hide his smile. He glanced up to find Tish watching him, looking amused. "What?"

"Nothing." She grinned. "Just, this is going to be interesting."

Cal sure hoped so.

# 11

Eliza had thought she was too old for this. Composing flirty texts, obsessively checking her phone . . . But now she felt like a teenager all over again, her stomach turning an excited flip every time she heard the telltale buzz of a new notification.

*So when do we try round two?*

*What, chicken pox?* she typed back.

*I was thinking a bout of flu, but I'm a flexible guy.*

*Oh, really?*

*;-)*

The messages flew back and forth all day long, while Eliza tried to pull herself together. Nothing had happened, she told herself. Not really. Nothing except one epic kiss, days ago, and a strange night together on the bathroom floor. It didn't make sense that her heart was beating faster, and she felt a quick-silver anticipation just remembering the way he'd looked at her over the breakfast table . . .

*Argh!*

Eliza despaired. She'd meant to scratch the itch and get him out of her system for good, but now, she only wanted him more. Which was crazy. Cal Prescott was living on another planet, the kind inhabited by glossy blonde women with trust funds and ponies and perfectly plucked eyebrows—the last twenty-four hours had proven that in spades. It was dangerous to get caught up like this, when she knew it would never lead anywhere.

Except . . .

Cal wasn't like that.

As much as she wished she could write him off as the arrogant playboy she'd thought he was, Eliza knew better now. Sure, he was a Prescott, and had grown up with all the wealth and privilege that that name meant, but there was more to him, too. The space his parents' death had left, his sense of duty and obligation. His playful spirit, and that razor-sharp mind . . .

Eliza felt shivers all over again just replaying their whip-fast conversations. She couldn't pick which turned her on more: that taut, toned body, or his wicked tongue. Together, they were a deadly combination.

*Don't forget the mayonnaise.*

Eliza stopped, confused, before she checked the message sender. It was her mother. Linda had thankfully been out at the library when Eliza finally arrived home in all her disheveled glory, and she'd rushed out again straight after cleaning up to avoid any interrogation. But she couldn't hide out in the *Caller* office forever, so Eliza braced herself and headed home.

To find a very familiar sedan parked out front.

Cal's.

Her heart did that inconvenient skip again. "Hello?" Eliza tried to sound casual as she ventured into the house.

"We're back here!" her mom's voice came.

Eliza paused a moment in the hallway to check her reflection. Clean hair, cute shirt . . . Compared to last night, she could be wearing a fresh burlap sack and she'd still make a better impression, but she still felt a flicker of nervous anticipation as she headed through to the back porch, where Cal and her mom were sitting in the evening sun.

"Eliza, sweetie, there you are. I was getting ready to send out a search party." Linda beamed at her, looking like the cat who got the cream. Or rather, the mother who had the most eligible bachelor in town held captive with a cup of tea.

"Sorry, I didn't realize we had company." Eliza shot Cal an apologetic look. "Have you been waiting long?"

"Just a half hour or so." Cal smiled at her. He was looking effortless and handsome again, in jeans and one of those button-down shirts. He'd always looked good, but now that she'd caught a glimpse of what was underneath that cotton—

*Nope.* She wasn't thinking about that—especially not with her mother sitting right there.

"I was just telling Calvin about your very first newspaper gig," Linda said proudly. "When you were ten."

Eliza groaned. "You didn't!"

"What? It was so charming," Linda continued, giving Cal a doting smile. "She wrote up reports on the neighborhood pets, with news on the anti-littering campaign."

"A Pulitzer prize-winner in the making." Cal's eyes were teasing.

"You know, Calvin here has all kinds of connections in the media," Linda continued. "I'm sure he would be able to introduce you to some people if you asked. Eliza is between jobs," she continued, oblivious about their history. "But someone would be lucky to snap her up. She's hard-working, smart, beautiful . . ."

"Are you trying to get me hired or pimp me out?" Eliza couldn't help asking.

Her mom gave her a look. "Eliza!"

"Sorry." She took a deep breath and tried to relax. "Why don't you put another pot of tea on, Mom? So I can see what Cal wants. Alone." She gave her mom a meaningful look. Linda leapt to her feet.

"Of course! You know, I owe Debra a call . . ."

"It was lovely chatting with you, Mrs. Bennett," Cal said smoothly, getting to his feet.

She blushed. "Oh, call me Linda, please!" She hovered a moment longer. Eliza nodded to the door, and finally her mom disappeared into the house.

Eliza exhaled. "I'm so, so sorry. Let me guess, she quizzed you about your prospects and intentions?"

Cal grinned. "Don't worry, I passed with flying colors."

"It's not you I'm worried about." Eliza took a seat and scoped out the tea table. "Wow, you really are her new favorite person. She keeps these fancy biscuits under lock and key."

"See, there are perks to dating me." Cal offered her the plate, but Eliza hesitated.

"Is that what I'm doing?"

"If I have my way with you, yes."

Their eyes caught, and a surge of heat rolled through Eliza, slow as golden molasses. She flushed. "Here on the porch?" she quipped, looking away. "My mom might have a few things to say about that."

Cal laughed. "Well, then for your mother's sake, I can wait."

Eliza took a cookie and tried to think of normal conversation that didn't involve tearing each other's clothes off. "Your cousin seems nice."

"She is." Cal's expression relaxed.

"Is she staying with you long?"

He laughed. "No. Tish's style is more room service and 24-hour concierge. She's at a hotel just up the coast. The Sandy Lane hotel?"

"I know it." Eliza nodded. "My friend, Brooke, is the manager."

There was a pause. She glanced up and caught his gaze again. They both laughed, almost awkward. At least she wasn't the only one feeling self-conscious after the other night.

"I believe I owe you a date," Cal said smoothly. "One that doesn't end in total disaster. When are you free?"

"How about now?"

Cal looked surprised, and Eliza remembered too late that she was supposed to be playing it cool, or hard to get, or any of the other things to disguise her real feelings. But she'd never been one for games. Somehow, they'd arrived at this strange, delicious connection, and she didn't want to let it slip away.

"But we do this my way," she added quickly, thinking of another stuffy restaurant. "No more Michelin stars."

Cal smiled. "I can live with that."

"OK." Eliza's pulse skipped, and she got to her feet. "I'll be right down."

She hightailed it up to her room and quickly changed her clothes. This time, she took her sister's advice, and pulled on a pretty set of matching lingerie in peach silk before yanking a loose sweater dress over her head. She shoved a light jacket in her bag, then she paused, before adding a fresh pair of underwear, deodorant, and a toothbrush.

Maybe she was planning too far, but this time, she would be prepared. And if one thing led to another . . . ?

At least she would be fresh and fragrant come morning!

THEY TOOK ELIZA'S CAR, AND EVEN THOUGH IT WASN'T AS luxurious as Cal's, she felt a shot of confidence taking her seat behind the wheel. This time, she was literally in the driver's seat. No feeling out of her depth, or over her head, or any of the other dozen metaphors she could use to describe the off-kilter sensation she got around him.

"So, where to?" Cal asked, sounding amused, and Eliza realized she hadn't even turned on the engine yet.

She flushed, and turned the key in the ignition. "I figured I'd give you a tour of some of my favorite local spots," she said, backing up and driving up the bumpy lane. "Lobster rolls at Pete's, drinks at the Shipwreck, and then the bakery for dessert. Summer does a mean mud pie."

"You got your appetite back, then?" Cal laughed.

"You can't keep me down long."

Eliza turned on the old AM radio, and found her favorite station of country classics. It was clouding over, that crackle in the air that spelled a storm, and as she breathed in the salty air, she felt the anticipation, just as electric in her veins.

"This is a great car," Cal remarked, relaxing back in his seat. "A classic."

"If by that, you mean old and temperamental, then sure." Eliza patted the cherry-red frame affectionately. "I worked three summers slinging popcorn at the local movie theater saving up for her. Mom threw a fit, of course, but me and my dad fixed her up ourselves. He always joked that this way, everyone would see me coming."

"I didn't."

Eliza turned and caught a heavy-lidded gaze from Cal. *Wow*. She blushed again, and fixed her focus on the road.

"He was a professor, wasn't he? Your father."

She nodded. "He taught history. He had a thing for nineteenth-century botanists."

"Really? That's . . . specific."

Eliza grinned. "I know. I always figured he was born in the wrong era. He was one of those gentleman scholars, spectacles and tweed. He loved hiding away with his books, or in the greenhouse. God, that greenhouse." She smiled at the memory. "He built the whole thing from scratch in our backyard. It drove Mom crazy. She always complained that if there was a fire, he'd save his notebooks first, then the seeds, then her."

"What about you and your sister?"

Eliza laughed. "Dad always figured we were smart enough to take care of ourselves."

"He sounds like a great guy."

"He was." Eliza swallowed back the well of sadness in her throat. "He'd like you."

"He would?" Cal seemed surprised.

"I think so." Eliza could just imagine them, sitting around, talking about some obscure Victorian botanist. "Or you'd argue in circles, but he liked that too."

"So that's where you get it from."

"Hey!" Eliza laughed. "You can talk. You love arguing. And I'm probably the only one who gives you a hard time."

"You're right about that." Cal paused, almost rueful. "I tell everyone to be straight with me, but, well . . ."

"Nobody's going to point out when you're crazy if you're the boss," Eliza finished for him.

"Exactly."

She turned down the winding, leafy road that led to Pete's: a bare-bones shack overlooking the water, set beside the mini-golf course. "Don't be fooled by the paper plates," she told Cal, pulling up in the already packed parking spot. "Pete serves the best lobster rolls in town."

"Don't let Declan hear you say that," he teased, getting out of the car. Eliza joined him, and they took a place in line along with the other locals, and a few early-season tourists in the know.

She snorted. "Are you kidding? The guy thrives on competition. I told him his coq au vin was *almost* the best I'd tasted, and he spent the rest of the afternoon locked in the kitchen, working on more."

"I'll have to remember that move," Cal said. "Maybe if I remind him Bobby Flay has a dozen restaurants, he'll finally agree to expand our empire."

She turned, surprised. "You're an investor?"

"Just for fun," Cal replied, casually. "He was always going on about the kind of place he'd open, so I told him to put my money where his mouth was."

"Oh." Eliza blinked. She didn't know much about the restaurant trade, but she had an idea how much investment it took to get somewhere like Sage open—and how risky the whole endeavor was. Cal was talking about it like he'd wagered five bucks on a bet, not six figures.

"Uh-oh," Cal said suddenly. "You've got that look again."

"What look?"

"The one like you've just remembered I'm a rich asshole." He grinned, looking so sunny and un-self-conscious that Eliza had to laugh.

"No," she protested. "Well, OK. Kind of. I just forget sometimes, how different we are."

Cal held her gaze. "No," he said, with an unreadable expression on his face. "We're the same, you and me. That's why we can't stay away from each other."

And then he leaned in and kissed her, right there in the line, sandwiched between a screaming toddler and a couple of high-schoolers, with the scent of fried food wafting in the breeze.

Hot, and swift, and *right*.

His lips only brushed hers for a moment, but it was enough to send her world spinning off its axis all over again.

"Next!"

A yell broke through her daze, and Eliza stumbled back to

find the guy at the counter waiting—and the line rumbling behind them.

Cal looked around and chuckled. "To be continued," he murmured before stepping up to the window. Eliza flushed and tried to focus, but the last thing she cared about was food.

Would it be rude to drag Cal back to the car right now and find a quiet spot to park?

*Down, girl,* she warned herself. She was trying to get to know the man, not just ravish him. Even if his kisses left her reeling, she could pull it together long enough to have a conversation.

Besides, it wasn't just food—it was fuel. For what hopefully was a long night ahead.

Eliza stifled a smile at the thought as they carried their trays over to a picnic table overlooking the shoreline. Between them, they had quite a spread, with lobster rolls, fries, and cups of the corn chowder she could never resist.

On a meal like this, they could last all night.

"Do I even want to know what that smile is about?" Cal asked, nudging her shoulder as they sat side by side.

"That depends." Eliza grinned. She felt like a kid on Christmas Eve, full of delicious anticipation for the fun to come. "Play your cards right, and maybe you'll find out."

"Now those are fighting words," Cal chuckled, giving her a wolfish look. "Because you should know, I never back down from a challenge."

"Oh really?" Eliza said, dunking a fry in the cup of ketchup. She took a bite, savoring the crisp, hot taste. "How's your mini-golf game?"

"A little rusty, but I can bring it." Cal smiled. They were right beside the course, complete with faded windmill and a pair of devilish clown obstacles. Eliza had played every summer, going back as far as she could remember.

“Want to bet on that?” she asked, casual, as if she didn’t know every play by heart. “Winner takes all.”

“Done.” Cal grinned. “You need to work on your poker face,” he added, leaning over to steal a fry from her. “You’ve got ‘hustler’ written all over it.”

“Have not!” Eliza protested.

“I don’t mind.” Cal gave her a look. “Something tells me losing to you might be the most fun I’ve had for ages.”

# 12

Cal was going crazy.

Confident, argumentative Eliza already sent his blood boiling with red-hot lust, but this Eliza—flirty and bold, full of teasing half-glances and lingering touches—had just about robbed him of coherent thought. She tormented him all through the game of mini-golf: brushing casually against him and leaning over to make her shot. She'd won easily, of course, and it had nothing to do with his game. It was all he could do to keep stringing two words together, trying his hardest to block the X-rated thoughts that flooded his treacherous mind.

He was a gentleman, dammit. His parents had raised him right. And fantasizing about laying her down right there on the mini-golf green was not something a gentleman would do.

"What do you think?" Eliza's voice pulled him back to reality, to their second stop of the night. The narrow bar was crammed on a back street in Provincetown, and Eliza swore it was the best spot for a drink. It was starting to rain, just a light splatter of drops as they approached the entry, and they hurried their pace.

"I like it." Cal ducked under the low doorframe and looked around. "Very . . . private." The place was dim and divey, with dark walls and cracked leather booths that had seen better days.

"I like Riley's," Eliza continued. "But sometimes, it's nice to be anonymous."

He agreed. He could only imagine the gossip if they were at a local haunt—and he was looking at Eliza like he wanted to slowly strip her naked.

"What do you want?" Eliza asked.

*You,* he wanted to reply. *Now.*

"Whiskey," he answered instead. "On the rocks." A drink was the last thing he needed when he already felt drunk on her, but this was a date, and he was finally getting it right this time.

"Coming right up. Winner buys." Eliza winked and headed to the bar, her hips swinging.

Cal tried not to notice how half the men in the bar turned to check her out. He couldn't blame them. He picked a table instead, a booth half-hidden in the shadows, and tried to pull himself together.

How long could he politely wait before dragging her to bed?

It had been an hour at least since he'd kissed her, and Cal was already in withdrawal. He'd never felt like this before, craving a woman with such a raw, animal need. Her touch. Her kiss. A smile. He was a red-blooded man, sure, but Eliza set something in him burning out of control, and he was just about ready to give up on fighting it.

The only question was, did she feel it too?

"Here you go." Eliza arrived back with their drinks. "It's a 25-year," she added, sliding in beside him. "They don't put it out for the tourists, but Mackenzie told me to ask special."

"She's the artist." Cal tried to keep it straight. "Dating Jake? And Summer is the baker, she's with the guy from the bookstore. Grayson."

"That's right." Eliza broke into a grin. "But you can relax, there won't be a quiz."

"But I want to know about your friends." Cal looked around the cozy bar, a world away from the fancy designer places in the city. "You've built a life here."

Eliza paused. "I guess so." She looked thoughtful. "I always thought Boston was home, but I've been spending so much time here this past year, it's sort of crept up on me."

"Do you think you'd ever settle here full-time?" Cal asked, remembering Tish's questions about long-distance romance and the future. He'd laughed it off at the time, but now he found himself leaning in to hear her answer.

Eliza took a sip and slowly licked her lips.

"Maybe. I always pictured it, but when I was older. Retiring down here, splitting the beach house with Paige like two old spinsters," she said, smiling. "What about you? Fancy taking on the Pink Palace for good?"

Cal tried to think straight. "Maybe. Who knows? Sometimes life can send you in . . . unexpected directions."

Like the back booth of a dive bar, hanging on every word from a pair of cherry-red lips. Eliza smiled, her eyes sparkling in the dark, and Cal had to reach for her. He took her hand in his and slowly caressed the hollow against her thumb.

Eliza's lips parted. Her gaze met his, and he saw the silent inhale of breath as her cheeks flooded with color.

God, she was beautiful.

Eliza glanced down and threaded her fingers through his. Slowly, almost shyly, she stroked her thumb over the smooth curve of his palm.

Cal felt it like a thunderbolt. One touch, and his body was demanding more.

He knocked back the rest of his drink in a single swallow. "Let's go," he said, his voice emerging harshly. "Now."

Eliza's eyes widened. "What about dessert?"

He leaned in, whispering in her ear. "I'm going to taste you. Slowly."

She met his eyes, and the desire he saw there took his breath away. Eliza nodded, wordless, and Cal pulled her to her feet. He threw down some bills and then practically dragged her to the exit. He needed to be somewhere alone with her, now, before this spark between them blazed out of control.

Outside the bar, the street was empty in the rain, street-lights reflecting off the wet cobblestones. "Where did you park?" Cal looked around. Eliza pulled out her keys and hit the lock button, and he heard the distant sound of a beep.

"Over there!" They took off at a run, the rain coming down harder now, cold and wet. But even the showers couldn't dampen his lust. He yanked on her hand, tugging her back to him, and kissed her, right there in the middle of the street.

The sparks caught, and just like that, he was on fire.

Eliza's mouth was hot, searching, and Cal drank her in. She clutched his shirt collar, pulling him down to meet her as his hands gripped her waist and their bodies pressed closer. She tasted like whiskey and chocolate, sweet and smooth and smoky, and he couldn't get enough, her body soft and sinful under his roving hands, and his tongue plunged deep between her lips, demanding more.

Eliza dragged her mouth from his. "Wait," she panted. "Not here."

"Eliza . . ." Cal groaned, too far gone to stop now.

"Do you want us to catch pneumonia?" she challenged. "Because with our track record . . ."

He paused. "Good point."

Cal managed to keep his hands to himself until they were safely back in her car. She started the engine and put the heaters on full.

"You're wet through," Cal said, his eyes drawn to the way her damp dress hugged her skin. "I need to get you out of those clothes."

Eliza laughed. "For the sake of my health?"

"Absolutely."

Eliza leaned in and kissed him again, hot and swift, and Cal cursed whoever hadn't invented teleportation just yet. He needed this woman. God, his whole body was craving her. But somehow, he had to keep it together long enough for her to drive them back down the coast, while he sat there beside her, his hand resting on her bare thigh, stroking idle circles on her skin.

"Don't." Eliza moved his hand aside. "I can't focus with you touching me."

He drank her in with his eyes instead, her profile flushed in the dark.

She shivered again. "I can't focus with you *looking* at me."

Cal had to smile. "Eyes on the road," he said, and dragged his gaze away. How did she do this to him? Just the presence of her beside him in the driver's seat was enough to make his blood boil, hot with desire. He said a silent prayer of thanks as the crossroads came up ahead of them, and she made the turn towards his place. Any farther, and he might have had to make her pull over and park in the woods, like they were a couple of randy teenagers.

She parked haphazardly out front and bolted from the car, but Cal was faster. He unlocked, flung open the door, and dragged her inside.

"Clothes. Off," he demanded, already reaching for her.

He didn't need to ask twice.

They stumbled down the dark hallway, shedding clothes and stealing kisses, until Cal lifted her clear off her feet and set her down in the bathroom. Eliza was stripped down to her underwear now, and he turned the shower on, filling the room with hot steam.

"I was kidding, about the pneumonia," she grinned, breathless.

"I'm not taking any chances." Cal kissed her, hot and deep. She moaned against his mouth, and God, he couldn't have wanted her more. He pulled her back into the shower stall, still half-dressed, and kissed her harder, up against the tile with the hot water pouring down on them.

Eliza tugged at his damp shirt, fumbling with the buttons until she let out a low curse and ripped it open instead. "Whoops," she said, wicked there in the dark.

"I'll live." Cal pushed off his jeans and buried his face against her neck. He tasted her, licking against the tender hollow of her throat and kissing lower, over the lacy swell of her breasts, as Eliza gasped and pressed against his mouth, wriggling free of her bra.

"Cal," she moaned softly, and damn, if it wasn't the sweetest sound he'd ever heard. His hands devoured her, caressing every inch until he found the heat between her thighs, and Eliza's breath hitched, and her voice caught, and he dropped to his knees.

But Cal already knew a taste would never be enough.

Eliza was in heaven. Or hell. She couldn't tell which, because the things Cal was doing to her were so devilishly divine, she could barely manage coherent thought at all.

"Cal . . ." she moaned aloud, flushing to hear the blatant need in her voice. But God, she couldn't help it, not with his hands on her, and his mouth, and that *tongue*.

The things he could do with his tongue.

Cal murmured against her, licking deeper, and it was all Eliza could do to sink back against the tile and try to keep standing. The water beat down on her, hot and slick, and she clutched his shoulders for balance, her fingers tangling in his wet hair. Over and over, he licked against her, teasing with his lips and fingertips, until she was wound tight, gasping, strung out on the edge.

But still, somehow, she couldn't fall.

Eliza tried to relax, but it was *him*. Cal Prescott. She shouldn't want him like this. She shouldn't let her guard down, moaning and begging in his arms, a world away from the polished, lady-like women he must be used to dating. She didn't want to let him see her, out of control with nothing held back.

*Be quiet,* she ordered herself. *Just relax, and let it go.*

Of all the times to go overthinking something.

But now the thoughts were rattling in her brain, she couldn't shut them off. What was he thinking? Was she being too loud? Or not loud enough? Eliza could feel the heat slipping away as she lost the moment, until Cal paused, and glanced up.

"Everything OK?" He gave her a lazy smile, his fingertips still circling on her inner thigh.

"Great!" she replied, too loud. "A-plus effort."

Cal laughed, looking surprised. "I didn't realize we were grading."

Eliza burned. "Sorry, I just meant . . ." She gulped. "Good work."

He rose to his feet and brushed wet hair back from her face. "I feel like I lost you back there."

Eliza cringed. "Sorry. It's not you. My brain switched on, and . . ." She gave a helpless shrug.

"Well, how about we try switching it off again?" Cal leaned in and kissed her again, slow and unhurried, and Eliza melted into his embrace. "Better?" he whispered, kissing slowly down her neck.

"Mmmhmm."

He nibbled on her earlobe, his breath sending hot shivers down her spine. His hands teased over her again, teasing against her curves, and Eliza slowly exhaled. Now they were talking. She ran her fingertips over his chest, exploring the expanse of taut muscle and smooth, tanned skin, and Cal shivered beneath her touch, his body pressing hard against her.

She tugged his face down to kiss him again, the spark igniting, low in her belly. Harder, deeper. Cal shut the water off, and they stumbled back, out of the shower. He grabbed some towels, enveloping her in the softness, and guided her down the hallway, stealing kisses until she was breathless again.

"Don't think," he murmured in her ear, his hands teasing her breasts and over the slope of her stomach. "Don't think about this, just feel. My hands on your body," he continued, his voice low and thick with desire. "Feel how much I want you. God, Eliza . . . You make me crazy. Since the day we met, all I've wanted is you."

Cal was poised above her, illuminated in moonlight through the window. The look in his eyes sent shivers right through her: hot, and wanting, and somehow, so real.

This time, she didn't have to listen to her secret insecurities; Cal's kiss blotted them all away. His body was hard against her, pressing her back into the mattress with a delicious weight.

She wrapped her legs around him, urging him closer, writhing now with a fresh, sharp need. His mouth grazed lower, kissing and sucking her nipples into stiff peaks, as his fingers dipped into her wetness, making her clench and moan. He lifted himself, reaching for the nightstand, and then Eliza surprised herself, rolling them so she was straddling him, on top.

She took the condom from him and slowly rolled it over his hard length. Cal shuddered under her hands, watching her with a look of pure, glazed desire.

She felt invincible. Beautiful.

In control again.

"Remember," she whispered, lowering herself against him. "Winner takes all."

Cal's eyes fell shut, and he groaned as she began to move. His hands gripped her thighs, and he rose to thrust with her, urging her on. This time, Eliza didn't hold back. She moved with him, chasing the sweet itch that curled, tempting, right in the heart of her. Over and over, she surged against him, determined.

And then Cal rolled them, flipping her onto her back beneath him, and she realized her sense of control was an illusion. Because she could never hold back, not when he felt so good, moving deep inside her. Everything melted away, and it was just the two of them: damp bodies and hot, bone-melting kisses, and everything inside her unravelling to let him in. Cal drove into her, and Eliza opened for him. No games, no defenses, just the look in his eyes taking her higher, making her gasp his name in pleasure until they both hurtled over the edge, and she came apart around him with a cry.

*Free.*

# 13

Eliza caught her breath. Cal was collapsed beside her, and her skin was still flushed with pleasure, her climax melting away. "Well . . ." She stretched with satisfaction. "That was . . . *something*."

"Mnugh." Cal made a satisfied noise, face-down in a pillow.

Eliza grinned and nudged his bare chest. "That's it? Wow. I never thought I'd see the day. Cal Prescott, lost for words."

Cal emerged from the covers. "Easy there, woman." He draped an arm around her, yawning, his eyes still closed. "Give me two minutes, and I'll have something to say. Multi-syllabic, and everything."

"Only two minutes? I'll have to try harder next time." Eliza dropped a kiss on his shoulder, and then took a light bite. His eyes shot open.

"Hungry?" Cal pulled her suddenly into his arms. Eliza laughed but the sound was swallowed as he kissed her: a slow, sweaty kiss, as if they had all the time in the world.

She melted into him. Man, this guy could kiss.

When they finally came up for air, her head was spinning. Cal grinned. "See? Two minutes. I told you so."

She laughed and playfully hit him with a pillow. "Down, boy. I'm going to need refueling. I didn't get dessert, remember?"

"We'll see about that." Cal leapt out of bed, and Eliza was treated to a glorious eyeful as he found a pair of sweatpants in the dresser and tossed her a robe. "Like what you see?" he asked with a wink.

"Maybe." Eliza shrugged and nonchalantly slid out of bed. Well, as nonchalantly as she could, while trying to remember where her underwear went. After a quick scan of the room, she admitted defeat and tied the robe tighter. "Moonlight is very forgiving."

"Ha!"

Cal's laughter followed her down the hallway to the kitchen. She poured a glass of water from the filter and gulped it down, standing at the counter. Outside the windows, the ocean was glinting silver in the moonlight, and the whole bay was bright with the cloudless sky.

She heard Cal approaching, and then his arms wrapped around her from behind. She exhaled and relaxed back into his embrace, loving the feel of him, warm and solid. She couldn't explain it, but a feeling of rightness settled over her.

This was exactly where she was supposed to be.

Cal dipped his head to drop a kiss on her shoulder. "I knew we'd get it right eventually."

She turned, still in his arms. "You mean, us, dating? Either that, or someone would have wound up dead."

Cal chuckled. "My money's on me. You've been doing your research."

She laughed. "I don't know . . . Sometimes, I'm putty in your hands."

Cal met her gaze, reaching to brush hair from her face, and Eliza had to look away. It suddenly felt too much. Too close.

Too vulnerable.

She scooted out of his embrace, over to dig in the refrigerator. There were slim pickings. Bottled water, beer, some suspicious-looking leftovers . . . She made a face. "Where's a whole cake when you need one?"

"Oh, ye of little faith." Cal opened the freezer compartment and pulled out a pint of ice cream with a flourish. "I know what women want."

"Double chocolate fudge?" Eliza pressed a hand to her forehead and pretended to swoon. "Why, Mr. Prescott. You're too good to me."

Cal found a pair of spoons and led her to the back-porch swing, adding an extra blanket against the cold. Eliza snuggled there beside him, savoring the cool sweetness of the dessert as she watched the dark shadows of the ocean.

It was peaceful out there, with just the moonlight and the distant sound of the waves. Slowly, her breathing steadied and her pulse slowed. Cal was silent beside her, but it was a calm, easy silence.

Eliza nestled her head against his shoulder.

"You don't let your guard down often, do you?" Cal's voice was low, and when she glanced up at him, he was watching her with a thoughtful expression.

She shrugged, suddenly self-conscious. "No."

"Me neither," Cal admitted quietly.

Eliza thought about his life, which on the outside seemed so effortless and easy. But the more she got to know him, the more she realized the weight Cal was carrying, just out of view. "It can't be easy, being the one in charge."

Cal looked cautious, as if he wasn't sure if she was teasing him again, but then he relaxed. "I can't complain. I know I have all this privilege . . . But actually being CEO?" He gave her a lop-sided grin. "I don't know if I'm cut out for it. Tish should be the one running things," he added. "She's got that steely determination, she can just switch off. Look at the numbers on the page, and not think about all the lives they represent."

"You say that like empathy is a bad thing," Eliza smiled.

"For this job? I don't know." Cal sighed. "I just don't want to let anyone down. The work we do at the Foundation is so important, but it couldn't exist if the Prescott Group wasn't thriving. Sometimes, I wish I could just quit everything else and focus on that full-time."

"Heavy sits the head that wears the crown," Eliza quoted lightly.

He smiled down at her. "Sorry, I'm complaining."

"You're allowed."

"Really? Even as a *summer person*?"

Eliza winced. "OK, maybe I jumped to conclusions about you. Just a little. But in my defense, losing that job . . . it really hurt."

"I know. And I'm sorry." Cal squeezed her shoulder. "Do you want it back?"

Eliza blinked. She pulled away from him, searching his face. "Are you serious?"

Cal gave a bashful smile. "I mean, I am the owner now. If I called the editor and told him to reinstate you . . ."

Eliza's mind raced. She could be back in the newsroom by first thing Monday morning, working on features, part of the team again . . .

Except . . .

She deflated. "No. You can't," she said, realizing with a heavy heart just how impossible that would be. "Everyone would know it was just because we were dating. They'd never respect me again."

"Are you sure?" Cal checked.

"Yes," Eliza said, miserable. But it was true. People got parachuted in all the time—interns, the son or daughter of someone important—but the regular staffers kept them at a distance. They hadn't earned their spot with work or talent, and everybody knew it. She could only imagine the gossip if she showed up there again—only for word to slip that Cal had pulled strings to get her in. "I'll figure something out on my own," she said reluctantly. "But thank you, for offering."

"You'll find something," Cal said, sounding more certain than Eliza felt. "You're too talented to stay out of the loop for long."

"Tell that to LuAnn's Manners. It's my new project," she explained, seeing his confusion. "The local newspaper. I'm whipping it into shape."

"Unearthing the big news scandals in Sweetbriar Cove?"

Eliza laughed. "Not so much. The first edition should be back from the printer tomorrow."

"Put me down for three copies."

Cal pulled her closer and dropped a kiss against her forehead. She snuggled back against him. She was getting sleepy now, the sound of the ocean lulling her half-asleep. "This is nice," she whispered, and felt Cal hold her tighter.

"I know. I don't think I've ever been with someone like this . . ."

He stopped, and Eliza saw again the strange, conflicted emotions she felt written all over his face.

"We're the same, you and me," she whispered, and she leaned up to kiss him softly. "That's why we can't stay away from each other."

Cal smiled in recognition. "Gee, that sounds familiar," he teased. "Somebody really smart must have said that."

Eliza smiled. "He has his moments."

She yawned and Cal got to his feet. "C'mon, sleepyhead. The news won't break without you. Time for bed."

~

THE NEXT MORNING, CAL FOUND ELIZA SILENTLY MOVING around the bedroom, pulling her clothes back on. He watched under half-shut eyelids, playing at being asleep as she pulled her messy, rain-curled hair up into a top-knot and wriggled into her dress.

Damn, she was beautiful.

He didn't think he'd ever spent a night like that with somebody before. Guard down, open, wanting her so much it lit the world on fire. Already, he craved her all over again: not just her sinful body, but that late-night conversation, holding her close, feeling for the first time like he was out of his depth. That he'd found the one who understood his crazy, complicated world, whose mind raced fearlessly ahead, who lived life on her own terms.

Eliza retrieved a sandal from beneath the bed and slowly tiptoed towards the door.

"Sneaking out?" he asked, and she leapt with surprise.

"What? No!"

Cal grinned to see her cheeks flush. "Don't tell me you're the love 'em and leave 'em type," he teased. "A trail of broken hearts strewn up and down the Cape."

Eliza laughed at that. "I wish. No, I just thought . . . You know . . ."

"That we shared too much, and things might be weird and awkward in the harsh light of day?" Cal finished for her. Eliza's smile turned rueful.

"You need to stop reading my mind."

Cal sat up in bed, wide awake now. If Eliza was feeling

anything like he was, she was still reeling from the epic night they'd shared. But he didn't want to lose this, to have it just become one single, precious memory.

They were still teetering on the edge of each other. He needed this to become something real.

"How about coffee?" he suggested, not wanting her defenses to slam back down. "There's nothing weird and awkward about going to get coffee."

Eliza paused. "I have to get to the newspaper office," she said, sounding regretful. "I need to check the issue and hand them off to the delivery guy."

"Then I'll meet you there. You can show me your new empire." Cal got out of bed and went over to her, caring less about the fact that he was stark naked, and more about giving her a gentle good-morning kiss. Eliza sighed happily against him, her lips soft in the morning light, and when he pulled back, she was smiling at him, the way she'd looked in the moonlight.

To hell with coffee, he had everything he needed right there. Cal was just about to pull her back to bed and spend the morning worshipping every inch of her, when Eliza gave a nod.

"OK," she said. "I'll see you there. Town hall, top floor. I take mine black with sugar."

She kissed him again, swift and hot this time, and then whirled out the door before he could say another word.

Cal grinned. Ravishing may have been his first choice of activities, but coffee and newsprint was a close second. It sounded like a perfect Sunday morning to him.

HE SHOWERED AND DRESSED AND TOOK THE BACK ROAD,

strolling into town. And he had a magnificent woman waiting for him.

OK, so Eliza probably didn't wait on anyone, but that just made the invitation more of a victory. Slowly, surely, he was peeling back those layers and learning more about her, and every minute they spent together only made him want her more. Stubborn and brilliant, beautiful and completely unexpected; Cal knew he was getting sappy, but damn if the morning skies didn't seem brighter and the colors in Sweetbriar more spectacular as he stopped by the coffee shop and picked up her order, just the way she liked it.

"Are you . . . whistling?"

He turned. Declan entered the café behind him, looking like he'd just stumbled off a two-day bender. He had dark sunglasses on and winced when the radio started playing.

"You look terrible," Cal said, taking him in. "Do I even want to know?"

"Let's just say, it involved two girls, a bottle of tequila, and my late-night puttanesca at 2Am."

Cal laughed. "Chef Michele wouldn't put up with that," he said, naming Declan's old boss.

"Perks of running your own kitchen." Declan flashed the girl at the counter a pained smile. "Black coffee, please, mate. Big as they come." He turned back to Cal and gave him a swift once-over. "You look far too bright-eyed and bushy-tailed. We need to get you out on the town, see some action of your own."

"That won't be necessary," Cal said casually.

"Oh really?" Declan waggled his eyebrows. "Who's the lucky lady?"

Cal wasn't about to kiss and tell, but he couldn't stop the grin from spreading across his face. "Eliza," he admitted.

Declan hooted with laughter. "You're a brave man," he said. "Lucky, but brave."

Cal didn't feel brave. Now that he'd seen the sweetness behind Eliza's smile, he wondered why he wasn't beating every guy in the Cape away to get his place in line.

Probably because Eliza had already sent the pretenders scattering.

"Does this mean she's going to be skipping work to make mushy eyes at you?" Declan sighed dramatically. "Just when things were running smoothly."

"I think Eliza's more than capable of handling her own schedule," Cal replied. "Don't let her hear you talking like that."

"Good point." Declan slapped him on the back. "We should all get a drink sometime. I'll bring one of my friends." He paused, clearly imagining Eliza's reaction if he rolled up with one of his perky coeds. "Or maybe not. Either way, just say the word."

"Will do."

Cal took their coffees and strolled across the square. The Town Hall was a creaking, classic building, and—three flights of stairs later—he found the office, tucked away in the attic space. The door was open, and for a moment, he just stood in the hallway, watching Eliza at work.

She was behind a big wooden desk, covered with papers and stacks of newspapers. She'd changed into jeans and a pale linen shirt, knotted loosely at her waist. Her hair was still damp, twisted up in a knot that was secured by a couple of pencils, and she had another between her lips, idly nibbling on the eraser as she scanned the pages in front of her.

"Special delivery," he said, tapping the open door.

Eliza looked up. "Hey." She smiled at him, and just like that, Cal felt something unfurl in his chest.

"So this is where the magic happens . . ." He stepped inside and looked around. There were old cabinets and furniture. Shafts of sunlight streamed through the dusty windows, and high above the square, it felt like they were hidden on top of the world.

Eliza looked bashful. "I don't know about that. It's a long way from the newsroom."

He could hear the wistful note in her voice, and was reminded of the choice she'd made, last night. It would have been easy for him to call her old editor and insist she get her job back, and even easier for her to accept it. Most people would have, but he was learning Eliza wasn't most people. She cared about doing things the right way, with integrity. Half the Prescott board could learn a few things from her.

"Black, extra sugar, as the lady desires." He deposited her coffee on the desk.

"Thank you!" She grabbed it and took a long gulp. "Ow, hot!" She winced—and then kept right on drinking. "I didn't stick around long back at the house," she added. "Mom was yakking up a storm with Aunt June, and I wasn't about to walk into the middle of *that* interrogation."

"Your mom seems sweet," Cal argued. He pulled up a chair and took a seat beside her. "She clearly cares about you."

"Say that again, after she's spent twenty years telling you to marry well." Eliza gave him a look.

He smiled. "Can't your sister distract her with a wedding and babies? Paige is older than you, right?"

Eliza nodded. "Just a couple of years. And, yes, things were on track with this one guy, Doug. But they broke up a few months ago, she won't even say why. Just that it didn't work out." She made a rueful look. "You can imagine how Mom took that. Paige is almost thirty. Practically a spinster," she added in a teasing voice.

Cal laughed. "If it makes you feel any better, my Uncle Arthur's been reading me the riot act too, about settling down.

'A man my age should be starting a family,' " he added, mimicking his uncle's stern tone.

"We should put them in a room together, let them wear themselves out." Eliza grinned, but Cal could only imagine what his uncle would make of Linda and her eager questions about their summer home and property back in Boston. And as for Eliza . . .

He shook off the thought and turned his attention to the desk. "So, this is the famous *Cape Cod Caller*," he said, surveying the pages.

"Yes!" Eliza brightened. "I picked up the samples from the print shop. I was just checking them for errors. Not that it would matter," she added. "They've already printed five thousand copies. The delivery guys are already on their way out."

"Looks good." Cal scanned the headlines: a mix of local news and soft lifestyle stories.

Eliza made a sound, something like a snort. "It's OK, you don't have to pretend," she said with a wry smile. "I know it's a long way from a real newspaper."

"No, I mean it," Cal protested, but Eliza didn't seem convinced.

"I picked it up last-minute after Wilber moved south—long story. Anyway, they were going to stop running altogether, but I couldn't let it just fold. How else would the good citizens of Sweetbriar Cove find out about the two-for-one on malt shakes at the coffee shop, or that the lighthouse is celebrating its 120$^{th}$ anniversary?"

Eliza's voice was clearly affectionate, but there was a defensive note there too. Cal could imagine that going from a Pulitzer-winning big-city paper like the *Boston Herald* to this shoe-string affair might feel like a step down in the world. But seeing the interesting collection of articles, the bold layout, and the lists of local events, Cal really was impressed.

"What's the circulation?"

"It's quieter now in spring," Eliza said, "but when the summer season kicks in and all the tourists arrive, that's when things really heat up. You know, real-estate ads, special event calendars. I found the print orders," she added, flipping through some files. "And come June, the circulation goes up to thirty, forty thousand."

"That's not bad," Cal said thoughtfully, his business brain already ticking over. "There are probably hundreds of small, local newspapers like this, all over the country."

"Thousands." Eliza nodded. "But they're dying out. I mean, there's no money in it, and unless you happen to have someone willing to pitch in and do it all for free . . ."

"But a lot of the writing isn't necessarily about Cape Cod," he said, looking at the pages with fresh eyes. "I mean, gardening columns, recipes, cartoons . . . Those could run anywhere. You could build out each issue from a central template, then you'd really only need to slot in local events and classified ads, and it could be distributed all over the country. *The Boise Independent,* or the *Santa Clarita Record.*"

"Yes," Eliza said slowly. She narrowed her eyes at him. "But you'd still need to print and distribute, and those are the costs running everyone out of business."

"Not if you went online." Cal felt inspiration strike. "Think about it: a central news portal, for each small town or region. The same syndicated columns, but then limitless space for ads or local color. You would only need a small, main staff and some local freelancers, you'd cut the costs way down, and—"

"Whoa. Stop," Eliza interrupted, frowning. "The whole point of the *Caller* is a print edition."

"Why?" Cal asked, feeling pumped. "You said it yourself, between print costs and getting the issues out, there's no money in it."

"Yes, but it's a newspaper," Eliza repeated. "Pages, print."

"Papercuts." Cal grinned, teasing, but she didn't seem to lighten up. "Going digital would solve all your problems."

Eliza shook her head stubbornly. "Maybe I don't see them as problems. Come with me," she said abruptly, getting up. She took his hand and dragged Cal determinedly out of the office and back downstairs. He wasn't going to object. Holding hands with her made him feel like a teenager again, and even though he could tell she was annoyed, Eliza was distractingly sexy as she strode across the town square.

"Are we going far?" he asked as they turned down a country lane. "Because we missed the road to my place . . ."

"You'll see," is all Eliza would say, until they reached the familiar frontage of the bakery. The bell sounded over the door as Eliza led him inside, and the finally, she paused for breath. "See?" she said, gesturing around the café.

Cal looked. There was a line at the counter, and every table was full of locals enjoying a cup of coffee, a pastry, and . . .

The *Cape Cod Caller*.

Browsing over coffee, absent-mindedly turning pages—the whole room was poring over the new edition.

"Great work, Eliza." One of the older women looked up from her paper. "I was wondering if they'd ever finish the rose pruning guide."

"Thanks, Debra," Eliza replied, smiling proudly. "Maybe you could do a guest column next time. Theater or movie reviews, maybe."

"I don't know if your opinion on those blockbusters is fit to print," the woman answered with a smirk.

Another man stopped to pat Eliza on the back, querying her on the crossword clues, and a group of young moms suggested including their playgroup in the next issue. Cal had to admit he was surprised. His numbers showed that newspaper circulation was plummeting all across the country, but here, it seemed like the *Caller* was must-read material.

Eliza snagged a free table in the corner and sat down with a thump. "It's not about what's in the issue," she explained to him. "You think anyone here couldn't find gardening tips or event schedules in five seconds using google if they wanted to? It's about opening up the pages and taking ten, twenty minutes to read. The ritual of it, everyone getting involved."

The baker, Summer, swooped by their table and deposited a plate of pastries. "Just a little something from the 'best, must-taste baker on the Cape.' " She leaned down and gave Eliza a hug. "Thank you! I mean, I know I said to say nice things, but you gave me a whole page review!"

"It's your fault," Eliza replied, smiling. "You make too many delicious things. I couldn't pick only one."

"Just for that, I'm going to whip you up some of that quiche you love so much."

Eliza gasped happily. "With the extra bacon and three cheeses."

"Coming right up." Summer winked and headed back to the kitchen.

"Featuring your friends, hmm?" Cal teased, breaking off a corner of a croissant and popping it into his mouth. "Isn't that journalistic bias?"

Eliza laughed. "People travel from New York to taste her cakes. I think she's a safe choice. Besides, that's the point of the *Caller*," she added, digging into a delectable sticky bun. "To let everyone know all the great businesses in the area."

"Part magazine, part PR campaign." Cal was beginning to understand.

"Exactly." Eliza sat back and looked around, her expression turning wistful. "My dad and I would have the same routine, every Sunday during summer. We'd pick up two copies, fresh from the presses, and go for breakfast, just the two of us. The bakery wasn't around then," she added. "So we'd go to this little café up in Provincetown by the water. He'd get a bacon sandwich, and I'd have donuts, and we'd both promise not to tell Mom. And then we'd sit and read it cover to cover. Just the two of us."

She stopped, and Cal could see the heartache in her eyes. He reached across the table and squeezed her hand.

"It was our thing." Eliza gave a self-conscious shrug, looking down.

"I get it," Cal said gently. "He would be glad you're carrying on the tradition."

"Do you have any?" Eliza asked, glancing up again. "Traditions. From your parents."

Cal thought, then he smiled. "Tollbooths," he said, remembering. "My father would always drum on the steering wheel, like a fanfare, every time. When I was a kid, he would make a big deal at the window, too, asking permission to cross, like he was a knight crossing the troll's bridge."

Eliza smiled. "You still do that?"

"Just the fanfare part," Cal chuckled. "I don't think the poor tollbooth guy would think it was so charming with a full-grown man."

"I don't know about that." Eliza's smile turned flirty. "I think you could pull it off."

Cal couldn't resist. He leaned over and kissed her, capturing her mouth in a slow, luxurious moment that seemed to make everything melt away. Her lips were soft and parted for him, sweet from the pastry, and he could smell the scent of her shampoo, something light and floral lingering in the bakery air.

It was a vacation, a moment of absolute calm, the bright sunshine breaking through clouds on a winter's day.

Eliza drew back, looking breathless. "People will talk," she whispered, her eyes sparkling.

"Let them." Cal smiled and kissed her again. As far as he was concerned, they could put it on the front page.

He was crazy about this woman, and he didn't care who knew it. But as he sank into the moment, chasing the warmth, that little voice in the back of his head was warning him.

Even vacations had to end sometime.

He'd put the real world on hold, his problems at arm's length. But what would happen when it was time to get back to reality, and the rarefied, pressure-cooker world of the Prescott Group? He was son, heir, CEO. And a renegade like Eliza . . .

Would she want to fit in that?

# 14

Eliza spent the morning at the bakery with Cal, leaving it to the last minute before leaving for her lunch shift at work.

"What are your plans?" she asked, kissing him goodbye.

"I have my appointment with June, to look at some houses," Cal said. "We're meeting at noon."

Eliza laughed. "Good luck. Watch out for any wandering hands!"

She headed over to the restaurant, arriving with a moment to spare. She kept a spare hostess-ready outfit in her locker there, and she quickly changed in the back room, but her mind was still at Cal's place, breathless and naked under the sheets.

God, that man was *good*.

"You look way too happy to be serving salads."

Eliza looked up. Jenny was just stashing her bag and tying on an apron. "Good weekend?" the other waitress asked.

"Pretty good," Eliza answered, unable to keep the smile from her face. "You?"

Jenny made a face. "I got stood up by a guy I didn't even

want to go out with in the first place. So, yeah, my self-esteem is about this big." She held her thumb and forefinger about an inch apart.

"Ouch, I'm sorry." Eliza was sympathetic. "Clearly, he's crazy. And blind."

"Thanks." Jenny smiled. "But it's the off-season, slim pickings out there until summer starts."

"And then your dance card will be full?" Eliza asked.

"From dawn until dusk." Jenny winked. "I like the city guys the best. There's something about a man in a suit, gets me every time."

Eliza murmured her agreement, picturing Cal in his smart dress shirt, with the sleeves rolled up over those tanned, muscular forearms . . .

She flushed. That was definitely not a work-friendly train of thought, but as her shift got underway, she couldn't shake it. Thoughts of Cal flooded her mind, even as she greeted diners and showed them to their tables.

Cal kissing her passionately on the street last night, out there in the rain.

Cal pressing her back against the wet tile and sinking to his knees.

Cal poised above her in the moonlight, eyes dark with desire as he moved inside—

*Ahem.*

Eliza shook her head and turned to greet the next party of ladies who lunched, certain that her skin was burning bright red. "Hi. Welcome to—"

"Eliza?" Tish emerged from the pack of perfect, glossy blondes. "It's me, Letitia. Calvin's cousin."

As if their meeting wasn't burned into Eliza's mind. "Hi, Tish," she said, then paused. "Sorry, is that a private nickname?" she checked. "It's just, Cal uses it all the time."

"No, it's fine. Great to see you again." Tish smiled, dressed in a chic navy sundress this time, with a sweater looped elegantly around her shoulders and oversized sunglasses pushed back on the top of her head. "Are you here for lunch? Cal said it was the best around. I know," she said, brightening. "Why don't you join us? Eliza's dating Cal," she added to her friends, who made an assortment of approving noises.

Eliza felt her skin redden even more. "No. Actually, I work here," she answered.

The group's expressions changed.

"Oh. Whoops." Tish flashed an apologetic smile. "And here I am, holding you up."

"No, it's OK." Eliza wished she didn't feel so embarrassed. So she had a job? There wasn't anything shameful about that. "Party of six, right?"

"The reservation's under Prescott," Tish added, and sure enough, it was right there in the book. If Eliza hadn't been so wrapped up in her X-rated memories, she might have seen this coming, but instead, she had to grab menus and lead them across the room feeling flustered. She bolted for the kitchen, but still, she wasn't fast enough to ignore the amused looks and whispers around the table.

The double doors swung shut behind her, and she let out a breath.

"Angry mob today?" Declan joked from behind the stove. Eliza gave a weak smile.

"Something like that."

She peeked back into the dining room. Tish and her friends were all deep in conversation, and Eliza could guess exactly what—or who—they were talking about. She wished it didn't bother her, but it made her feel like she was in prep school all over again: the scholarship kid working weekends, while her moneyed classmates had trust funds to spare.

It was easy to forget she and Cal were worlds apart until that golden, glossy world was right in front of her, needing water refills and their appetizers fetched.

She braced herself and walked back out, heading to her hostess station.

"Excuse me! Lizzie?" A voice came from Tish's table. Eliza detoured over.

"Everything OK?" She tried to keep a smile on her face. She recognized one of Tish's friends now as the blonde they'd run into at dinner in Provincetown. Susie, or Sukie, or something like that. But Sukie stared blankly at Eliza like they'd never met before.

"We're ready to order," she said, sounding impatient.

"Sukie!" Tish interrupted. "Sorry," she said to Eliza with a smile, then turned back to her friend. "Eliza's the hostess. A server will take our order."

"So?" Sukie shrugged. "They all work here."

Eliza kept the smile plastered on. "I'll make sure someone is right out," she said, but Sukie wasn't done yet. She held up her glass.

"We asked for bottled, but this is tap water. I can taste it."

"The water's fine," Tish interrupted again, and she shot Sukie a look.

"But—"

Tish glared. This time, Sukie deflated a little. Clearly, Tish was the Queen B of the group, but the politics didn't matter to Eliza, not when she was the one way out of the loop.

"New water. Coming right up." Eliza walked away, counting under her breath. Luckily, a new group of diners arrived, and she didn't have time to check on Tish and co. for the rest of the afternoon. She was just straightening up the hostess station when the group filed past, towards the exit.

Tish fell back behind the others. "Sorry about Sukie," she said, looking apologetic.

"Nothing to be sorry about," Eliza replied brightly. "She's right, we all work here. Did you enjoy your meal?"

"It was great." Tish paused. "I'm heading back to the city this afternoon, but maybe we could have a drink sometime. The three of us."

"Sure," Eliza said slowly. She searched Tish's expression for any hint of her friends' attitude, but Tish just looked friendly—and curious. "That sounds great."

"Perfect. I'll tell Cal and make a date." Tish beamed. "Because God knows if I leave it up to him, it'll never happen. You'd think that with an assistant and a secretary, he'd manage to keep his dates straight," she added with an affectionate grin, "but if I didn't call him the night before every dinner, he'd never show up."

"Good to know." Eliza smiled. She was just about to relax, and admit that maybe she shouldn't feel so defensive, when voices filtered through the open window beside them. Tish's friends, waiting for her outside.

"He can't actually be dating her," Sukie's voice came. "She's just a local side-piece."

"I haven't seen them together in town," another woman added. "He's hiding her out here."

"Of course he is." Sukie trilled with mean laughter. "I mean, can you imagine her at the club? Or any of the galas this season?"

"Not unless she's pulling waitress duty. I'm sorry, *hostessing*."

More laughter came.

"I'm sorry." Tish looked pained. "They can be bitches."

Eliza narrowed her eyes. "It's fine," she said shortly. "I get it. I'm not his usual type."

"Which is a good thing."

Tish seemed as if she wanted to say something else, but maybe she could tell Eliza didn't want to make a scene over it. "Anyway, we'll get that drink. See you soon, I hope." She departed. The gossip outside the window immediately stopped, and Eliza could hear the group move off.

Well, that had been fun.

Eliza tried to forget the comments as she finished up her shift, but the voices echoed in her mind, polished and smug. She knew, logically, they were probably just jealous. After watching Sukie fawn all over Cal at the restaurant, it was clear he was Bachelor #1 in that world. How could he not be? He had the Prescott name and fortune behind him, as well as those heart-stopping good looks. And now, Eliza had to admit, she knew that he was kind, and sweet and smart.

Not to mention spectacular in bed.

And in the shower.

And—

*Down, girl.*

But even though Eliza tried to brush off their comments, her insecurity flickered, all the same.

Was she fooling herself?

It had started out of nowhere; she'd told herself a million reasons why Cal was all wrong for her, but now the thought of being just his side-piece, his little vacation fling, made Eliza's chest clench. Cal would never think like that or use those words, but he'd said it himself—this was a break from him, away from his regular life.

Would that life have a place for her in it? Or was she being naïve to even think that way?

SHE FINISHED UP HER SHIFT AND HEADED BACK TO THE HOUSE.

Cal called to check in, but Eliza didn't tell him what had happened. It felt like she would be tattling, and besides, it would only force a conversation she wasn't sure they were ready to have.

"So, no drama over the lunch service today?" he asked.

"Nope," Eliza replied lightly. "What about you, how was the house-hunting? Or is this call really just to tell me that you're running off with Aunt June?"

"Well, I wanted to tell you in person . . ." Cal's voice couldn't hide his laughter. "But now that you mention it . . ."

"The heart wants what the heart wants." She smiled, unlocking the front door. "But don't even joke. Rumor has it her new beau is all of thirty-eight."

"He'll be lucky to keep up. She had me all over the Cape today."

Eliza snorted with laughter, and Cal quickly added, "You know what I mean."

"Uh huh. So, do you want to do something tonight?" she asked. "Or did June wear you out?"

"I can always find the time for you." Cal's voice turned intimate. "Come over. I'll cook."

Eliza got a flash of Cal, shirtless, cooking for her, and was about to agree. Then she paused. "How about we go out?" she suggested instead, hearing Sukie's voice in her head—and hating herself for it.

*"I haven't seen them together . . . He's hiding her out here."*

"We could grab a drink at the pub," she continued. "You can get to know everyone."

"Without them shooting daggers at me this time?" Cal teased.

"I'll protect you," she joked back. "What do you say?"

"Sure, sounds good," Cal replied. "On one condition."

"Name it."

"That I get you naked in somebody's bed by the end of the night."

Eliza sucked in a breath. Her stomach curled, and she couldn't deny the heat that rolled through her just to hear him say it.

"I think that could be arranged," she said softly. "Meet you there at seven?"

"I can't wait."

Eliza hung up and paused a moment, the phone against her beating chest. It didn't sound like he was hiding anything.

Everything was OK, she reassured herself. She was over-thinking this, that was all. Sukie and her friends were jealous, and Eliza just needed to forget their petty sniping, and focus on the gorgeous, brilliant man promising to ravish her senseless.

It sounded like a pretty good plan to her.

"Eliza?" Her mom emerged from the back of the house. "I didn't hear you come in."

"I just finished work," she explained.

"Do you have a moment?" Linda asked. "There's something we need to talk about."

Eliza winced. She'd been hoping her nights spent sleeping over at Cal's had gone unnoticed, but she should have known: Linda Bennett saw everything. She wasn't in the mood for one of her mom's "giving the milk away for free" talks, so she wrapped her in a quick hug and then bounded for the stairs. "Can't stop! I'll be out late again tonight. We can talk tomorrow!"

CAL HAD TO ADMIT, WALKING INTO THE PUB TO MEET ELIZA that night felt like walking into the line of fire. Her friends had made it clear that they were watching out for her, and they'd probably heard the worst of it from when he'd first arrived in town. But stepping through the doors, he realized that holding a grudge was the last thing on anyone's mind.

They were singing. Loudly.

"Karaoke night," Eliza said by way of explanation, greeting him with a kiss. She dragged him to the bar, elbowing her way through the crowd. "I totally forgot the place is always packed for this."

"Why?" Cal asked faintly, watching a couple of older women tunelessly belt out "Memories." "Are you all gluttons for punishment?"

Eliza playfully thwacked his arm. "It's fun. We're all terrible," she continued, smiling. "I can't hold a note, and Mackenzie's even worse. Cooper's the only one with a voice," she said. "But he won't do it unless Poppy bats her eyelashes."

"Sounds like a fun night," Cal said, but he wasn't even lying. Eliza was right there beside him, poured into a pair of jeans that were making him lightheaded. He reached out and tugged her closer, closing his arms around her waist and breathing in the scent of her; the heat. "Hey," he murmured, loving the way her cheeks flushed as she tilted her head up and smiled at him.

"Hey."

"I knew it." They were interrupted by the bartender, Riley, grinning at them with a smug look on his face.

"Knew what?" Eliza asked, reaching over to swipe the glass of beer he set on the bar.

"Knew that the way you two were bickering, you'd be madly in love by the end of the month. Or calling me to help hide the body." Riley winked.

"Don't speak too soon," Cal said. "I bet you have the perfect spot all picked out," he added to Eliza, and was rewarded with a sunny grin.

"The marshes, past Black Gull Pond," she said without hesitation. "With a few weights, you'd sink right to the bottom, and nobody would ever see you again."

Riley laughed. "Watch out, buddy!"

"It actually wasn't my idea," Eliza said, turning back to him with a sweet smile. "It was Brooke's pick."

Riley laughed even harder.

"What's this?" Brooke herself joined them, slipping an arm around Riley's waist.

"Eliza was just filling me in on your murder plans," Riley said, squeezing her with clear affection.

"Oh, the marshes!" Brooke exclaimed. "Good call, right? You've got the dirt road for driving, but it's secluded, away from the main road . . ."

"Nobody around to hear their cries for help," Eliza agreed.

Riley caught Cal's eye. "We sure know how to choose them," he said, grinning.

"Amen to that," Cal agreed. Riley slid another beer across the bar, and Cal took a gulp, feeling more relaxed than he had since . . . the last time his arm was around Eliza, and he was listening to the delighted sound of her laugh.

He looked around the room. The "Memories" pair had been replaced by a guy singing Montgomery Gentry, complete with cowboy hat, and he recognized more of Eliza's friends in the corner. A server passed with a platter of tacos, and Cal's stomach rumbled.

Eliza laughed, and patted his belly. "Is that a hint?"

"More like a demand. Any chance of some food?" he asked Riley, who was already back, trying to serve the crowd. "When you get a moment."

Riley flashed a thumbs-up, so they headed across the room, where Jake was sitting with his girlfriend, an auburn-curled woman with what looked like paint speckling her pullover. "You must be Mackenzie," he greeted her.

"And you must be Calvin Archibald the fourth," she said with a wicked gleam in her eye.

He groaned. "You told them?"

Eliza smirked. "It's a lovely name."

"Only my grandmother calls me that," Cal said with a wince. "Usually when I've done something wrong."

"It's OK," Mackenzie reassured him, making space for them at the table. They crowded in just as Riley materialized with a platter of food. "My middle name is Leafie. Hippie parents."

"Ryan," Jake offered. Cal turned to Eliza.

"What about you?" Eliza shook her head. "Come on, now I have to hear it," Cal grinned. "Let me guess, Rachel. Kristen. Anne-Marie."

"Gertrude," Mac pitched in. "Sue-Ann. Dot."

"I hate you," Eliza said to Cal, but she had a smile on her face. "Fine, I'll tell you, but you all have to promise not to laugh."

"Cross my heart," Cal agreed.

"OK, OK," the others chorused.

Eliza paused. "It's Elisabeth."

Cal blinked. "Eliza Elisabeth Bennett?" His lips twitched despite himself, and he had to cover it with a cough.

"You promised!" Eliza elbowed him.

"I know, it's just . . ."

"Unusual," Mackenzie finished tactfully.

Eliza sighed. "Mom's mom was called Eliza, and Grams on my dad's side was Elisabeth, but for some reason, instead of combining them like any sane person would, they decided to keep it, to the letter."

"I think it's sweet," Cal said loyally, leaning in to kiss her forehead. "And it could have been worse."

"How?"

"You could have been Eliza Elisabeth Lizzie." He grinned, and she broke into a smile.

"Good point . . . Archie."

He shook his head firmly. "Nope."

"Arch?" she tried, fluttering her eyelashes.

"No way."

"Hmm, we'll work on that." Eliza leaned in and kissed him. When they broke apart, Cal noticed Mac and Jake watching them—and trying hard not to look like it. He coughed, self-conscious, but Eliza didn't seem to mind.

"Eyes on the stage!" she ordered them playfully.

"What, or we'll miss Bert's rousing rendition of 'Bat Out of Hell'?" Mac shot back, smirking. "Tell me you can carry a tune, Cal. We're all hopeless."

"I don't sing," Cal said it firmly. He could already tell these guys didn't take no for an answer, but he had no intention of making a fool of himself up on stage. Somebody would have a camera phone, and then he could just imagine the viral video clips: "Prescott Heir Murders Showtunes."

That wouldn't be so easy to disappear in the marshes. He took a taco instead, and let Eliza and Mac chat away, awarding points for style and originality—and, occasionally, tunefulness—as the rest of the town took their turn. It was more entertaining than any big A-list concert, and soon, even Cal was clapping along.

"Tell me this is a regular thing," he said when finally there was a break in the performances. "I want to see Eliza up there—even if it is just to play the tambourine," he added, when she shook her head so violently, her hair spun out.

"It's usually once a month," Jake replied. "Or whenever the girls bug Riley into 'finding' the karaoke set."

The air quotes made it clear the set went missing a lot.

"But just wait for the summer JamFest!" Mackenzie exclaimed.

"Music or canned preserves?" Cal joked, but she just grinned.

"Both. It started as a jazz festival," she explained, "but then one year a whole busload of Swedish tourists arrived, expecting to find food, so Franny and Debra whipped up a few batches, and ever since, it kind of spiraled out of control."

Eliza leaned in. "A lot of things spiral in Sweetbriar Cove."

Cal smiled back at her. "I'm beginning to figure that out."

"Anyway," Mackenzie continued, "the mix just stuck, and now there's a whole weekend of music, canning contests. Who doesn't like their Coltrane with a side of lingonberry spread?"

"I know I do." Cal sipped his beer. "I'll be there."

"Will you be in town for that?" Eliza asked, and Cal thought he saw a flicker of tension on her face. "You must be getting ready to head back to Boston. You were only staying a couple of weeks."

"Can't wait to get rid of me, huh?" he joked, but Eliza's smile didn't reach her eyes.

He realized it was a loaded question. They hadn't talked about the future, or where this was going. As if he could spend just one night with her. Or two, or three.

He already knew that would never be enough.

Cal dropped his voice. "Plans change," he said, and he took her hand, giving her a reassuring smile. "Even if I do need to go to the city for meetings, I can drive back. Or maybe June will have found me a place by then."

"That's right," Mackenzie spoke up. "I heard you were looking. Did the Asher place strike your fancy?"

Cal chuckled. "What did she do, send out a news bulletin after?"

"Actually, she was live-tweeting the tour," Mac grinned.

"That sounds about right. And no," Cal added, taking a swig of beer. "It didn't feel like me. I think I would want to be right on the water," he said, imagining waking up every morning to the blue horizon—and a view of Eliza beside him, if he was lucky. "Your place has a great location," he said, turning to her. "It's pretty small, but June said it's a double lot, right?"

Eliza nodded. "Grandpa had plans to build on it, but we never got around to it."

"Still, it means your mom will get a great price," Cal continued, reaching for another taco. "June said you had some developers ready to make an offer. They could tear it down and build a real showstopper."

There was silence.

When he looked up, Eliza was staring at him blankly. "What?" he asked.

"Our house isn't for sale," Eliza said slowly.

"Sure it is," Cal replied, confused. "June showed me the listing. She pitched it pretty hard, but I don't know if I want a big project like that . . ."

He trailed off, seeing her expression, and suddenly, everything made sense. "You didn't know," he said, his heart sinking.

"No, I didn't." Eliza's jaw clenched.

Across the table, Mac cleared her throat. She and Jake bobbed to their feet. "We're just going to get another round," she said uneasily, and they quickly retreated, leaving Cal and Eliza alone.

Cal exhaled. "I'm sorry you had to hear it from me." He squeezed Eliza's hand. "Maybe she was just waiting for the right time to tell you?"

"You mean, after you and every realtor on the Cape?" Eliza shot back.

Cal silently cursed Linda, and June too. He hadn't realized

he was wading into a messy family situation. "I'm sure if you just talk it out . . ."

"Before or after someone rips down the house?" Eliza asked, her voice thick with sarcasm. "Like you said, someone could build a real showstopper. Never mind the years of memories, or the fact that the house has been in my family as long as I can remember."

"I'm sorry," Cal said again, feeling useless. "I know that house meant a lot to you."

"*Means* a lot to me," Eliza corrected him, still looking angry. "It's not gone yet."

"I know." Cal felt like he was navigating a minefield. "It was a bad choice of words."

Eliza shook her head. "You know what? Forget it, you wouldn't understand."

There was something dismissive in her tone, but Cal tried to keep his voice even. "Why not?"

"Because you could buy our house without even thinking twice," Eliza said icily. "You could tear it down, and put up some fancy mansion, and all you'd have to do is snap your fingers to make it happen."

"Well, the permits would take longer than that," Cal tried to joke, but he could tell the minute the words left his mouth that it was the wrong thing to say. He winced. "I'm sorry, that was insensitive," he added, but the damage was done.

"Thanks for nothing." Eliza got to her feet and grabbed her jacket.

"Wait—" Cal tried to say, but she was already storming towards the door.

Damn.

He got up and quickly followed, catching up with her outside. "Eliza, stop."

She kept striding down the dark, empty street. He fell into step beside her.

"Look, I know you're mad, but this isn't my fault." Cal stopped again. Couldn't he say anything right? "I just mean, this is between you and your mom. You guys will figure it out."

"How?" Eliza whirled on him. "I don't live in your world, where a house is no big deal. You rolled up to Sweetbriar Cove and thought, 'Gee, maybe I'll spend a million dollars on a weekend getaway,' but do you even know what that means? Or have you spent so long in the Prescott bubble that you've forgotten what it's like for the rest of us?"

"That's not fair," Cal replied, fighting to stay calm.

"Welcome to the real world," Eliza said, and she started walking again.

This time, Cal didn't follow her.

# 15

Eliza walked all the way home, tears stinging in the back of her throat—and anger burning hot in her chest. How could Cal be so oblivious? Acting like it was no big deal that her childhood home was about to get ripped down and cleared away, probably to make room for another multi-million-dollar mega-mansion, for some rich guy like him to visit for a few weekends every summer. Well, not everyone had a trust fund and could go impulse-buy a whole freaking house anytime they chose. And not everyone could waltz around having hundred-dollar lunches, sneering at the help for daring to pay the damn bills with an honest job.

Eliza swiped angrily at her face. Her blood was running hot and angry, but as she left the lights of the town square behind and strode on, down the dark, familiar streets, her rage slowly faded.

What was she doing?

She knew, deep down, that her mom putting the house up for sale, and Sukie and Co.'s bitchy comments, had nothing to do with Cal, but still somehow they all swirled together in a painful mess of insecurity and bitterness inside.

Everything was changing. First she'd lost her dad, then her beloved job. Now all of this?

It felt like she'd spent the past year spinning in a strong, cruel wind, and now, just when she was finally getting back to something like normal, it all was blowing away again. But even worse than feeling so untethered was the quiet fear that maybe she was the one screwing everything up. She'd chosen to write that bombshell of an article, just to prove something to herself. She'd chosen to run away and hide here on the Cape, rather than keep grinding to find a new job back in the city. She'd chosen to keep her mom at arm's length, cutting her off anytime she'd wanted to have a real conversation, and she'd chosen to blow up at Cal back there, rather than have an adult talk and share all the emotions whirling in her chest.

Sure, things were hard and confusing in her life right now, but she was playing her part to make them worse.

Sometimes, she could be her own worst enemy.

By the time she reached home, Eliza was ready for a fight. The lights were on, but when she unlocked the front door, she found the door to her father's old study open, and her mom inside—sitting in Dad's old chair by the window, flipping through some of the old photo albums Eliza had set aside.

Her anger dissolved in a heartbeat. She swallowed. "Hey," she said softly from the doorway, and her mom's head snapped up.

"Oh. Sweetheart. I thought you were staying out tonight." Linda dabbed at her eyes, and Eliza felt a twist of guilt for intruding on her private moment.

"No, we cut things short." Eliza swallowed, and stayed, lingering in the doorway. "Cal told me you put the house on the market."

Linda looked away. "I know, I should have talked to you girls first, but June and I were chatting, and she mentioned it was the perfect time to sell."

"But do we have to?" Eliza moved closer. "I can pitch in more, especially since I'm staying here. I could get another job, pay real rent—"

But her mother shook her head. "That's sweet of you to offer, but it won't help. The truth is things have been difficult for a while now. The medical bills ate up pretty much everything we had."

"I thought there was insurance." Eliza took a seat beside her.

"There was," her mom sighed. "But with co-pays and limits, there was still so much to pay. I've got your father's pension now, but between the upkeep here and the mortgage back in Boston . . . Well, I sat down with our advisor and the budget, and something has to give."

Up close, Eliza could see the tired lines on her mother's face. She'd thought it was just grief she was wrestling with, but it turned out there had been an even heavier burden to carry.

"I know you and your sister love this place." Linda squeezed her hand. "I loved it too. I always imagined passing it on to you and your families. But I've been trying to make the numbers work, and nothing else makes sense. I'm sorry, sweetheart."

"No, don't be." Eliza shook her head. "Of course we should sell, if it means you won't have to worry anymore. I just wish I was able to help out. But my career doesn't exactly bring in the big bucks," she added, rueful.

"You know I'm proud of you," Linda said with a smile. "You and Paige both. You're good girls. I'd just like to see you settled with your own families. Safe and secure."

Eliza hid a grin. Of course her mother couldn't help slipping that one in. "We'll be fine."

"You'll need someone to take care of you."

"I can do that just fine on my own," Eliza reassured her. "Besides, I have you to look out for me, too."

"You never know what life has in store." Linda squeezed her hand tighter. "I thought I'd have another twenty years with your father, and then . . ." She stopped.

Eliza leaned closer and kissed her on the cheek. "So, I guess this means we'll have to pack up the house, then?" She looked around with a sigh. "At least I got a head start in here."

"We won't have to move out right away," Linda told her. "I said to make it a condition of the sale, that we stay for the summer."

"Our last summer," Eliza said with a pang. She couldn't stop things changing, no matter how hard she tried. "We'll just have to make it count."

ELIZA HEADED UPSTAIRS TO BED, BUT SHE WASN'T TIRED AT ALL. She lay on top of the covers in the dark, staring at the ceiling, speckled with the faint glow from decades-old glow-in-the-dark stars. Her dad had stuck them up there one summer when she'd had a nightmare and didn't want to be left in the dark. And behind the dresser, she knew there would be a scrawl of crayon, twenty years old. There were memories everywhere in this house, but still, it felt like they hadn't spent enough time.

There was a sudden tap at the window. Eliza sat up.

The noise came again, the rattle of a pebble.

She got up and opened the window, leaning out to see. Another rock came up out of the darkness, and Eliza had to duck out of the way. "Hey!" she yelped.

"Damn. Sorry!" a loud stage-whisper came. Eliza squinted, and there he was, standing down below on the back lawn.

"Cal?" She gulped. "What are you doing?"

"Trying not to wake your mom," he call-whispered up. Eliza exhaled.

"Look, it's late," she said, still feeling tangled up in the past. "Can we do this tomorrow?"

"My father taught me to never go to bed angry," Cal insisted, stepping closer. "Let's just talk a moment. I brought brownies," he added.

Eliza paused. She didn't feel ready to face him again after blowing up like that, but he'd come. Even after she'd lashed out at him, he'd shown up to talk it out. "Wait right there."

She ducked back inside and pulled on a sweatshirt, then tiptoed downstairs. Cal was waiting on the front porch, and when she felt the chilly breeze, she beckoned him inside.

"Shh," she whispered, leading him quietly upstairs to her bedroom. She closed the door gently behind them. Cal looked around.

"Cute," he said, crossing to look at the framed photo on the dresser of Eliza and Paige as kids, posing in their frilly polka-dot bathing suits. He offered up a takeout box. "For you."

Eliza took it, still feeling wary. "Where did you get brownies at midnight on a Sunday?"

"Let's just say I have my ways." Cal gave a cautious smile. "Riley had a batch in the kitchen, fresh from the bakery. I begged some. In a manly fashion," he added, then his expression turned serious. "I'm really sorry, Eliza," he said, taking a step closer. "I know this house is important to you, and you're right, I forget sometimes, not everyone is as lucky as I am. I understand why you got mad at me. I shouldn't have been joking about this."

Crap. Eliza felt a pang. That was a really good apology.

And he brought her peace-offering brownies, too.

Cal was looking at her with such an expression of sincere apology on his handsome face, that she had to take a bite of brownie to keep from reaching for him. "I'm sorry too," she mumbled around a mouthful of chewy batter. She braced herself and swallowed. "I know this wasn't about you, I just . . . needed to get angry. And you were right there."

"But you're right." Cal reached out and pushed a strand of hair from her eyes. "I've never had to worry about making the next mortgage payment, or finding rent."

"No, but you worry about all your employees keeping a job." Eliza felt the need to defend him. "That's stressful in itself." She exhaled, wishing she could explain the raw nerves she had when it came to him and his background. "I know you care, and you work hard. It's just . . ."

"The Khaki Effect," Cal said wryly.

Eliza broke into a smile. "The Khaki Effect," she echoed. "Forgive me?"

Cal blinked. "That was easy," he said. "I had a whole speech planned."

"You don't need speeches when you have brownies," Eliza said lightly, and Cal laughed, pulling her into his arms. He felt solid and stable, and Eliza swayed closer, savoring the touch. He held her a moment.

"So we're OK?" he asked against her hair.

"We're OK."

Eliza felt him exhale, and although she still felt guilty over making this a fight, it still warmed her to know he'd worried.

He cared.

Cal moved her hair from her shoulder and kissed the bare skin it revealed. He followed the curve of her neck, whisper soft, making her shiver, every nerve sparking to life.

"Remember my mom is down the hall," she warned breathlessly. Cal kept on kissing.

"We'll just have to be quiet . . ." he said, tipping her back onto the bed.

Eliza landed on the bedsheets, and Cal followed, covering her with his body and claiming her mouth again. This time, she didn't hold back. She kissed him hard, an all-out, backseat kind of a kiss that pulled them both under and made her blood run hot. He moved against her, peeling her sweatshirt over her head, and then her tank top to follow.

His mouth found her bare breast, and Eliza shuddered. "Oh God," she murmured, and Cal lifted his head with a wicked look in his eyes.

"Shh," he ordered her, smirking. "You want your mom to come see what the noise is about?"

She grinned and silently shook her head.

"Good girl." Cal lowered his mouth to her again, and Eliza bit her lips to keep from moaning. His tongue teased her nipples into stiff peaks, and his hand trailed lower, sliding under the waistband of her loose pajama pants. She giggled, thinking he was just teasing. He wasn't going to do that here, with her mom just twenty feet away. He was polite, a gentleman—

Not that much of a gentleman.

*Oooh.*

Eliza gasped as his fingers brushed against her, stroking, then dipped inside. Cal chuckled, and then he began crawling down her body, dropping kisses and giving teasing bites that only wound her tighter, so by the time he helped her wriggle out of her pajamas and settled between her legs, she was already panting.

"Remember," Cal murmured, biting softly on her inner thigh. "Quiet."

He licked against her, and Eliza buried her face in a pillow to muffle the sound of her pleasured moan. Dear Lord, was he trying to get them caught? She flushed, writhing, captive to his wicked tongue but loving every minute of it as he curled his fingers higher and matched every stroke with a slow, lavish lick.

Eliza sank into the sensation, God, the pure luxury of his mouth and hands, and the relentless pleasure. It felt forbidden and naughty, like two reckless teenagers breaking curfew, but already, she wanted more. She grabbed a handful of his shirt and yanked him back up to meet her lips. "Off," she whispered, pulling it over his head. Cal stripped quickly, and they tumbled under her covers, giggling, pausing only for her to lean out of bed and snag her purse, rummaging for her wallet until she found a condom.

"Girl scout, huh?" Cal grinned, nipping at her neck.

"I have badges and everything," Eliza told him with a flirty grin. She rolled it onto him, pulling the covers over their heads to muffle their voices. The white linen tented over them, and for a moment, it felt like they were totally alone in the world.

Then Cal spread her thighs and pushed inside of her, and there could have been the whole town listening on the other side of her bedroom door, and Eliza wouldn't have cared.

God, he felt so good. So right.

This was how it was supposed to be. Playful and teasing, hot and sweet. They kissed, tongues as tangled as their bodies in the sheets as her hands slid over his torso and his mouth took her to heaven and back. She was cresting, every thrust of his body taking her higher, faster, *deeper*, and she couldn't get enough.

Then Cal caught her wrists and pinned them above her head. He moved into her again, torturously slow. Eliza panted, biting down on his shoulder and bucking desperately against him. She needed more. God, she was so close.

But Cal didn't break pace. He thrust into her, deep and slow, over and over until she was almost crazy with the thick, sweet friction. She didn't notice when she gave up fighting him and just surrendered to the pleasure, but they were moving as one now, and every stroke seemed to fill her deeper, thicker, driving her higher until she was gasping in his arms.

"Cal . . ."

"I'm here, baby," Cal groaned softly against her. His body was slick with sweat, his breathing labored. He rose up, driving slowly into her again, and Eliza nearly lost her mind. She arched to meet him, clutching the bedsheets as Cal leaned down and licked into her mouth, so sensual, her body shook. "I'm right here."

He caught her face in his hand, poised there above her. Eliza couldn't look away; there was nowhere to hide, not with his body possessing her, and his blue eyes fixed, seeing everything, seeing *her.* She lost herself in the tenderness of his gaze, open to him, coming apart. She shattered with a cry that Cal swallowed in his kiss, as he surged into her again, and then she felt him break, and they were both falling, into each other, holding on for dear life.

It was a revelation.

Afterwards, Eliza lay breathless in his arms, reeling from the feel of him. She had only ever glimpsed it before: this sense of true connection, completely letting go. She'd never taken that step, or maybe she'd never been with a man who made her feel like he was worth the risk. But there in Cal's arms, she was completely herself—and it was safe. He didn't think she was too stubborn or too smart, too argumentative or too *much*. He was just as bad as her, only they didn't feel like bad parts of herself with him, something to try to soften or hide.

She'd tasted what that felt like now, and she knew in her heart there was no going back or settling for second best again.

She was hooked.

## 16

The last place Cal wanted to be at nine a.m. on Monday morning was sitting in a conference room on the fourteenth floor, staring at a table full of Prescott board members and a platter of executive pastries. He'd had to drag himself—quietly—out of Eliza's bed at dawn to get on the road in time, and leaving her sleepy, smiling body under the covers alone after the night they'd shared was just about impossible.

Now, he fought to pay attention to financial reports and new business proposals when, just a hundred miles away, Eliza was still snuggled in bed without him.

And to add insult to injury, those croissants had nothing on the ones in Sweetbriar Cove.

"The next quarterly projections show some promising trends out of the Northeast." Their numbers guy was reviewing the thick folder of data Cal was currently trying to focus on. "But with rising costs in other regions, the new revenues . . ."

Cal's phone silently buzzed in his pocket, and he surreptitiously pulled it out, holding the handset under the table to check the message.

*On a scale of 1-10, how bored are you?*

He smiled, feeling a ray of sunshine despite the stuffy environment.

*12,* he typed back. When he looked up again, he caught his uncle glaring at him from across the table. Uh-oh.

"Would you agree we need to shift resources to these new markets?" Arthur spoke up, interrupting. "Cost-cutting in the Midwest, for example."

"I thought we were tabling that idea," Cal said evenly.

"He just said the projections are way below where we need," his uncle replied.

"They're still just projections. The factory could turn things around."

Arthur gave an indulgent smile. " 'Could' isn't a sound strategy. What do the numbers say, Leonard? Closing the factory entirely would solve the problem, wouldn't it?"

The numbers guy paused and shot Cal a nervous look. "Well, it's not as simple as that . . ."

"We're running a loss. Killing the factory would remove that loss." Arthur shrugged. "Seems pretty simple to me."

Cal tried to keep his temper. He should have known Arthur would use the meeting to ambush him. Aside from Cal and Tish, the rest of the board were all older Prescott relatives or corporate representatives. They were there to rubberstamp leadership decisions—and cash their dividend checks.

"Well, that's an interesting idea, Arthur," Cal said evenly, as if they'd never discussed it before. "We'll table it until we can run some more specific models. What's next on the agenda?"

"The gala next week," Tish piped up. Cal shot her a look of relief. "The publicity plans are all in place, and with our permit application still pending on the South Bay development, it will be perfect timing to show city council what a philanthropic organization we are." Tish nodded to her assistant, who began passing out yet another binder. "I've put together the main talking points on the project and how it will revitalize the neighborhood . . ."

Tish launched into her PR overview, and the rest of the meeting thankfully passed without any more argument before they broke for lunch. Cal made sure to see everyone out, chatting and shaking hands with every last member until finally, the room emptied. He sank into the chair at the head of the table and exhaled. Through the open doors, he could see Uncle Arthur huddled with a few people by the elevator. He could only imagine what kind of mass layoffs they were discussing.

"You've got to stop fighting Dad in the open like this." Tish followed Cal's gaze. "You know he just digs his heels in, especially for a crowd."

"So what do you suggest?" Cal asked, feeling like he'd just run a marathon, not sat through a simple corporate get-together. "I just give in, and let him cut his way through our workforce?"

Tish sighed. "No, dummy. You fight him on the details."

"How?" Cal looked back at her, confused.

"He wants to cut costs, so find some to cut. Ones that don't involve people's wages." Tish gave a brisk shrug. "There's always fat in the budget, you just need to get creative, that's all."

"I already told them operating expenses are way too high," Cal replied. "They came down five percent, but it's nowhere near enough."

"Do they know the whole factory is on the line?" Tish retorted.

Cal made a face. He hadn't wanted to make threats like that, not when people needed stability.

Tish sighed again. "Look, you can try being warm and fuzzy, but sometimes that does more harm than good. Go down there, meet face to face, and get real about the situation. Tell them you're fighting for them, but they need to get in the ring, too. You'd be surprised how people can go that extra mile when they know the stakes."

It made sense, however much he wanted to avoid bringing the hammer down. "You're right," Cal said reluctantly. "Of course you're right."

"Obviously." Tish grinned. "Come on, we'll be late for lunch with Mom. Do you want your club sandwich with a side of lecturing or fake concern?"

"Don't even joke." Cal laughed, following her out of the room. "You know they'll pull the double act."

SURE ENOUGH, WHEN THEY ARRIVED BACK AT TISH'S PARENTS' house, his aunt Sylvie greeted him like he'd been wandering the desert. "Look at you," she cried, smothering him with a hug. "You've been gone so long, I was getting worried."

"It's Cape Cod," he reminded her lightly. "Not the mountains of Nepal."

"But still, you missed my arts tea and the annual Groundhog Day trip. Come, I had the chef make his chowder, I know it's your favorite." Sylvie led him through the house and out to the huge glass conservatory, where the table was set for lunch amongst her prize orchids and tropical foliage. Arthur had beaten them home and was already at the table, but he barely glanced up from his phone as Cal and Tish took their seats.

"Arthur, honey, not at the table."

"Just a moment."

Sylvie rolled her eyes indulgently. "The whole point of getting together *after* the board meeting is so you've already dealt with work." She turned to Tish, beaming. "How are the gala plans coming along? What are the flowers?"

"You'd have to ask the event planner," Tish replied, reaching for a roll. "I think they said something about roses? Or gardenias?" She shrugged.

"Well, do you know what you're wearing yet?"

"A dress?" Tish saw her mother's disappointment, and grinned. "I'm sure it'll be lovely. I had my personal shopper pick something out. You know I'm too busy to worry about that stuff."

"I know, but you need to take a break, enjoy yourself. Date," Sylvie added meaningfully, and Cal had to smile. Eliza's mom would approve. But Tish caught Cal's look from across the table and smirked.

"You know who's dating? Is there something you want to share, Cal?"

Sylvie gasped. "You are? Don't tell me, is it the Vanderwhalen girl? I know you two hit it off at the Christmas party."

"No, Sylvie, it's not Luce." Cal shot daggers at Tish, but she only stuck her tongue out at him. "I've been seeing someone. It's still early, but . . . I think it could be serious."

Sylvie clapped her hands together in joy. "When can we meet her? You must invite her to dinner. Or a party. I've been wanting to host, when the weather's warmer, and we can do it outside. Just a small gathering, a hundred people, maybe. I could do a sit-down dinner, and then dancing—"

"Sylvie!" Cal interrupted, before she could go wild and book a full orchestra. "Relax. Like I said, it's still early days."

"Well, tell us about her," his aunt insisted, beaming. "What does she do?"

Cal cleared his throat. "She's a writer," he said, shooting a cautious look at his uncle. "She's visiting her mother on the Cape at the moment. We met out there."

"Oh." Sylvie gave a knowing smile. "Now it makes sense. I've been wondering why you've stayed out there so long. I'm so glad. I can't wait to meet her."

"That might be a while," Cal said, thinking fast for an excuse. "I mean, our schedules, work . . ."

"Don't be silly, Cal," Tish's voice piped up again. "You can bring her to the gala next week."

Cal glared again, but it was too late, the damage was done.

"Perfect!" Sylvie declared.

"I don't know if she can make it . . ." Cal hedged, but his aunt wasn't hearing it.

"Why not?" Sylvie talked over him. For a petite woman, she could have all the force of a bulldozer. "I'm sure she'll want to support you and meet everyone. It's settled. Arthur?"

"Hmm, what?" his uncle looked up, still distracted.

"Cal's new girlfriend," Sylvie beamed. "We're all meeting her at the gala next week."

"Excuse me," Cal said, bolting up from his seat. "I just remembered, I need to make a call. Boise," he added to Arthur, then slipped out before they could object.

Cal escaped back into the house. He had calls to make and could have used the time to get through some of them, but instead, Cal found himself texting Eliza again.

*When can I see you?* he asked, already imagining the feel of her body against him.

*When will you be back?*

*I have some things to take care of at the office, but I can be home by 6.*

*Then that's when you'll see me :)*

Cal smiled. He could make it through lunch, and an afternoon of meetings, if he knew Eliza was waiting at the end of it.

He lingered there in the hallway for as long as was polite, then reluctantly headed back through the house. He wondered what Eliza would make of this place—full of formal rooms decorated with antiques and magazine-ready furniture. Arthur had always been the stuffy traditionalist, even back when his parents were alive, and he could only imagine the fights he and Eliza would get into if they got talking about, well, anything.

Note to self, he would need to keep them a ballroom apart next week.

"Calvin."

He was passing his uncle's study when Arthur's voice summoned him. Cal braced himself and stepped into the room. It was lined with full-length bookcases; his uncle sat behind a heavy, antique desk. Arthur looked up from some papers, but Cal decided to pre-empt him.

"I'm going to look at cost-cutting in the Midwest," he said quickly. "You're right, we need the numbers to work."

Arthur paused. He'd clearly been expecting a fight. "Oh. Well, good."

"It was Tish's idea," Cal added. "You know, she's wasted in PR. I could use her on this stuff more."

"Let's all just play to our strengths," Arthur said dismissively. "But that isn't what I wanted to talk to you about." He circled the desk. "I've been worried about your attitude. We all are."

Oh. It was one of *those* talks.

"If this is about me taking a vacation—" Cal started, but his uncle cut him off.

"It's not about one thing, Calvin. But the little things add up. I'd hoped by now that you would embrace your role as head of this company. But I can see you're still fighting it. It's time to think about what kind of man you are, the life you want to build," Arthur said, a note of impatience in his voice. "The legacy you want to leave behind. Because none of this," he said, gesturing around the ornate study, "was built by chance. It took a vision, and determination to make that vision real."

Cal bit back a smart reply about luck and timing. He knew his uncle meant well. Arthur had looked up to his older brother, Cal's father, and hadn't planned on taking over as the head of the family.

They all meant well, in their way. Which only made Cal's own doubts about his role harder to carry.

"I'll think about it, Uncle Arthur," he said, resigned. "I know there's a lot riding on my decisions. I promise, I only want to do what's right for the company."

"I know you do." Arthur slapped his back. "You'll do the right thing. And about this girl—"

"Woman," Cal corrected him.

Arthur raised an eyebrow, but he didn't comment. "We're looking forward to meeting her," he said instead. "The right partner is crucial for a man in your position. As many deals are done over dinner as they are in the boardroom."

Cal coughed. "Right. Sure."

He headed back to the conservatory, trying to imagine Eliza in pearls, playing hostess the way Sylvie had done beside Arthur all these years. Maybe not. But then the image shifted in his mind. Eliza, right there beside him at a dull function, making things brighter just by being there. Eliza, in his bed every night. Waking up beside him in the morning. Bickering over the morning newspaper and smiling back at him with a mug of coffee.

It was intoxicating. Cal drifted through the rest of lunch and his meetings back at the office, impatient to get back to the Cape. He damn near broke the speed limit on the way there, feeling his tension melt away as the highway wound down the coastline and the ocean glittered, just behind the trees. He called Eliza before his cell signal dropped. "I'm almost back. Want me to come pick you up?"

"I'm just finishing a shift," she replied, and he could hear the restaurant noise humming in the background. "See you at the Pink Palace?"

"Soon."

Cal hung up with a smile. He recognized the spot up ahead where he'd pulled over with that flat tire, weeks ago now, and Eliza had come barreling into his life. He'd known from the start that she was trouble, but he knew so much more now: her loyalty, her strength, the sweetness she let slip when she felt safe enough to open up. There were so many layers she kept hidden beneath that whip-smart surface, and even with another hundred years, he wasn't sure he could discover them all, but damn, it would be an adventure to try.

He stopped at the store in Sweetbriar Cove to pick up some groceries and wine, and then he headed home. As he pulled into the drive, he was rewarded with the sight of Eliza, sitting cross-legged on the front steps. She was reading a book in her lap, head bent, her hair burning at the edges in the last rays of evening sun.

She looked like she belonged there.

"Hey." Eliza looked up and greeted him with a smile. "How was your big meeting?"

"Let's pretend like the last eight hours didn't happen," Cal replied.

Eliza got to her feet and slipped her arms around his waist, pulling him into a kiss. "You look tired," she said, gently pushing his hair back. "Everything OK?"

"It is now." Cal kissed her again, and he felt the world click back into place. Her mouth was cool and sweet, and for a moment, he just savored her, soft in his arms. "What about you, good day?"

"Good enough," Eliza replied. Cal unlocked the door, and she helped him with the groceries. "The numbers on the first new edition of the *Caller* came in really strong, so I might get to bump the page count for the next one."

"That's great." Cal headed for the kitchen, and Eliza peeked in the bags.

"Steak, wine, chocolate cake . . . ? Why, Mr. Prescott, are you trying to seduce me?" She batted her eyelashes at him, and Cal laughed.

"If I wanted to do that, I would have cut straight to the chocolate." He winked. "I thought we could stay in tonight. I'll cook."

"That sounds like an offer I can't refuse," Eliza smiled.

"See? My plan's already working." Cal took his time pouring them a glass of wine. "You sit down and relax."

"Now you're really talking dirty," Eliza quipped. She hopped up on a stool by the counter and let out a sigh of relief. "We had a big party in from New York, I was on my feet all day."

"Trade you?" Cal said, only half-joking. "Next time, you sit through all the financial forecasts and passive-aggressive comments from my uncle, and I'll take the lunch rush."

"Deal," Eliza said immediately. She gave him a sympathetic look. "That bad?"

Cal shrugged. He didn't want to complain, not when he knew his uncle was only looking out for the family. "I'll figure it out. The gala is next week, so hopefully everyone will have some fun and relax before the next meeting." He paused, looking over at her. "Would you maybe want to go with me?"

Eliza grinned. "Are you, like, inviting me to prom?"

Cal laughed. It did feel that way. "I know it's not your

scene," he said quickly, "and I need to play host. But I'd really like it if you'd be there with me."

Eliza bit her lip. "You mean, meet all your friends and family?" She looked nervous for a moment, so Cal put down the chopping knife and moved closer.

"They'll love you," he reassured her.

Eliza raised an eyebrow.

"OK, so maybe Aunt Mindy will hold a grudge," Cal admitted. "But I promise, their bark is worse than their bite. It would mean a lot to me," he added, and Eliza exhaled.

"Then of course I'll be there." She tilted her head up to him for a kiss. "I'm guessing the dress code is fancy-pants?"

"Super-extra fancy-pants, actually," Cal corrected her, smiling.

"Noted."

Cal went back to the food prep, and Eliza sipped her wine. She looked around. "You know, I'm going to miss this place. When does your godmother get back?"

"Not for a few weeks." Cal laid the steaks in a simple olive oil and rosemary marinade and turned his attention to the vegetables. "She's actually the one who taught me how to cook this," he added. "She said every man needed to be able to wow in the kitchen."

"I like her already," Eliza said, and Cal couldn't resist pausing to round the counter and kiss her again. This time, she slid her arms up around his neck, possessive, and teased his mouth with her tongue until his blood was pounding.

He lifted her in a single move, wrapping her legs around his waist. He started walking her towards the bedroom.

"But . . . dinner . . ." Eliza sounded breathless. Her cheeks flushed, and her body arched as she held on tight.

"The marinade needs thirty minutes," Cal said, leaning in to nip at her neck. Eliza shivered against him.

"Well, in that case . . . How will we spend the time?"

Cal grinned and pressed her back against the nearest wall. "I have a couple of ideas," he murmured, capturing her mouth again and feeling her body rise.

Dinner could wait. He had more important things to taste.

# 17

"I need your help," Eliza greeted Mackenzie and Brooke later that week, meeting for lunch in Provincetown. They'd all been so busy she hadn't seen them since karaoke night, and they'd set aside the time to catch up, eat, and enjoy a lazy afternoon in the sun. "I know we planned on a spa day, but I have an emergency."

Brooke's forehead wrinkled in concern. "What kind?"

"A shopping emergency."

Her friend laughed. "That's my favorite kind. Right there with 'Oh no, all the ice cream will melt if I don't eat it' emergencies."

"And 'Whoops, my boyfriend surprised me with a tropical vacation' emergencies," Mackenzie agreed, smiling. "What's the problem?"

"Cal invited me to be his date for the Prescott Foundation Gala," Eliza replied. She'd had days to mull it over, and her early excitement had faded clean away. "I'm going to need a dress. A fancy, formal, snooty, gorgeous gown, so I can mingle with all of Cal's rich friends without feeling two feet tall," she added. "Do you think we can find something here in town?"

"Challenge accepted," Brooke declared. "Trust me, I know every designer in a twenty-mile radius. This town is full of cute formalwear."

"And she'd know," Mackenzie laughed. "Didn't you have to find replacement bridesmaid's dresses on zero notice?"

"The bride suddenly decided they looked too good in blue," Brooke said, rolling her eyes good-naturedly. "They wound up in a hideous salmon color, but the best part is, it clashed with the bride's skin tone, so she looked even worse!"

"No salmon, thanks," Eliza said. She paused. "The gala . . . This is serious. I saw the photos from last year, it's like the who's who of Boston's social scene. I don't know if I'm cut out for that."

"Sure you are," Mackenzie said, frowning. "Where's this coming from?"

Eliza shrugged. It had only taken long enough for her amazing orgasms to fade for the reality of the situation to slap her in the face. "Just . . . my last few run-ins with these people haven't exactly been great. I don't want to let Cal down. This would be the first time he's brought me to anything," she added. "You know, as a date."

"Awww." Brooke looked excited. "You really like him!"

Eliza flushed. "Maybe. Or maybe I just don't want to get humiliated in front of a whole ballroom full of important people."

"She likes him." Mackenzie grinned. "Don't worry, we'll find something spectacular. You'll be the belle of the ball."

"I'll settle for blending into the crowd, thanks," Eliza said. "Although, in this crowd, that might be above my pay grade. Crap, I'm going to need shoes, too," she realized. "And a bag. And jewelry . . . There goes my paycheck for the week."

Brooke shook her head. "We're the same size," she said. "You can borrow something from me. And the lost and found at the hotel is like a fashion closet of cute accessories."

"Would that be OK?" Eliza checked, not wanting to cause any trouble.

"Sure," Brooke grinned. "I figure if nobody's claimed something in six months, it's fair game."

"Thank you. You're a lifesaver," Eliza told her gratefully, but as they finished up their food and started strolling the cute cobbled streets downtown, she still couldn't shake the feelings of trepidation when she thought about the gala.

She tried to brush it off, but clearly, she was a bad actress, because they were browsing the first boutique when Mackenzie nudged her gently. "What's really going on?" she asked. "I thought you loved an excuse to get dressed up and hit an open bar."

"I do, usually," Eliza said. She flipped through the racks, trying to find something Sukie and the glossy blonde crowd would wear. "But this isn't just a fun night out. All of Cal's family and friends are going to be sizing me up. Judging me." Eliza's nerves returned.

"Since when do you care so much about random strangers?" Mackenzie looked puzzled. "The Eliza I know doesn't give a crap what people think."

"This is just different." Eliza shrugged, self-conscious. "The fundraiser is a big deal to Cal, and I'm just not part of that world." She paused on a plain black cocktail dress. "What do you think?" she asked, pulling it down.

"Boring!" Brooke called, sing-song, from across the room. "But this would look amazing on you." She held up a red silk gown with draped neckline. "Can you just imagine this with old Hollywood curls, red lipstick . . . Va-va-voom!"

The dress was gorgeous, a showstopper. Which is exactly

what Eliza didn't want to do. "Va-va-nope," she replied. "It would be like walking around with a neon billboard screaming, 'Look at me!' "

"Because you'd be a knockout." Brooke and Mackenzie exchanged a look.

Eliza caught the concern in their eyes, but she didn't know how to explain. She *wanted* to blend in and be invisible, so she didn't embarrass Cal. She needed the night to be a success for him and the Foundation, and the last thing he needed was to have her sticking out like a sore thumb, or, worse still, looking like she didn't belong. "Let's just find something gorgeous *and* understated," she said instead, turning back to the racks. "Think 'work function,' not 'wild weekend in Vegas.' "

"Their loss." Brooke shrugged and set the red dress down again. "But anytime you want to wow, you know where to find it."

TWO HOURS LATER AND ELIZA HAD TRIED ON WHAT SEEMED LIKE every formal dress in town. Cocktail, floor-length, lacy, and satin, she'd paraded them all to Brooke and Mackenzie, but nothing was making her feel like a million bucks.

Hell, at this point, she'd settle for feeling like fifty bucks and change.

"OK, here's the last one," she said, emerging from the dressing room of the fifth boutique. This dress was a demure navy sheath with an asymmetrical neckline and knee-length skirt. "I figure it's between this, the black, and that gray one."

"First of all, I refuse to allow you to buy a blah gray dress for this," Mackenzie said, folding her arms. "Second, you look like you're going to a job interview in that."

"And third, the black was so boring, I can't even remember what it looks like," Brooke finished.

"Guys!" Eliza looked in the mirror in despair. "This isn't funny. I need to pick *something*."

"Ahem, the red," Brooke fake-coughed.

"Something appropriate," Eliza insisted. She took in her reflection: the dress hugged her figure, at least, and didn't flash too much skin. With pumps and a pretty clutch, she would blend right in. She checked the tag. "And it's on sale." She brightened. "Ding-ding-ding, we have a winner."

"If you say so," Brooke muttered. Mackenzie elbowed her.

"You look great," she added loyally. "Cal won't know what hit him."

"Thanks." Eliza smiled. "You guys have been awesome."

She changed back into her regular clothes and took the dress to the register. "I owe you both drinks," she said. "And dessert, too."

"Raincheck?" Brooke checked her phone. "I better get back to work."

"Me too," Mackenzie said. "I just got a big order for a set of my new collection."

"That's great. What is it this time?" Eliza asked, as the clerk rang her up. "Drowned sailors? Mythical beasts?" She loved Mackenzie's work, and her friend was famous for her delightfully odd ceramics.

"Close." Mackenzie grinned. "The Salem witch trials. Only in my pieces, the witches turn on the mob and hunt them down with burning torches."

Eliza laughed. "That sounds amazing. I'll have to come by the studio and see."

"Swing by anytime. I messed up a bunch of bowls last week in the kiln," Mackenzie said cheerfully. "And you know what that means."

"Smashing time," Eliza chorused with Brooke. "Hold that

thought until next week," she added. "I'll probably need to blow off some steam after the gala."

"Keep up posted." Brooke gave her a hug. "And let me know what you need to finish the outfit!"

Eliza's phone buzzed just as Brooke and Mackenzie departed. She picked it up, expecting Cal, but instead it was Riley's voice on the other end of the line. "All clear?" he asked in a hushed voice.

She'd almost forgotten their plans. "Yup, Brooke just headed back to work."

"Perfect," he said, and gave her an address just a few streets away.

"Be there in a sec."

Eliza walked over, swinging her bag with the new dress inside. She wished she could have been more excited today: happily trying on outfits and gossiping in anticipation with her friends. So why did it feel more like she was gearing up for an appointment at the dentist than a fabulous gala? It wasn't the formal ball itself; she'd attended plenty of fancy parties before. On the features beat at the newspaper, she'd been the one covering charity fundraisers and big events. She usually had a great time, getting into the swing of things so she could write up every detail and give her readers the inside scoop.

But this wasn't an assignment, and she wouldn't just be an anonymous face in the crowd. She would be on Cal's arm—on display. And something about the thought of walking into that room full of strangers, looking at her—judging her—made Eliza's usual confidence wither away.

*It will be fine,* she told herself. She would play nice and stay quiet, and they would sail through the night without any problems. Cal had blended in just fine with her friends, she could at least try to do the same for him.

When she arrived at the address Riley had given her, she found him loitering outside a jeweler's, looking nervous.

Eliza looked from him to the window display of gorgeous engagement rings and back again. "Really?" she squealed, her problems suddenly seeming far away. "Congratulations!"

"Whoa, there." Riley looked bashful. "I haven't asked her yet. And she hasn't said yes."

"But she will," Eliza beamed. She'd had her doubts about Riley in the beginning—and with his playboy reputation, who wouldn't?—but he and Brooke had turned out to be the perfect fit. They were crazy about each other, and Eliza knew that taking the next step in their relationship had always been just a question of when, not if.

And when, it seemed, was now.

"Let's go inside," Riley said, glancing nervously around. "I don't want anyone to ruin the surprise."

Eliza was about to tease him for being paranoid when she caught a glimpse of Aunt June at the other end of the street. "Quick!" She yanked him through the door and ducked out of sight, before Riley's shopping expedition could wind up front-page news.

Inside, the store clerk greeted Riley like an old friend. "You've been here before?" Eliza asked.

"I narrowed it down to a few choices," Riley said. He pushed back his messy blonde hair, looking more excited now. "I have one that I like best, but wanted a second opinion. This is the ring she's going to be wearing for the rest of her life, after all. Unless I screw things up," he added with a grin.

"Hey, stop that." Eliza hit him lightly. "Nobody's messing anything up. Besides, you think Brooke would let you?"

"Good point," he chuckled.

The clerk brought out a tray with three rings displayed. "What do you think?" Riley asked, nudging it closer.

Eliza leaned in. They were all beautiful choices, but one leapt out at her as being exactly Brooke's style. "This one," she said immediately, pointing to a simple platinum band with a princess cut diamond. "It's classic, elegant . . . perfectly Brooke."

Riley grinned wider. "That's my pick, too. I just wanted to be sure."

"She's going to love it." Eliza hugged him. "But you better do it soon. I don't know if I can keep the secret for long!"

Riley laughed. "I've got it all planned out, next weekend," he confided. "I'm taking her out on the boat for a sunset cruise. It was how we spent one of our first dates. Back when we were pretending to be just friends," he added, smiling.

"I remember," Eliza laughed. "And I also remember telling her to just go for it. So, you can thank me."

"Thanks." Riley grinned. "I know it's a cliché, but, she makes everything better, you know? I feel more like myself—my best self—just being with her."

Eliza felt a pang. "Didn't you worry though, starting out, that you guys were just too different?"

Something must have given her away in her tone, because Riley gave her a sideways look. "Me and Brooke, or you and Cal?"

"Both. Neither. I don't know." Eliza let out a sigh. "It's just . . . One minute, I feel like I can let my guard down with him and put it all out there. That we're connecting, for real. But then I remember who he is and where he comes from, and I wonder how we could ever make it work."

Riley turned, frowning. "Is this coming from him? Because if he's said anything to make you feel like you're not good enough—"

"No," Eliza stopped him quickly. "It's not about him. This is just my stuff."

"OK." Riley seemed to relax. "Because you say the word, and me and Grayson can pay him a visit."

Eliza couldn't help but smile. "Oh yeah? What are you two going to do, threaten to hack his computer and take his bookshop privileges away?"

"We'll take care of things." Riley gave her a nod. "Besides, you already told me where to hide the body."

Eliza laughed. "Easy now. Anyway, like I said, it's not his fault. I'm the one who doesn't fit in with the whole society thing."

"Bullshit," Riley said firmly. Then he paused.

"What?" Eliza prodded.

"Look, I don't have anything against the guy, he seems nice enough," he started, looking reluctant. "But if being with him makes you feel this way, then maybe he's not the right guy for you." Riley shrugged. "You deserve someone who makes you feel amazing, just being yourself. Not like you don't measure up, or that you need to be careful, in case you get hurt. Before Brooke, I was with someone, and it felt like putting on a show," he added. "You know, like I had to be on my best behavior, living up to the man I thought she wanted. That's not real. You can't be with someone, really be with them, if you're pretending to be something you're not."

His words struck Eliza, too close to home.

She swallowed. "I know," she said quietly, and Riley gave her a hug.

"But I'm not worried about you."

"You're not?" she asked.

Riley chuckled. "You'll be fine. If anyone knows who they are, it's you."

Eliza looked at him and felt something snap back into place.

He was right. She'd always known exactly who she was—

and been proud of it, too. Something about being with Cal had shifted her center of gravity. No, she'd *let* it shift. But that wasn't her, and it wasn't how she could live her life.

Bending over backwards to try to fit into Cal's world would never work. Either she did this her way, or it wasn't worth doing.

"Thank you," Eliza said gratefully. "Is it OK if I take off? There's something I need to do."

"Of course. Thanks for the help," Riley said.

"Brooke's going to love the ring!" Eliza ducked out of the store and walked determinedly back the way she'd come. All this second-guessing and insecurity had nothing to do with Cal himself. He thought she was perfect, even when she was showing up to fancy places in jeans and a worn-out shirt.

Well, she could do a little better than that this time.

Eliza opened the door to the clothing boutique.

"Can I help you?" The clerk looked up and recognized Eliza. "Oh, hi. Did you forget something before?"

"Yup." Eliza deposited her bag on the counter with a thud. "I need to make an exchange."

# 18

"I've got a surprise for you."

Eliza glanced over from the passenger seat. The day of the gala had arrived, and Cal was driving them into the city, his backseat full of garment bags, shoe boxes, and the weekender tote of beauty essentials she had packed to get ready.

"Let me guess," she said, trying to ignore the tangle of nerves forming in her stomach. "We're going to bail on the gala, and drive to Mexico instead. Just you, me, a beach, and two of those drinks with little umbrellas in them?"

Cal chuckled. "Close. No, I booked us into a hotel for the night. I have to be there early to make sure everything's running smoothly. I figured you could relax and get ready in style."

"That's sweet, thank you," Eliza said, even though secretly, she would have preferred the grand escape. "But are you sure it's not just an elaborate plot to stop me from seeing your apartment? Don't think I haven't noticed you're keeping me away from it. What's the big secret," she teased, "notches on your bedpost? Lime-green bedsheets? Or is it a frat-house den of debauchery?"

"None of the above." Cal flashed a grin as they reached the downtown core. "OK, so maybe my housekeeper is on vacation this week."

"I knew it!" Eliza smiled. "Well, I guess I'll just have to settle for room service and pay TV. You think they'll have a steam iron, so I can shake out my dress?"

Cal looked amused. "I think they'll find one for you."

When he pulled over, Eliza discovered why. "The Drake," she said, swallowing. The fanciest, most luxurious hotel in the city.

"Of course. It's my favorite spot to stay in town."

The valet opened the car door for her, and when she reached to help with the bags, he shooed her away. "I have this, ma'am."

"We're in the Prescott suite," Cal said, slipping him a folded bill. "Please be careful with the garment bags."

"Yes, sir."

Eliza blinked. "You have a suite named after you?"

Cal gave her a grin. "Long story, but it involves my great-grandfather, a poker game, and shares in the East India Company."

"Of course it does," Eliza said faintly. Something told her she was going to have to get used to stories like that, especially if she was going to make it through the night.

She followed Cal inside the opulent lobby and up to the penthouse suite. There was a sitting room, bedroom, and library space, all with stunning views of the city. "Think you'll manage here?" Cal asked, looking around.

"I'll be brave and try. This place is gorgeous." Eliza placed her handbag on the coffee table, where it looked very small surrounded by the swathes of antique rugs, plush upholstery, and glittering chandeliers. "What do you say we give that king-sized bed a test run?" she beckoned, flirtatious, and Cal smiled, sweeping her up in his arms and depositing her on the mattress with a bounce.

Eliza kissed him, loving the kick of adrenaline in her veins and the way her body seemed to arch to him of its own accord. But Cal only kissed her for a moment before sitting up and straightening his shirt. "I wish I could stay," he said, looking reluctant. "But I've been fielding calls from the event planner all day. I better get over there."

"OK." Eliza hid her disappointment and tugged him down for one last kiss. "But this bed is getting a workout, so don't make me have to use it as a trampoline."

Cal grinned. "After the gala is done, we won't get out of it all weekend," he promised. "They'll just wheel room service right in."

"Now you're talking."

Cal got up and grabbed the garment bag with his tux. "I'll call when I'm on my way over. We'll have fun tonight, I promise."

"Go." Eliza flopped back into the impossibly soft pillows. "Be a titan of industry. I'll be here, raiding the minibar."

"Go crazy," Cal said with a grin, and then he left her, the door to the suite clicking shut behind him.

Eliza exhaled, gazing up at the brocade canopy on the four-poster bed. She felt her nerves creeping again about tonight, so she leapt up and went to explore. There was a complimentary iPod docked in the living room, so she set it to blast some upbeat rock, and set about discovering exactly what kind of perks the Prescott name provided.

The answer was, a lot.

She toured the suite, inhaling the scent of the fresh-cut roses on every surface, and sampling the chocolates displayed on a silver platter. There was fresh fruit and finger sandwiches, and a thick card propped against a bottle of wine. *"With compliments of the Drake,"* she read aloud. *"Best wishes, as always, from your home away from home."*

Maybe she could get used to this.

"You will not believe this place," she said, calling Paige from the marbled bathroom. "The tub is like a lap pool, with views all the way to the river."

"Fancy," her sister laughed.

"Are you sure you don't want to come tonight?" Eliza checked. "Cal said he could get an extra ticket."

"And play third wheel? No thanks."

"More like wing-woman," Eliza argued. "I feel like I'm going to need backup walking in there alone."

"You won't be alone," Paige reminded her. "You have Cal. Anyway, I can't, I have a blind date tonight."

"Ooh, with who?" Eliza perked up. She started running water into the tub and selected a whole bottle of rose-scented oils to fill the room with bubbles.

"My co-worker's cousin just moved to town, and she thinks we'll hit it off." Paige sounded uncertain. "We're having dinner, then going to an art exhibit I want to see."

"That could be fun," Eliza said encouragingly. She knew Paige hadn't been dating since her breakup, so it was good she was finally getting back out there again. "Maybe he'll sweep you off your feet."

"Maybe," Paige agreed, but she didn't seem convinced. "Anyway, how about brunch tomorrow? Bring Cal. I need to actually meet the guy properly, if this is serious. Is it?" she asked.

Eliza found herself smiling. "It is. OK, brunch then. And have fun tonight!"

"You too."

Eliza rang off. She brought in the champagne and chocolates, setting them on a little stool by the tub, then stripped off and slipped into the hot, steamy water.

Ahhh . . .

She sank back, looking out at the city, and tried to feel calm. She was nervous about tonight, but excited, too, a flutter of delicious anticipation dancing in her stomach. Meeting all of Cal's friends and family was already intimidating, and tonight, the stakes seemed even higher: making their debut as a couple to all of Boston's social elite.

Eliza wondered, did Cal know that kind of pressure was enough to make her break out in hives? There was nobody else she would do it for, but when Cal had asked, she had barely hesitated.

This was for real. She wanted to be there for him, support him—and then drag him back to this hotel room and spend the weekend barely coming up for air.

She flushed, just imagining the things they could do in this bathtub . . . But more than that, she wanted to curl up beside him at night and wake up with him to do it all over again.

*This was the real thing.*

Eliza inhaled in a rush. It was a quiet voice, steady and calm, but she still wasn't ready to listen to it just yet. It felt too soon, too precarious, to be feeling this way.

*One day—and night—at a time.*

She got out of the tub and toweled off, wrapping herself in an illegally fluffy robe. She went to get her things to start getting ready—

Her dress!

Eliza's heart stopped. No, no, no! She searched frantically

through the bags, even checking the closet in case the bellhop had hung it up, but there was no sign of it. Had Cal taken the wrong bag with him?

The doorbell sounded. Eliza flung it open, flustered, to find a uniformed butler—with her dress bag cradled in his arms. "I took the liberty of taking it to be steamed," he informed her. "Is there anything else you'll be needing?"

Eliza exhaled in a whoosh. "Oh, thank God. I was having a serious meltdown," she said, grabbing it from him.

"I can send a doctor to prescribe some Xanax, if you wish."

Eliza had to search his face to see if he was even joking. His lip twitched in a smile. "Oh. No, thanks." She laughed.

"Very well." The butler leaned in with a wink. "I find a glass of the '58 Chateau works nearly as well."

"Good tip."

Eliza closed the door and sank back, her heart still racing. Maybe she would open that bottle.

TWO HOURS LATER, ELIZA WAS DRESSED, STYLED, SPRITZED, AND perched on the couch, trying not to wrinkle her dress while she watched old Housewives reruns and waited for Cal to come pick her up.

And waited. And waited.

At half past seven, her phone finally rang. "I'm sorry," Cal said, sounding apologetic. "I totally lost track of time. People have already started arriving, and I need to be here to greet them."

"Oh." Eliza's heart sank. "No, I understand."

"Jump in a cab, and I'll meet you here," Cal told her. "Just look for the guy in a tux trying to keep the wheels from falling off."

"You've got this," Eliza reassured him. "I'll be right there."

She hung up and collected her purse: a small, jeweled clutch that, sure enough, Brooke had managed to save from the hotel lost-and-found. Eliza hoped that the real owner didn't mind her borrowing it for the night, even though she felt reckless trading her usual messenger bag for a tiny square that barely held lipstick and a breath mint. She gave herself a final look in the mirror and smiled. Her friends had been right: the red dress was stunning, and she felt ready for battle in the brilliant silk armor.

She pulled on her coat, headed downstairs, and caught a cab to the gala venue for the night, the grand Public Library building in Copley Square. She'd loved to visit the grand, Renaissance-style building when she was a kid, but she'd never seen it look like this: spotlights illuminating the impressive frontage, with a red carpet leading up the front steps, and press and photographers lined up in front, their cameras flashing at the procession of guests in gowns and tuxedos making their way inside.

Eliza took a breath, steeling herself, then joined the line. Security kept careful watch at the doors, and a brisk-looking woman in black approached her with a clipboard, wearing a headset and a stern expression. "Name?"

"Eliza Bennett," she said.

The woman scanned her list. "Bennett with a B?" she asked.

"Is there any other way?" Eliza cracked, but her joke fell flat.

"I'm sorry, I don't see you. Do you have the invitation?"

"No, sorry," Eliza said. "I'm supposed to meet Cal here. Calvin Prescott," she added. "He's the one hosting this whole event."

"I know who he is, but I don't see you on the list," the woman repeated. "I'm sorry, could you move aside? People are trying to get through. Welcome, names?" she said, already stepping around Eliza.

Eliza fumbled with her clutch and pulled out her cellphone. It rang and rang, but Cal didn't pick up. He was probably busy inside—with the guests who weren't being turned away at the door. Perfect.

"Excuse me." Eliza tapped the door-woman on the shoulder. "Hi, sorry, but if you can't let me in, then I need you to go find Mr. Prescott. He'll vouch for me."

"I'm a little busy right now." The woman glared.

Eliza held her ground. "Then I'm sure you can find someone else."

"You need to move aside." The woman looked around, then beckoned to security. "People need to get past."

Eliza was just about ready to roll up her coat sleeves and throw down when a voice came from behind her on the red carpet.

"Eliza?"

She turned. It was Tish, waltzing past the line in a gorgeous green gown and fake-fur cape. "You look amazing," Tish said, greeting her with air kisses. "Sorry, lipstick. I hate the stuff," Tish added. "I always forget I'm wearing it and eat the canapes, and it winds up smeared everywhere."

"Hi," Eliza said, relieved. "Maybe you can help. Cal didn't put me on the list, and now I'm about to get carted off in chains for trespassing."

Tish arched an eyebrow. "Kelly, what's going on?"

"I'm sorry, Miss Prescott," the door-woman said, suddenly looking anxious. "We were told nobody gets in without an invite."

"Eliza's not nobody," Tish said, linking her arm through Eliza's.

"I'm so sorry," Kelly groveled again as they moved past.

Eliza exhaled. "Thanks," she said, stepping inside. "Cal's not picking up."

"He's probably busy playing host." Tish looked around. "He always gets nervous over these things."

"Cal, nervous?" Eliza didn't believe it.

Tish gave her a smile. "Between you and me, that charm only goes skin-deep. The Foundation means a lot to him, so it's important this night goes perfectly."

Was it just Eliza's imagination, or was there a note of warning in Tish's voice? She brushed it off. "Well, this place looks amazing. I'm sure it'll be great."

Tish checked her phone. "I have to go see a guy about a permit, but I'll see you around later?"

"I'll be here."

Tish whisked away, leaving Eliza alone to take in the party for the first time. The building had been taken over with a cherry-blossom theme, and huge displays of pink origami flowers fluttered in every corner, suspended from the ceiling in oversized art installations. Waiters circulated with delicious-looking trays of food, and in the main ballroom, she could see there were several full bars set up, their counters filled with expensive champagnes.

How much of the event budget could have just been sent directly to the charity?

Eliza pushed down her cynical thought. Cal knew far more about getting rich people to open their wallets, and if it took lavish parties and a ten-piece orchestra on the balcony, then she was sure it was worth it.

She found the coat check and peeled of her heavy woolen coat. The hallway was warm, but she still shivered, catching a glance from a passing couple—all in black. In fact, looking around at the guests, the tones were all muted and sophisticated: blacks, navy blue, a few daring pastel chiffons. Well, if she was going to wear this red, she might as well *wear* it.

Eliza took a deep breath, squared her shoulders, and walked in.

~

CAL FINALLY HAD EVERYTHING UNDER CONTROL. THE EVENT planners had done a spectacular job, the venue looked great, and—most important of all—his VIP donors were already opening their checkbooks and signing up for the silent auction.

One of the guests, a high-profile tech CEO, checked the listing and whistled. "Owner's box at the playoffs? How did you swing that one?"

"Let's just say I called in a favor." Cal smiled. "And there's a trip to London your wife will like: private tours at Buckingham Palace."

The man shook his head, but he was smiling—and reaching for the nearest pen. "I can already tell you'll give my wallet a workout tonight."

"Hey, it's all for a good cause!" Cal slapped him on the back and moved on: greeting, mingling, and making sure everyone was having a good time. Still, despite the crowds, he kept one eye on the entrance, wondering when Eliza would arrive. He wanted to introduce her around; there were a few big editors and publishers in attendance tonight, and he was certain that just five minutes with her and they'd be jumping to add her to their teams. He was just reaching for his phone, ready to call, when he caught a flash of red out of the corner of his eye.

His jaw dropped—and he wasn't alone.

"Wow," he heard a man murmur behind him. Sure enough, every head in the room had turned to watch Eliza walk in.

She was magnificent. There was no other way to describe her, gliding into the ballroom in a floor-length red gown that set Cal's blood boiling and his heart beating right out of his chest. The silky fabric pooled around her curves, draped modestly at the neckline, but when she turned, he could see it fell in a low swoop across her back.

He forgot how to breathe.

"There you are." The look on Eliza's face was pure relief as she emerged from the crowd. "I didn't know where to find you."

She took in his slack-jawed expression and paused, looking down. "Is the dress OK? I wasn't sure if—"

"It's perfect." Cal finally found his voice. "I love it. Never take it off."

Eliza arched an eyebrow, her familiar confident smile returning. "Never?" she said, leaning closer so only he could hear. "That would be a shame, you'd never get to see what I'm wearing underneath. Or not wearing," she added, her lips grazing his earlobe.

Cal felt like he'd been hit with an anvil. Dear God, did she want him hard, right there in the middle of the gala?

He knew he should still be on hosting duty, but he needed to touch her right now. Without an audience.

"Let me give you the tour," he said, then took her hand and pulled her after him, moving fast to the edge of the room.

"Cal, wait. Heels!" she protested, and Cal managed to slow long enough for her to find her footing again. He ducked out of the main ballroom and down the hall, searching for a quiet spot. Finally, he reached the exit to the courtyard, where a fountain was burbling and tiny tea lights were strung up, making a dim, romantic, retreat. "What's the rush?" Eliza asked, looking breathless.

Cal moved her back against the wall and kissed her without a word.

*Yes.*

Her mouth was sweet and hot, and she melted against him. Her dress was silk under his palms, and he skimmed over every last curve, making her moan into his mouth.

"You look incredible," he murmured, finally breaking away. "Every guy here couldn't take their eyes off you."

"I don't care what every other guy thinks." Eliza gave him a sultry smile. "Except one. The man with the dessert tray," she added, teasing, and Cal laughed.

"Damn pastry chef. How am I supposed to compete with that?"

"Hmm, you'll think of something." Eliza swayed closer and kissed him again. "I like you in a tux," she said, smoothing her palms down his lapels. "Very James Bond."

"I'll spare you my bad British accent." Cal took a breath, trying to rein in the desire thundering through him, but it was no use. He wanted to steal her away to some dark, secluded room and make her moan his name over and again. He wanted to possess her with a fierceness that shook him to his core, but this wasn't the time. And it definitely wasn't the place.

"We have to go back to the party now," he said regretfully. "But just know you're driving me crazy right now. And when this is all over? I have plans."

Eliza's eyes sparkled. "Good. Because I've got a few of my own."

Cal groaned and pulled her back against him. He kissed her hard, until they both were gasping. "OK, now we really do have to go back," he said. He stepped out of the corner, and—

"Calvin, there you are!"

Cal gave thanks that he'd had a two-second head start before his uncle and aunt stepped into the courtyard. It wouldn't have been the best first impression in the world if they'd caught him necking with Eliza, but luckily, she was only slightly flushed as Cal presented her. "Sylvie, Arthur, this is Eliza Bennett."

"It's lovely to meet you," Eliza said, politely holding out a hand to shake.

"Finally, the famous Eliza!" Sylvie exclaimed, and pulled her into a hug. "We've been dying to meet you. Cal won't say a thing about you, so I'm coming in blind, I'm afraid. You're a writer?"

"Journalist," Eliza replied, but before Cal could change the subject, she continued, "Most recently at the *Boston Herald,* but I'm freelancing now."

His uncle frowned. "Bennett? Wait, aren't you the one who wrote that hit piece on Mindy Kensington?"

Eliza blinked. "I profiled her, yes. Are you friends?"

Arthur glared. "She's my sister."

Cal sighed. He should have warned Eliza ahead of time not to mention her time at the newspaper. "Eliza's really sorry about any problems the article caused," he said quickly. "She caught Mindy on a bad day. I think everyone regrets the incident."

"Do we?" Eliza asked, giving him a look.

"We should get back inside." Cal quickly steered them towards the ballroom. "Drinks, anyone?"

Luckily, Aunt Sylvie was a pro at changing the subject to easy small talk, and soon, she was chatting away with Eliza about Cape Cod, her social diary, and the Foundation. "We're all so proud of Cal," she said with a doting smile. "It's so wonderful seeing him carry on his parents' good work."

"I know he works hard." Eliza squeezed his hand. "Everything looks great here tonight."

"As long as you're not planning any more articles," Arthur said, still looking annoyed. Sylvie gave an awkward laugh.

"Oh, he's just joking. Water under the bridge!"

Cal cleared his throat. "I want to introduce Eliza to some people," he said quickly, taking her arm. "We'll see you at dinner."

"Great meeting you," Eliza added, before Cal led her away.

She exhaled. "We're going to need a safeword," she said, and Cal promptly choked on his drink.

"Shh!"

Eliza laughed. "For parties, I mean! How about 'canapes'? When conversations get awkward, I can just say I'm dying to get something to eat, and we can make our escape."

"That wasn't awkward," Cal lied. "Uncle Arthur is like that with everyone. Besides, you knew they weren't happy about your article."

"Funny how everyone's mad about what I wrote, but not the fact that Mindy was screaming at her poor nanny," Eliza said, giving him a look.

"You're lucky, she couldn't make it tonight." Cal scanned the room. "And the Mayor won't be staying for dinner. So we should get through the rest of the evening without another scene, as long as you don't mention it again."

Eliza pressed her lips together. "Any other topics of conversation you'd like to be off limits?"

Cal thought fast. "Good point. You should be fine, as long as you steer clear of the upcoming elections. Well, politics in general," he added. "Oh, and when I introduce you to Bill Keller, don't mention the Red Sox. He just lost a bid for the team and he's not happy about it."

"Should I write it all down?" Eliza asked, and Cal smiled.

"Don't worry, I can do all the talking."

Eliza gave him an odd look. "So I just stand here and look pretty?"

Cal was distracted by someone across the room. Ted Chambers. One of the publishers he wanted to introduce her to. "Yup, you're doing great," he said hurriedly. "Ted!" he called to get the man's attention. "How the hell have you been?"

"Calvin." Ted greeted him with an enthusiastic handshake. "And who's your lovely lady friend?" he asked, taking in Eliza. "If Julie wasn't here somewhere, I'd have to steal this one away."

Cal chuckled. "Ted Chambers, Eliza Bennett. Eliza's a great journalist," he added proudly.

"Oh yes?" Ted asked. "What kind of things?"

"Lifestyle, features, mainly," Cal answered for her, in case Eliza went off track. "She'd be great someplace like Chambers, you're launching another fashion title next year, aren't you?"

"Now, that's supposed to be under wraps," Ted mock-scolded him.

Cal grinned. "Word travels fast."

"Yes, it does. Great meeting you, Eliza. Cal, we'll talk." Ted winked and moved on.

Cal turned to Eliza, grinning. "You did great," he said, pleased.

"I didn't say a word," Eliza replied, frowning.

"That's fine, I'm sure he thought you were just nervous," Cal said, wanting to reassure her. "I'll call him Monday and mention you again. I bet I can get an interview set up by the end of the week."

"Wow." Eliza looked taken aback. "That easy?"

"He owes me a favor," Cal said. "Trust me, we'll have you back in a new job in no time."

Eliza opened her mouth to reply, but the music stopped,

and the conductor tapped a glass for attention. "Dinner is served," he announced.

Everyone started moving to the next room, but Cal took a moment to look around. He'd done it. The event was a success, the Foundation would raise the money it needed, and even better, he had Eliza at his side.

Everything was going to plan.

## 19

Eliza took a deep breath and tried to keep smiling. They were seated at the head table for the dinner portion of the night: Cal, Tish, his aunt and uncle, and half a dozen other members of the Boston elite, sipping champagne and toying with the four-course meal served by waiters in starched uniforms. The beautiful dining hall was filled with the hum of happy conversation and the ring of silverware.

Eliza wanted to scream.

"The powder is great in Aspen," Cal chatted away, oblivious beside her. "But you're right, Telluride is the new spot."

"Where do you like to winter, Eliza?" one of the other women asked.

"My job usually keeps me in the city year-round," Eliza said pleasantly. "I never learned how to ski."

"That doesn't mean I can't teach her to après-ski," Cal added, and the table laughed.

Eliza couldn't take any more. She dabbed her lips with her napkin and rose to her feet. "Excuse me," she said, "I'll be right back."

She exited the room fast, and wandered blindly down a hallway until she reached the restroom. It was a cool expanse of pale marble, blissfully empty. Eliza put her clutch down and leaned against the counter. She had a headache coming on.

Who was this guy seated beside her, and what had he done with the real Cal?

Eliza didn't understand what the hell was happening. The funny, sincere, real man she'd fallen for had been replaced by a patronizing stuffed shirt. OK, so this was an important event for him. She knew he needed to charm the donors and make sure things ran smoothly, but that didn't mean he could treat her like arm candy—pretty much telling her to stand still and look pretty, and not ruffle any feathers by daring to have a thought or opinion in her mind.

Who did he think he was?

If it was any other guy, she would have told him where the hell to go. But this was Cal, *her Cal,* and she wanted so desperately for the night to be a success for him. So, she bit her tongue and laughed along, and barely said a meaningful word to anyone all night.

But inside, she was boiling.

What was she doing? This wasn't the man she fell for.

This wasn't a guy who seemed to know her at all.

Was this really what he wanted in a partner? Eliza wondered, feeling a chill. A pretty, sweet mannequin to parade around at parties like this? Because if it was, then he had no business chasing after her. She was the last person in the world who would ever sign up for a relationship like that.

But here she was, touching up her lipstick, all the same.

The door swung open, and a trio of blondes in designer black dresses sashayed in. "Lizzie!" a high-pitched voice caroled, and Eliza braced herself. It was Sukie, her hair twisted up in some complicated braid, revealing huge diamond earrings that glittered under the lights. "Oh my God, you look . . . *so cute*," Sukie gushed. "Doesn't she look cute, girls? You'd never guess she was a waitress. Well, in Vegas, maybe," she added with a smirk.

Eliza forced herself to smile.

*Take the high road. Take the high road.* "That's so sweet of you," she said, matching Sukie's syrupy tone. "And congratulations! When are you due? It must be soon, now that you're already starting to show."

Yes, it was petty. Yes, she should have taken the higher ground. But it was worth it to see the look on Sukie's face.

The other women burst out laughing. "I'm not . . . It isn't . . ." Sukie spluttered, but Eliza was already heading for the exit.

"Toodles!" she called behind her as the door swung closed.

ELIZA'S VICTORY WAS SHORT-LIVED. BACK AT THE TABLE, CAL barely paused to smile in her direction as she took her seat again. "It's shaping up to be a great year for the company," he was saying.

"I hope this means you'll be back in the city full-time now," Arthur said, his disapproval clear. "You've been out of town for far too long."

"Although, we can see the appeal," Sylvie added, smiling at Eliza.

"Actually, I might stay a while longer. I've found some interesting business opportunities down there," Cal said, taking a sip of wine. Eliza turned, surprised.

"Since when?"

"Yes, Calvin." His uncle looked just as surprised. "Do tell."

"It was Eliza's idea, actually," Cal continued, looking modest. "She showed me there's a market in smaller, local publications. The small fish that get overlooked, they're all struggling to stay in print. But if we consolidate, bring them under one digital umbrella, we could develop an infrastructure that works all over the country."

His words sliced through Eliza. Was he serious right now? She turned in disbelief, but Cal was focused on his uncle.

Arthur looked thoughtful. "I like it. Have you run the numbers?"

"It's early days," Cal replied. "But I can ask our people to start looking into it."

"Good idea," Arthur said with an approving nod.

Cal's blue eyes were full of pride, but Eliza's anger reached boiling point.

"Cal," she said, trying to stay calm. "Didn't we talk about this? I showed you why it's a terrible idea."

"I get it, you have an attachment to the printed page." Cal patted her hand dismissively. "But the business model is sound."

Eliza took a breath and slowly removed her hand. "Could we talk somewhere for a moment?" she asked quietly. "Alone."

Cal's smile slipped. He glanced around and cleared his throat. "We're in the middle of dinner."

"Yes," Eliza said, keeping her voice low and a fake smile on her face. "Which is why I'm doing you a favor and not having this discussion at the table right now, in front of all your important friends."

Cal looked annoyed, but the steel in her voice must have shown, because he got to his feet. "Please excuse us," he said to the others with a chuckle. "Official business."

Eliza silently followed him out of the dining hall and down the hallway, back out to the courtyard, which was now deserted. A couple of hours ago, she'd been out here kissing Cal like it was all that mattered in the world, flushed with happiness and desire. But now, looking at him, Eliza felt off balance, like she was at the edge of a precipice, and one wrong word could send her tumbling into freefall.

"Well?" Cal demanded, when they were finally alone. He looked back at the party impatiently. "What's so important, we had to be rude to everyone at the table?"

"Really?" Eliza asked, incredulous. "You're going to pretend you don't know what this is about?"

Cal didn't meet her eyes. "The newspaper thing is only an idea," he said evasively, looking away. "Uncle Arthur just needed to hear I'm still focused on the company. I was going to tell you later, you didn't have to interrupt everyone."

"That's right, I forgot," Eliza said, her voice dripping ice. "I'm supposed to just stand here and look pretty."

"I was joking. Come on, you know that's not what I meant." Cal took a step towards her, flashing that charming smile, but Eliza wasn't fooled this time.

"Were you? Because you haven't let me get a word out all night. You answer for me, talk over me, *apologize* for me," she added angrily.

"You're mad about that? I was just trying to smooth things over," Cal argued. "I didn't want you making a bad first impression."

"I'm sorry if I'm embarrassing you," Eliza said, stony.

Cal tensed. "You know that's not what I mean."

"How am I supposed to know?" Eliza cried. "You're steering me around like some kind of prop, but God forbid I tell people anything about who I am or what I do."

"You know you can be . . . difficult sometimes," Cal said, looking frustrated now. "I just don't want you making a scene."

His words sliced through her, a dull, hot blade.

"Is that really what you think of me?" Eliza whispered, stunned.

Cal paused, just a split second, but it felt like an eternity to Eliza—and it told her everything she needed to know.

She wasn't good enough. Not to him.

Her most private insecurities came roaring to life. She stepped back, suddenly dizzy.

"I'm not an idiot, Cal," she said, tears stinging in the back of her throat. "I know tonight is important. I wasn't going to ask Ted Chambers why he fired half his editorial staff last month, or go three rounds with your uncle over the environment. But you don't even trust me enough to speak for myself."

"You're taking this all wrong." Cal looked confused, his expression conflicted. "I just want them to like you, for you to be a part of the family."

"But not the real me," Eliza said, feeling that ache again, like something inside her was breaking in two. She'd gotten dressed up for him. Put on the fancy dress and the makeup, bit her tongue all night so hard she probably had teeth marks, taken the high road when she could have lashed out.

And that still wasn't enough.

*She* wasn't enough.

Eliza had walked through those doors feeling like she didn't belong here, but for some reason, knowing that Cal thought the same thing was more than she could bear. "What exactly were you afraid I'd tell them?" she asked, finally finding her voice. "That you fired me from my job? That I work part-time as a hostess in a restaurant and come from a family with no money or social standing?"

She wanted him to tell her no. That he didn't care about her background or job. Promise that he was proud to have her as his partner.

But instead, Cal just took a deep breath. "I can't have this fight with you right now," he said, straightening his jacket. "I need to go back out there before people start to talk."

"Let them!" Eliza exploded, her pain and insecurity finally igniting. "God, what are you doing, Cal? You have a good heart and a brilliant mind, but you're just going blindly along with what everyone else wants for you. When are you going to figure out what *you* want from life?"

Cal's gaze flashed with controlled anger. "You sound like my uncle."

"Well, I guess we have something in common, after all." Eliza looked at him, so disappointed she could hardly stand it. "You're a grown man, Cal. But all night, I've watched you schmooze and charm and bend over backwards for your uncle's approval."

"It's called being a polite guest!" Cal shot back.

"No, it's pretending to be something you're not." Eliza swallowed, fighting to keep it together. "And I won't do it, Cal. Not even for you."

There was a beat, her words landing hard on the cold ground between them.

Eliza gulped. It sounded so final out loud, more than she had even meant, and a part of her wished she could take it back. But it was the truth, wasn't it? That gnawing discomfort in her chest was there for a reason. Something inside her knew this wasn't how it was meant to be.

"So, that's it?" Cal said slowly, realization flashing in his eyes. "You're just ending this. Because we had one disagreement—"

"No," Eliza stopped him. "You still don't get it, do you? This isn't about the new business plan, or one stupid party, or even you patronizing me all damn night. You don't know who you are," she said, aching inside. Eliza wished that she could make him see, but even after everything, he was still out of reach.

"You don't know what you want," she continued, finally putting into words the feeling that had been swirling under the surface. "You're one man with me and a different guy with all of these people, and you switch it on so easily you don't even notice the difference anymore! But I do," she said, aching for him. For everything they could have been. "I know the difference, and I don't want *this*," she said, gesturing to his perfect tuxedo and the twinkling lights, and the ballroom full of people who didn't know him at all. "I want the other man. The one who laughed with me, and opened up to me, and brought me a blanket while I was puking my guts out on the bathroom floor."

"That's still me," Cal insisted. He pushed his hair back from his brow, a familiar gesture that made Eliza ache, but she couldn't back down. Not now, watching everything they had slowly crumble to nothing, right there on the petal-strewn ground. "Because that guy would have let me speak for myself and told Ted Chambers where to shove it. He would stand up to his uncle and make his own path."

"I'm trying to do a job!" Cal's voice rose in frustration. "I'm head of the company, the family. I have responsibilities. I can't just walk away and do whatever the hell I want!"

"Why not?" Eliza demanded.

"You tell me," Cal shot back. "You tried it. How's it working out for you?"

Eliza inhaled in a rush.

There was silence.

Cal's face changed, regret striking fast. "Shit, Eliza, I'm sorry, I didn't mean it like that."

"Yes, you did." She curled her hands into fists to keep her composure, her nails digging into her palms. "And it's working out great."

"You lost the job you loved, and you're stuck working as a waitress." Cal gave her a knowing look. "How is that great?"

"Because I believe in what I'm doing," Eliza shot back

fiercely. "Sure, the newspaper isn't a big, fancy operation, but it means something, It's a part of my community. And I know that working in a restaurant is beneath you people, but I'm paying my own bills, and I won't be ashamed of that!"

"*You people*," Cal echoed. He gave a bitter laugh. "You never could get over the Prescott name, could you?"

Eliza clenched her jaw. "I guess not."

There was silence, nothing but the distant hum of dinner conversation filtering from down the hall. Eliza was cold, and tired, and she didn't want to do this anymore: yell at a guy who felt like a stranger, while her heart broke quietly in her chest.

Maybe she'd been right from the start, that first day out on the highway. He was from a different world, and tonight, it was clear, he didn't think she had a place in it.

"So, that's it then." Eliza took a shaky breath.

"That's it," Cal echoed, his expression blank. "I guess it's better we did this now, before someone gets hurt."

"Right," Eliza echoed, hurting like hell. "I guess so."

He swallowed. "You can have the suite tonight, of course. I'll stay at my place."

"Thanks."

"And of course I'll tell my family you were feeling unwell and had to leave. I'll send your apologies."

Eliza nodded blankly. Cal Prescott, a gentleman to the bitter end.

He paused there a moment, like he wanted to say something. Or maybe he was expecting her to make the move. Apologize, beg, promise to smooth things over.

But Eliza had her pride, and she held onto it. She stood there, unmoving, as he turned to go, his footsteps fading on the polished hallway floor.

And then she was alone again.

Eliza turned and fled for the exit, the tears coming now, hot and sharp. She was used to it, she told herself desperately, she'd always been alone. But she already knew it was different this time.

Because this time, she knew exactly what she had just lost. Cal wasn't like the other guys she'd held at arm's length her whole life. She'd let him in: torn down her defenses and risked her heart to share everything she'd kept hidden inside.

But it still wasn't enough.

She wasn't enough for him.

The one man who had ever really known her had just walked away.

# 20

"Are you planning on getting off the couch today?"

Eliza lifted her head long enough to take in her sister's concerned expression. "Maybe."

"It's not that I don't understand wallowing is an essential part of post-breakup recovery," Paige added gently. "I'm just saying, you could do it in clean clothes. After a shower. Maybe even go crazy and wash your hair."

Eliza reached up to push a lock of hair out of her eyes. It was tangled and dull. OK, so maybe her sister had a point.

She pulled herself upright, feeling like a faded carbon copy of herself. "I'm sorry," she sighed. "I know I've been getting in the way."

"No," Paige insisted. "OK, maybe a little." She picked her way over the debris of throw blankets and empty takeout containers on the living-room floor and settled beside Eliza. "But I like having you here. It's weird being on my own again after living with a guy for years."

"This place is cute, at least," Eliza said, looking around the studio. "If you ignore all my mess, I mean."

Paige smiled. "It's just a sublet, until I figure something out. I don't know what I'm doing next."

"That makes two of us."

After fleeing the gala, Eliza couldn't face sleeping alone in that luxurious hotel suite. She'd picked up her things and arrived at her sister's to crash on the couch . . . which she'd barely moved from all week. She must have cycled from heartbroken to furious to miserable a hundred times, and she still didn't know how to feel. There was a jagged, raw place in her chest that ached whenever she thought about Cal, but even though she had her phone turned to loud, sitting ready on the coffee table, he hadn't called, not once. And every day, her last hope that they could work this out faded a little more.

It was really over.

Eliza swallowed. "Maybe he's been hit by a bus," she said, still watching her silent phone. "Maybe he ran out of the gala after me, got hit by a bus, and has been in traction all week, unable to call?" She exhaled with a rueful smile. "Wow, you know things are really bad when the best-case scenario involves a gruesome accident."

Paige squeezed her. "How about I order from that Thai place you love and we have a girls' night? You go freshen up, I'll take care of everything."

"Real smooth." Eliza managed a smile. "Don't think I didn't notice the shower part in there. But for you, I'll do it. I'll even put on clean sweatpants."

"Hallelujah!"

Eliza headed to the bathroom and stripped off, stepping under the shower. The water hit her tired skin, and in an instant, she was back at Cal's, sinking against the tile while his wicked mouth sent her to heaven and back.

Tears welled, and this time, she didn't stop them from falling.

Was it supposed to hurt this much?

Eliza didn't know; she'd never had a breakup like this before. Other guys, she'd always been the one to decide it was over, and even though, technically, she'd done the same with Cal, it felt different. Wrong. Like they'd been cut short when their story was only just getting started. She'd stepped off the edge, ready to fall—and hit the ground, hard.

Was she a fool for even trying? She'd seen the warning signs from the start, but somehow, Cal had made her believe that maybe they could make it, after all. That he wasn't just another preppy trust-fund guy, that there was so much more going on in his wounded, generous heart. They'd laughed together, loved, shared their secrets, late into the night.

But it wasn't enough. He'd retreated back into that staid Prescott world and left her on the outside again. They'd come close to something wonderful, only to have it slip from Eliza's grasp at the last minute.

And God, she missed him. So much.

WHEN SHE FINALLY DRAGGED HERSELF OUT OF THE SHOWER AND changed into clean clothes, Eliza stepped out of the bathroom and did a double-take. The studio was spotless, with gleaming surfaces and even fresh-cut flowers arranged in a pretty vase. "Did you have a group of woodland animals helping you in here?" Eliza teased her sister, toweling off her hair.

Paige grinned. "I had to take the chance while I could. Who knows when you're getting off the couch again?"

Eliza sat back down with a thump. "Don't worry, I know I can't hang around here forever. Mom needs help packing up the beach house, and Declan is begging me back to the restaurant. Apparently, things fall apart when I'm not there to keep him in line."

Paige raised her eyebrows, and Eliza knew her sister so well, she could tell exactly what she was thinking. "No," Eliza snorted. "Definitely not. Even if my heart didn't feel like it's been ripped out of my chest. What Cal and I shared was real," she added wistfully. "And now that I know what that feels like . . . a random fling with some guy just wouldn't be the same. Oh God," she groaned, burying her face in the couch cushions. "How am I ever going to date again after *him*?"

"Come on, the guy can't be too hard to live up to," Paige urged her, upbeat. "He drove you crazy, remember."

"Yes. Vividly." Eliza's lips curled in a smile, and Paige laughed, tossing a throw pillow at her.

"Give it time. You'll move on."

"Like you and Doug, you mean?"

Paige blinked. "You know, I forgot about him completely. We were together for three years, and it feels like we never dated at all!" She looked horrified. "I'm a terrible person!"

"Please, you're a saint." Eliza tossed the pillow back, as the doorbell rang. "Ooh, takeout."

She went to collect the food while Paige picked the movie, and soon they were sitting on the floor, with a feast spread on the low coffee table. There was Pad Thai, spring rolls, hot coconut soup, and . . . "Salad?" She blinked at her sister's plate. "How are you eating salad right now?"

Paige made a face. "I'm on another diet."

"Why?!"

"Because I'm thirty and single, and my skinny jeans don't fit."

"None of those things are reasons to starve yourself." Eliza shoved a delicious mouthful of noodles into her mouth. "Buy new jeans."

"Thanks for the tip." Paige lifted the remote. "Ready?"

Eliza nodded. Paige hadn't asked what she wanted to

watch; her sister didn't need to. As long as she could remember, the Bennett girls' favorite comfort watching had been *Pride & Prejudice*. Maybe it was destiny, after all, their mother had named Eliza after the heroine. The classic BBC version ranked top, of course, but when they didn't have six hours to spare, the Keira Knightly movie worked just as well. Eliza settled back and let the familiar soundtrack and arch, witty dialogue wash over her, knowing that soon enough, despite all their differences, Elizabeth and Darcy would find their happily-ever-after: true partners, each meeting their match.

The way she'd always wanted for herself.

The way she thought she'd found with Cal.

Tears welled up, and she tried to subtly wipe them away. Not subtly enough.

Paige hit pause. "Are you OK?" she asked softly. "We can just talk, if you want?"

Eliza shook her head. "What's there to talk about? Cal decided he'd be better off with some perfect, polished socialite who agrees with everything he says and never speaks her mind."

Paige furrowed her brow. "Did he really say that?"

"He didn't need to. You should have seen the way he acted at the gala. He didn't let me get a word in, he was so worried I'd embarrass him and make a scene."

Her sister paused.

"What?"

"Nothing." Paige hesitated. "It's just . . . you can be kind of stubborn sometimes. You get riled up about the principle of something, and then there's no stopping you."

"I stand up for what I believe in," Eliza corrected her. "We all should."

"Yes . . ." Paige made a face. "But there's a time and a place, and sometimes you make a big deal about it, just to prove a point. I'm not saying what Cal did was right," she added quickly. "But based on your experiences together so far, I can maybe see why he would be nervous, introducing you to that crowd. The newspaper article?" she reminded Eliza. "The thing with his tires?"

"That was before I knew him. I see how much the Foundation means to him," Eliza protested, feeling uncomfortable now. "I would never have ruined the night."

"But did he know that?" Paige asked gently.

"He should have trusted me." Eliza folded her arms. "And given me a chance before assuming the worst about me."

"The way you did for him?"

Paige's question made Eliza uneasy, but before she could answer, her cellphone rang.

Eliza's heart leapt.

"Well?" Paige asked, her eyes wide.

"You look. If it's Cal, I don't want to talk to him," Eliza lied.

Paige scooped up the handset. "It's not him," she said, and passed the phone. Eliza felt a swell of disappointment. She cleared her throat and answered. "Hello?"

"Eliza Bennett? This is Ted Chambers, we met at the gala last week?"

Eliza nearly dropped the phone. "Hi," she said, confused. "What can I do for you?"

"Listen, as Cal said, I'm putting together a new magazine." Ted's voice was jovial. "I'd love for you to come in and chat about some opportunities we may have for you."

"Um, sure," she answered.

"Perfect, I'll hand you over to my assistant to schedule the meet. Looking forward to talking more."

The line went silent, and then a brisk-sounding woman came on to set up an appointment for Eliza the next morning. By the time she hung up, she was more confused than ever.

"Well?" Paige asked expectantly. "What was that?"

"A job," Eliza said slowly. "Or at least, an interview. I think. At Chambers publishing."

"Yes!" Paige exclaimed. "Does this mean you might wear actual pants? Oh, I have the perfect interview outfit for you," she continued, leaping up. "This vintage pencil skirt with a cute silk blouse. Very *Desk Set*, you'll be great."

Eliza let her sister chatter as she pulled down clothing from her storage rails. Inside, her head was still spinning from the unexpected call. Did Ted Chambers know about the breakup? Had Cal put him up to it? Was this a favor, some way of letting her down gently?

But after the way they'd parted, she couldn't see Cal going out of his way to recommend her for a job. So that meant Ted still thought she was Cal's girlfriend—one of the in-crowd. He'd probably take one look at her resume and regret inviting her in.

Still, it was something. She had no idea what kind of work he was offering, but Eliza knew it was time to get off the couch. Literally. So, the next morning found her walking into the lobby at Chambers Publishing, hoping she looked more confident than she felt. Thanks to her sister's eye for fashion, she at least looked like she belonged as she stepped into the elevator with a cluster of other stylish women and was whisked to the tenth floor.

"Eliza Bennett, here for Mr. Chambers?" she asked the receptionist, but Ted was already striding across the office.

"Eliza, great to see you. Come, we're set up in the conference room. Wasn't that gala a blast?" he said, leading the way. "The Prescotts sure know how to throw a party. Did Cal meet the fundraising goal in the end?"

"I'm . . . not sure," Eliza said, hurrying to keep up.

Nope, he definitely didn't know about the breakup.

Ted led her into a comfy-looking conference room with views of the skyline. He took a seat at the table, and Eliza cautiously perched on a chair, too. "Tea, coffee, coconut water?" he offered.

She shook her head. "No, thank you."

"Straight to business, I love it. Now, let me tell you a little about the magazine we're launching," he said, leaning forwards with an enthusiastic smile. "*Glow*, the newest bible for women. Fashion, relationships, style . . ." Ted launched into his pitch, painting *Glow* as a must-read for every fashionable woman in America.

Eliza listened cautiously. She'd written for these kinds of magazines before, but she'd never worked there. One look at the glossy, polished office culture, and it was clear she and her sneakers didn't fit. But she wasn't about to turn up her nose at a real live job offer, especially one that could let her get back to her first love: journalism.

The question was, did Ted really know what he was getting himself in for?

" . . . indispensable reporting." Ted was finishing up. "So, what do you think? I have a staff writer slot open, great benefits package. You could be helping shape the magazine from the ground up."

Eliza paused, torn. "It sounds great," she agreed. "But, I have to be honest with you, I may not be the kind of writer you're looking for. I love features and profiles, but I don't write puff pieces. If you want someone to write a glorified press release of a new skin cream . . . that's just not me."

Ted chortled. "I've read your portfolio. I know exactly what I'm getting myself into."

Eliza exhaled in relief.

"You've got a voice, a point of view, and sure, it may ruffle a few feathers sometime, but that's what I need if I'm going to make this magazine stand out from the crowd." Ted leaned back and gave her a thoughtful look. "The question is, is *Glow* right for you? What do you want next from your career?"

Eliza blinked, thrown. It was the same question she'd thrown at Cal like an accusation, but now, it didn't feel so simple.

Ted grinned. "Why don't you take a couple of days to think it over? We'll email the offer details, and you can decide if we're the right fit."

"Thank you."

Ted stood, clearly not the guy to hang around on formalities like a real interview. Eliza followed him out to the reception area, then paused. She knew she should just take the offer at face value, but she couldn't make the decision without knowing the truth. "I have to ask, did Cal put you up to this?"

"Cal? No," Ted said, shaking his head. "I actually had your name on a shortlist before we ran into each other last week. I figured it was a sign. Loved that profile you did of Mindy Kensington," he said with a wink. "What I wouldn't have paid to be in the Mayor's house the day that hit!"

He strolled away, chortling, leaving Eliza by the elevators alone.

She should be happy that she'd earned the offer on her own merits, but she felt an inexplicable sense of disappointment instead. If Cal had set this up for her, it would have shown he was thinking about her. That he cared.

But Eliza needed to face the truth.

He'd moved on. No calls, no messages, no reason to ever see her again.

It was clear, as far as Cal Prescott was concerned, she was in the past.

# 21

Cal had a headache. A raging, pressure-cooker, five-day headache that had settled around his skull like a vice, squeezing almost hard enough to make him forget the bullet wound of a broken heart torn clear through his chest.

Almost.

"Christ, mate," Declan exclaimed. "If I'd known you were going to be such a buzzkill, I would have left you moping at home. You're seriously cramping my style."

Cal nursed his whiskey and glared. "Thanks for the support."

"You don't need my support, you need to get laid. Which is never going to happen with that scowl on your face. Look, the bar's full of beautiful women, and none of them will come near us." Declan looked mournfully around the busy city bar. "Some wingman you're turning out to be."

"I thought you were the one helping *me* get over things," Cal pointed out. " 'Come have a drink,' " he mimicked his friend. " 'Get your mind of Eliza.' "

Cal winced. Even saying her name was like a knife in his

gut. Was there any part of his body that wouldn't be hurting by the end of the night?

"Change of plan," Declan said cheerfully. "I know a lost cause when I see one. You'll do nothing but scowl all night, but me? I have possibilities. Like that blonde. Or her friend. Or both of them."

"Congratulations," Cal said, deadpan. "I've very happy for the three of you."

"Aw, come on, buck up. I mean, Eliza's great and all, but please, did you really see it ending any other way?" Declan drained his beer and gestured to the bartender. "You guys are like oil and water. It was never going to last."

Cal lifted his head. "You really thought that?"

"Nope, but I'm trying to make you feel better here," Declan grinned. "Is it working?"

"Not by a long shot."

"There's an idea," Declan said, smiling wider. "Shots. Can't mope around over a woman if you can't even remember your own name."

Cal couldn't argue with the logic, but he already knew it wouldn't work. Even after three shots of tequila, another two whiskeys, and a beer to wash it all down, he still couldn't get Eliza's teasing smile out of his mind. He rolled out of the cab back at his apartment and stumbled to the couch, collapsing onto the cushions and staring up at the ceiling as it spun.

Why the hell did he have to mess things up this time?

Eliza wasn't the kind of woman to hand out second chances; he'd known that from the start. But still, he'd been so wrapped up in the gala and impressing everyone, he'd forgotten that the most important person in the room was the one on his arm. She'd mattered more than any high-rolling donor or snooty society dame, but he'd steamrolled right over her, and behaved like one of those jackasses he'd spent so long trying to convince her he wasn't. Even when she confronted him, he hadn't realized what was on the line. It wasn't until he was sitting back at that table, the empty seat beside him, that it had hit Cal like a damn anvil.

She was gone.

That knowing, mischievous smile, the flash of challenge in her eyes. Her warmth, her smart mouth, and God, her incredible body. He'd driven it all away. But worse than anything he'd lost was the fact he'd made her feel like she wasn't good enough. He could see it now, that flash of misery in her eyes. It had cut him so deep, he knew there was no chance of saving them. Not after he'd gone and done that. It had hurt like hell to go along with her breakup, but damn, he deserved to hurt. And hurting he was, stuck in a prison of his own making, with nothing but time to count the mistakes he'd made.

And top of that list was falling in love with a woman who made him feel, for the first time, that he truly belonged.

Because now that he knew how that felt, he couldn't settle for anything else again.

"Get up."

Cal groaned. The sun was so bright it hurt his eyes, and his headache was back—with a killer dose of hangover.

"Get up, we're going to be late!"

Tish's voice pierced through his skull, and Cal rolled over in bed. "Go away."

"Believe me, there's a dozen other things I'd rather do besides drag your stinky ass out of bed, but we have that board meeting at eleven."

Cal squinted, confused. "We just had one."

"Yes, and if you'd been paying attention instead of mooning over your girlfriend, you'd know we tabled a bunch of things to this week." Tish yanked the covers away. "Jesus, did you drink a whole brewery last night?"

"I went out with Declan."

"Mystery solved." Tish sighed, then rummaged in her handbag. "Water. Aspirin. Emergen-C. Drink it all, and meet me in the car in ten minutes," she said, shoving the items at Cal. "Oh, and cuz? Breath mints are your friend!"

The last thing Cal wanted was to face the Prescott board right now, but he knew playing hooky wasn't an option. This was his responsibility, so he dragged himself into the shower and a clean set of clothes, and met Tish downstairs where—thank God—she was waiting with a cup of coffee. "Angel," he said, grabbing the cup.

She leaned in and sniffed suspiciously. "Better. Oh, I should warn you, Dad's on the warpath. Something about marginal growth estimates? Either way, watch out."

"Perfect." Cal massaged his temples with his free hand. "Anything else I should know?"

"That you're being an idiot and need to make up with Eliza."

"Besides that."

"Come on," Tish said, as they got into the waiting car. The driver headed downtown, while Cal tried not to burn his mouth on the coffee. "You know she's perfect for you. I don't understand why you're not halfway to Sweetbriar Cove to rent out the gazebo or hire a flash mob, or do whatever it is guys do when they have a ton of money and want to make a grand romantic gesture."

"Are you finished?" Cal asked.

Tish grinned. "Maybe. It depends. Are you going to take my advice?"

Cal shook his head. "It's no use. It's over."

"Quitter."

"You didn't see the way Eliza looked at me," Cal said with a heavy heart. "She's not the forgiving kind."

"Everyone makes mistakes." Tish frowned. "She didn't give you a chance to grovel at her feet and explain?"

"I didn't even try," Cal said. "What's the use? She told me it's over."

Tish thwacked his arm so hard his coffee nearly spilled. "Hey!" he protested.

"For a smart guy, you sure can be dumb sometimes," Tish said, looking exasperated. "How is she supposed to know you're in love with her if you don't even try to work things out?" She watched him, her eyes narrowing suddenly. "You did tell her you love her, right?"

Cal looked away.

"Honestly!" Tish exclaimed. "You're useless!"

"You and Declan should start a club," Cal said, managing a smile. "Unsupportive Friends Unite."

"You know I've got your back," Tish said, smiling. "And part of that means sometimes you need a shove."

"Off a cliff?"

"Maybe just a small staircase," Tish laughed. "Knock some sense into that thick skull of yours. Don't you even know what you want anymore?"

Her words brought back the echo of Eliza's voice. *When are you going to figure out what you want from life?*

Cal shook off the memory. He needed to focus, especially if he was going to make it through this meeting.

They reached the Prescott headquarters and headed up to the conference room, where Uncle Arthur was already waiting. "Calvin." He nodded approvingly. "I just got off the phone with the Midwest. He says you had a productive call. They've made a list of cost-cutting targets that should bring us under budget again."

"I'm putting together the full report," Cal replied. "You'll have it next week."

Arthur patted his shoulder. "Excellent work. And I've been hearing nothing but glowing reports about the gala. Excellent PR for the company."

"And the million dollars we raised for the cancer research doesn't hurt either," Cal added.

"I suppose not."

They headed into the meeting. Luckily, despite his late night, Cal had plenty of notes stored on his phone about current business, enough to bluff his way through the discussion. He'd thrown himself into work, hoping to smother the pain in financial projections. It hadn't worked, but at least he could hold his own today as the meeting got underway.

*You have a good heart and a brilliant mind, but you're just going blindly along with what everyone else wants for you.*

Cal tried to focus on the numbers in front of him, but Eliza was in his ear again, challenging him, making him think about questions he'd never had to answer. After all, his path was set. The Prescott heir, CEO, his father's son. He had a job to do and a name to live up to. That wasn't up for debate.

Was it?

Cal looked around the room, everyone deep in conversation. The decisions they made in here affected thousands of people. It was both a privilege and a duty, that's what he'd always been told, as if the whole company would fall apart without him at the helm. But he was just one guy, still learning the ropes. The only reason he was even sitting there was his last name, and if the past year had taught him anything, that name could do plenty of good in other ways.

*I believe in what I'm doing.*

And just like that, he knew exactly what he needed to do.

As if the decision had been made long ago, and he was simply waking up to what he'd already known.

Cal cleared his throat. "Can I please have your attention for a moment?"

The room fell silent. They all turned.

"There's an order of business," his uncle said, looking disapproving.

"I know, but this won't take a minute." Cal took a deep breath. His headache had lifted, and his mind was clear for the first time in days. "I'm resigning from my position as CEO, effective immediately."

There was an audible intake of breath.

"I'll still keep my seat on the board, but I'll be running the Prescott Foundation full-time from now on." Cal found himself smiling. "This year, we raised three million dollars for important causes, and next year, I plan to double that."

"Calvin—" his uncle started, looking furious. Cal cut him off.

"My decision's made," he said firmly. "And if you're looking to keep the CEO position in the family, my vote's for Tish. She'll do a better job than me."

"I will," Tish spoke up. "No offense," she added to Cal.

He grinned. "None taken."

There was a pause, and then one of the board members got up and rounded the table. "Congratulations," he said, reaching to shake Cal's hand. "I'm sure your parents would be very proud of you."

Cal was taken aback, and as the rest of them joined the chorus of well-wishes, he realized it was true. This felt right—a way to honor his parents' legacy, but doing it his way. The relief was incredible, and Cal knew he'd made the right decision.

His uncle arrived beside him. "I'm sorry," Cal said, and

meant it. "You've been a great mentor, and I've learned a lot. But I have to make my own path now."

"Who knows what this will do to the stock price?" Arthur grumbled.

"You'll weather it. And like you said, the Foundation is excellent PR," Cal pointed out.

Arthur brightened a little. "True. But where am I going to find a replacement?"

"Right in front of you," Cal said. He looked across the room to where his cousin was already schmoozing some of the board. "Give her a chance. She's better suited to this than I ever was."

"Hmmm." Arthur didn't say anything, but Cal thought he could see a hint of agreement in his uncle's expression. "We'll see." He turned back to Cal. "Does this mean you'll be moving out to the Cape? I take it this Foundation plan is something you cooked up with the Bennett girl."

"No," Cal said regretfully. "Eliza and I . . . aren't together anymore."

"Really?" His uncle looked surprised. "I would have thought this little speech had her fingerprints all over it."

"No sir, this was all me."

The version of himself Cal hadn't been brave enough to reveal—until Eliza urged him on. She'd known who he was even before he had realized it for himself.

Despite all their bad first impressions and preconceptions, she'd seen the best in him. The man he wanted to be.

With her.

Was it really too late? Cal wondered as they finished up the meeting and he said his goodbyes. He was needed back at the office—an announcement like this should be broken to his team in person, coordinated with PR, all kinds of work—but Cal needed a moment to himself to think.

He set out on foot, heading downtown through the financial district with the busy streets and towering office buildings. He remembered his morning strolls through the leafy back lanes of Sweetbriar Cove, and it felt like a lifetime ago. Part of him wanted to get in the car and just hit the highway again, make it back in time for lunch at the harbor and a beer at the pub.

But everything about that place was bound up in Eliza. Fresh breeze and bright ocean. The highway into town, where she'd appeared in his life like a tempting, troublesome siren, the garden at the pub, where he'd kissed her for the very first time. Walking on the beach together; getting morning coffee at the bakery. He could still see the look in her eyes on that rain-slicked street in Provincetown, pulling him down for a kiss that had stopped his heart dead in his chest.

What was he doing without her?

Cal looked around and realized he'd wandered close to the Public Library building. He climbed the broad stone steps and ducked inside, making his way down the hushed hallways to that small courtyard in the middle of the building, where it had all fallen apart for them.

Without the lights and decorations from the gala, the space was quiet, just a couple of people snatching a lunch break by the fountain. Cal took a seat on a bench, wrestling with the emotions still fighting in his chest.

He'd taken the easy way out.

Letting her go. Walking away. He replayed the fight over in his mind, and he saw half a dozen moments where he could have done it differently and stopped her in her tracks. Apologized, admitted he was wrong, insisted that she was the only one who mattered. Maybe he could have pulled them back from the brink, or maybe, Eliza was too hurt to even listen, but he could have tried.

He didn't try hard enough.

What had been holding him back? What was paralyzing him, even now? He'd almost called her every day since the fight. But he hadn't. Hell, he was sitting here, going over everything for the hundredth time in his mind instead of hashing it out face to face. He'd never been a coward, never shied away from doing the right thing. But for some reason, Cal was letting the best thing that had ever happened to him slip further out of reach, while he just sat there, watching her go.

He wished his parents were still around to tell him what to do. His mom would give him a scolding over Eliza, that's for sure. They would have got along like a house on fire. He smiled, just imagining the two of them, commanding the conversation at family dinners and driving Uncle Arthur up the wall. And his father . . .

Cal had never missed him more.

Losing them so young, Cal thought he knew about grief. What it felt like to need somebody, to have a space in his life that couldn't be filled. After that, he'd been determined nothing would ever hurt that much again.

Was that why he'd let her go so easily?

The realization landed hard, a jolt to his system. He'd had plenty of relationships before, but none of those women had challenged him like Eliza. None of them had called him on his bullshit, defiantly demanded more—and shown him just how it felt to connect with someone on a deeper level, all their defenses stripped away, leaving nothing but the raw, messy truth. It was exhilarating and passionate.

And scary as hell.

Because if he could hurt this much from losing her now, Cal knew it would only get worse. A year together, five years, ten. God, even the thought of it filled him with awe. A love like that could be a magnificent thing. It could change a man—break him, to lose it again.

He'd already been broken once before, that terrible day he'd opened his door and found Uncle Arthur on his doorstep, his face like death. But he was learning now there was a different kind of pain from losing someone you loved: the regret that was edged with a sharp edge of guilt, knowing it could have been different.

That it still might be, if he could get up off the mat and take that risk.

Cal rose, his turmoil finally giving way to determination. He didn't have the answers figured out just yet, but he knew he wouldn't find them here. And there was only one place he would find them.

It was time to take a drive.

# 22

Eliza drove down to Sweetbriar Cove, still mulling the offer from Chambers Publishing.

She knew that just a couple of months ago, she would have leapt at the chance. A big publisher, a fast-paced office, the status of a glamorous job to show everyone at the newspaper that she'd come out ahead—it all added up to what should have been an easy yes.

But now, she didn't feel so sure about it. The same questions she'd asked Cal echoed in her own mind. What did she want to do with her life? After her father had died, she'd thrown herself so deeply into work she didn't want to come up for air. Late nights in the newsroom, whole weeks a blur of coffee and cheap takeout. The only break from the grind was when she made the commute out to the Cape to see her friends and work on freelance articles—and then wound up driving back late Sunday night, ready to block out her feelings and do it all again.

Was that what she wanted this time around?

Now that she'd had a chance to take a breath, that single-minded drive to work was faded. Eliza didn't feel the same burning ambition. Yes, she wanted to write, and work, and share her stories with the world, but it wasn't all she wanted anymore. She wanted a life, too.

So would she find that life at Chambers Publishing?

ELIZA HAD ALMOST REACHED SWEETBRIAR COVE WHEN A CALL came through from Brooke. "Where are you?" she demanded, sounding happy. "Are you still moping in the city? Because I have big news."

Eliza smiled. Riley had made his move, then. "I'm ten minutes away, want me to swing by?"

"Oh, crap," Brooke laughed. "I better clean up!"

When Eliza arrived at Brooke's place, her friend bounded down the steps to meet her in the courtyard. "Big news, huh?" Eliza asked, trying to keep a straight face.

Clearly, she failed.

"You knew!" Brooke exclaimed, her eyes widening. "How?"

"A little bird told me." Eliza winked. "Congratulations! Come on, let's see it." She beckoned for Brooke's hand. "How did he pop the question? Was it epic and romantic?"

"Epically wet, yes." Brooke laughed. She proudly displayed the ring. "He took me out on the boat, I guess he was planning a big gesture, but we got caught in a storm."

"No!" Eliza exclaimed.

"Yup." Brooke was still grinning ear to ear. "So, we put down anchor in this cove and were just hiding out below deck, wind wailing everywhere, the cabin leaking rain. Riley looked so miserable, I decided to try and make us drinks, but I found the ring box he was hiding in a coffee jar. But then he proposed," she said, her eyes softening. "And it was perfect. There's nobody I'd rather be stranded with."

"Aww." Eliza hugged her. "That's how you know it's real. Anyone can stick around when it's smooth sailing. It's how someone acts when you hit rough waters that makes all the difference."

She thought of Cal and her, flat on the bathroom floor with food poisoning, and felt a pang.

"Oh God," Brooke laughed as they made their way upstairs to the apartment. "I'm going to be hearing nautical puns forever now, aren't I?"

"Just wait until I give my maid of honor speech," Eliza said, pushing her sadness aside. "Wait, I am going to be maid of honor, right?"

"Obviously," Brooke declared. She nodded to a stack of binders on the countertop. "I may have pulled a few ideas together about the wedding . . ."

"A few?" Eliza took in the pile. "Oh God, please don't turn into a Bridezilla."

"Never," Brooke vowed. "Well, maybe a tiny one. Babyzilla. We're thinking a winter wedding," she confided, opening a bottle of wine. "Snow, and horse-drawn sleighs, and candlelight . . ."

"It sounds beautiful." Eliza hugged her again. "I really am happy for you guys."

"But what about you?" Brooke's expression turned concerned. "I've only heard bits and pieces. Is it really over? I thought you and Cal were so perfect together."

"Not perfect enough." Eliza took a gulp of wine, but there wasn't any alcohol in the world strong enough to make the ache in her chest subside. She told Brooke about the gala event, and how Cal had been embarrassed to have her as his date. "He made it clear I don't belong in his world."

"I'm sorry." Brooke put an arm around her shoulders and squeezed. "I saw the way you were with him. You were . . . I don't know, more yourself. In a good way. But if he's too blind to see that for himself, then good riddance!"

Eliza knew she was trying to be supportive, but it didn't feel like a lucky escape. It felt like she was the one who'd lost out. "The worst part is, I miss him so much," she confessed. "I've almost called him a hundred times and asked to work it out. I always thought women were crazy going back to guys who didn't feel the same, but now I understand. A part of you just wants to be with them, no matter what the price." She caught Brooke's look of concern and managed a weak smile. "Don't worry, I didn't. I still have my pride."

Maybe too much. Eliza remembered her sister's words and felt an uncomfortable itch. Was she too stubborn to try to work it out?

"You don't think I'm . . . too judgmental, do you?" she asked Brooke suddenly. "Jumping to conclusions and not giving people a chance."

Brooke paused. "You know your mind," she said slowly. "But you're loyal and supportive, too."

"That's not a no," Eliza noted, her heart sinking.

Brooke gave another sympathetic smile. "Hey, don't let this thing with Cal make you question yourself. Maybe if he was trying to fix this and you wouldn't hear him out, that would be one thing. But you haven't heard a word, right?"

Eliza shook her head sadly.

"There you go. What's that you're always telling me?" Brooke said. "Sometimes a first impression is all you need. Maybe you were right about him from the start."

Brooke started making them lunch, chatting about wedding plans and the engagement party they were planning for the next week, but Eliza found it hard to focus; her thoughts slipping back to Cal.

Was she being too hard on him? She knew he was under

pressure at the gala, and maybe it wasn't the right time to try to talk, but still, she couldn't forget the way he'd treated her like an embarrassment, or how quickly the shutters had come down when she'd confronted him.

If he'd cared, wouldn't he have fought for her? Wouldn't he have reached out or done anything to try to make this work, even if it was hard and messy and painful?

Instead, she'd had silence. No sign at all that leaving had made a dent in his heart. Maybe he'd already moved on to one of the glossy, blonde girls who seemed to flock around him. Somebody suitable, who felt at home in expensive restaurants and knew the right things to say, and who wouldn't pick a fight and demand answers when he didn't treat her right.

Eliza hated her already. That girl wouldn't challenge him or know how much more he had to offer than his Prescott name, or the easy smile he wore to hide the struggle he kept beneath the surface.

*She* was the one who knew him. She was the one who missed him.

And she was the one who'd driven him away for good.

AFTER LUNCH WITH BROOKE, ELIZA HEADED TO THE BEACH house. She pulled up out front and braced herself for the chaos of moving boxes and packing tape her mom had promised inside, but instead, when she stepped through the front door, she found the place spotless, untouched.

Her mom was on the back porch, drinking tea with Aunt June. "Hi, sweetie," Linda said, smiling. "Was the drive OK?"

"Fine," Eliza said, shrugging off her jacket. "But what happened to packing? You said to bring supplies."

"That was before." Her mom beamed happily, and June looked just as delighted.

"Before what?" Eliza snagged a cookie from the table.

"Before this." June picked a slim file of papers from the table and passed it to Eliza, who skimmed over the dense contracts, confused.

"Can someone stop being cryptic and just tell me what's going on?" she asked.

"We're keeping the house!"

Eliza stared at her mom in shock. "What? How? I thought you were already talking to a buyer."

"We were," June answered for her. "They wanted a fast close, so the sale went through this morning. Signed and sealed. For a very nice price," she added, a note of pride in her voice.

"That's great," Eliza said, even as she felt a pang. "But you just said we're staying?"

"Well, we could. But I guess that's up to the new owner," Linda smiled. "What do you say, sweetie?"

"You're holding the title deed," June said helpfully. "Check the name."

Eliza looked at the papers again, curious who the buyer was—and why her mom was talking in circles. "It says the house belongs to . . . Me?!"

She stopped. It had to be a mistake, but there it was, her name written there in neat type. Now the owner of parcel 26 of beachfront land.

Eliza sat down on the porch swing with a thump. "But . . . how?"

"The buyer decided to sign it over to you," her mom replied, lifting her teacup with a smug smile. "I guess he changed his mind."

Eliza frowned. It didn't make any sense. Who would . . . ?

Oh.

"Cal," she said, everything becoming clear.

"It's so romantic!" Linda cooed. "Imagine being able to make that kind of gesture. Oh, Lizzie, I always knew the two of you were meant to be."

Eliza shook her head. "No."

"Of course, the two of you will still need somewhere else to live," Linda chattered happily. "June, did the Greystone house come on the market yet—"

"No!" Eliza leapt to her feet. "This is crazy. We can't accept this!"

"Honey—"

"No," Eliza swore again. She grabbed the folder and glared. "If he thinks he can just buy his way back into my life, he's wrong. Get the boxes ready, because when I get back, we're packing. For real this time!"

She stomped back out to the car, her heart pounding. She couldn't believe Cal's nerve! Did he really think writing a check would make everything better, like her heart carried a million-dollar price tag and was available for the highest bidder? He'd officially gone insane! Maybe that was how they played it in his world, where an expensive gift could wipe the slate clean, but Eliza couldn't be bought—no matter how high the bidding.

She drove the short distance to the Pink Palace in a rage, guessing that's where he'd be if he was back in town. She hit the brakes outside, stormed up the path and pounded on the door.

It opened. Cal stood in the doorway, looking so good it took her breath away.

*Focus!*

Eliza struggled to contain the emotions that came rushing to the surface.

God, she'd missed him.

"Hey." Cal smiled, his eyes crinkling at the edges. Damnit. Why did he have to be so handsome?

"What the hell is this?" Eliza waved the papers in his face. She refused to be distracted by those gorgeous blue eyes or the tanned arms she ached to have holding her.

"You got my delivery, then." Cal didn't seem surprised to see her there, which only made Eliza's temperature rise.

"I can't believe you!" she cried. "You thought that you could just write a check, and I would come falling into your arms again?"

"No." Cal looked amused. "I thought I would write a check, and you would come storming over to throw it in my face, and then maybe we could talk about us, and what we can do to fix this mess."

Eliza blinked, thrown. "So, you didn't mean to give me the house?"

"Oh no, that part's real." Cal grinned, infuriatingly calm. "It's all yours. For you and your family. No strings attached."

"No strings . . ." Eliza echoed in disbelief. "How can you even say that? There are always strings!"

"Not with me." Cal took a step closer and reached to cup her cheek in his hand. The touch ricocheted through her, and damn if Eliza didn't need him more than ever. "I promise," he said softly. "You could slap me in the face and walk away, and it wouldn't make a difference, as far as the sale is concerned. The deed is in your name now. It's done."

"But, why?" She gaped.

"Because that house belongs to you. You said it's where you have the happiest memories of your father." Cal gave a rueful shrug. "I can't bring him back for you, but I can keep him close."

"Oh."

Eliza found herself speechless, fighting the tears that were suddenly welling in her throat. He'd done that, for her?

Her rage melted away. "Thank you," she whispered, overwhelmed. "That was a very nice thing to do."

"That's it?" Cal asked, looking surprised. "I figured you would yell at me for a good half hour."

Eliza sniffed. "I'm trying to be a better person. Compromise more."

"Why's that?"

She looked up at him. "So I don't push the people who matter most away."

Cal swallowed. His eyes searched hers. "What if they deserved it? Could you maybe find a way to give a second chance?"

Eliza ached inside. She'd been going over things so long, she didn't know what to believe anymore. All she knew for sure was the way she felt when she looked at Cal.

Like she'd found her way home.

"I miss you," she whispered. "I've missed you so much. And I know it doesn't make any sense. We weren't together hardly any time at all, but still . . ."

Cal pulled her into his arms, and Eliza sank against him, holding on for dear life. The feel of his body against her, his strong, safe embrace. She breathed in the scent of him, and it was all so right, so real, it took her breath away.

"I'm sorry," she said, the tears falling now. "I know I should have given you a chance to explain, but you just pushed all my buttons—"

"I'm sorry," Cal insisted. He pulled back enough to gaze into her eyes, full of regret. "You were right, I acted like an ass, and I was too stubborn to see. But you're the best thing that ever happened to me, and if I lose you now, I don't think I could ever forgive myself." Cal took a breath and gave her that heart-stopping smile she felt all the way to her bones.

"I love you," he said softly, and Eliza's heart took flight. "I love you, Eliza Bennett," he said again, stronger this time. "And I know we're probably going to wind up driving each other crazy down the road, and we'll fight and get stubborn, and we'll both have our share of apologies. But I promise, I'll always be yours. I'll always believe in you, and be here for you—"

Eliza cut him off with a kiss. She couldn't help it; she couldn't be apart from him a moment longer. Their mouths found each other, and she fell into the embrace, a glorious freefall that left her breathless and gasping for more.

"I love you, too," she said urgently the moment they came up for air. Cal's face split in a smile.

"Just promise me one thing. Don't quit on me," Eliza said, clutching his shirt. She felt exposed, her heart raw and wide open to him. "I know I can be hard to take sometimes . . ."

"You?" Cal grinned, teasing. "You're a marshmallow."

She hit him lightly. "Hey! I'm trying to be serious here."

"I know." Cal pulled her in and kissed her neck. "Keep going."

"We're both going to have to compromise more . . ." Eliza gasped as Cal tugged her back over the threshold, still kissing lower along her shoulder. "And be honest when— Ooh," she moaned, as he found that sensitive spot along her collarbone.

"Honest, huh?" Cal slammed the door behind them, and lifted her, wrapping her legs around his waist. "Honestly, I need you. Now."

He smothered her in kisses, already carrying her down the hallway to the bedroom. Eliza laughed as he threw her down on the bed with a bounce. "Yes," she said, reaching for him.

"Yes to what?" Cal stripped his shirt over his head, and then moved to kiss her again.

"Yes to everything," Eliza said, pulling him closer, as close as she could. Her heart was singing, a wild, joyful tune.

This man. God, *this man*. He knew her completely, and still, he came back for more. Despite her sharp edges and raw wounds, everything that always made her feel too much. The things she'd always thought were the worst parts of her, somehow, he thought they were the best. She kissed him again, and she knew she would never let him go this time.

Whatever happened next, they would find a way through —together.

"Yes to you," she whispered, as the rush took them over. "Always."

# 23

Brooke and Riley's engagement party was planned for Saturday night. "Just a few people at the beach," Brooke had said. "Small and casual." But Eliza suspected "small" wasn't in Sweetbriar Cove's vocabulary. Sure enough, when they arrived at the beach she could already see at least fifty people down on the sand, with a bonfire burning, tables of food, and music filtering up from the speakers somebody had rigged in the back of a truck.

"Looks like a party," Cal said, pulling over to park. He turned off the engine and reached for her, and Eliza moved into his arms like it was the most natural thing in the world.

"Should be fun," she agreed, meeting his mouth with a satisfied sigh.

"We should get down there," Cal said, sliding his hands around her waist, teasing kisses down her neck. "Say hi to everyone."

"Mmhmm," Eliza agreed, shivering to his touch. "In a minute."

She kissed him again, savoring every moment. The party could wait a little while longer; for now, she had everything she needed in the front seat of that car.

The pair of them had barely come up for air all week, tucked away in their own, private world at the cottage—working, and kissing, talking late into the night. Making up for lost time and missed chances and unravelling in each other's arms. It had been bliss, but Eliza knew the real world was waiting. She had a dozen messages on her voicemail from Mackenzie and the group, all demanding the juicy gossip about Cal, and she wanted to celebrate all the good news with her friends. So tonight, they'd dragged themselves out to meet the world as an official couple for the first time.

But maybe the world could wait a little longer.

Eliza ran her hands through Cal's hair and gave a hum of satisfaction. "Did I ever tell you you have great hair?" she said, smiling. "You should be a TV doctor with this hair."

Cal chuckled. "Clearly, I missed my calling." He carefully smoothed down her shirt. "You look beautiful tonight. You always look beautiful," he added.

"Even in a ratty T-shirt and shorts?" Eliza teased, remembering their disastrous first date.

"Especially then." Cal grinned. "I spent that night on the bathroom floor, wishing I had the strength to seduce you out of them."

Eliza laughed. "It's a good thing you didn't try. Vomit isn't exactly an aphrodisiac."

"I don't know." Cal leaned in for one last kiss. "It worked out pretty well for us."

They got out of the car and made their way down the dunes to the party. "Eliza!" Poppy greeted them with a cry. "You made it." She turned to Summer and held out her hand. "Pay up."

Summer sighed good-naturedly.

"We had bets on whether you two would drag yourselves out of bed," Brooke explained, as Summer handed over five bucks. "We figured no way, but Poppy here thought Cal's manners would win out in the end."

Cal laughed. "Glad to be of service."

"Do you guys want a drink?" Poppy asked. She was showing even more now, her pregnant belly the size of a beach ball under her warm sweater. "Riley hauled half the bar down. And there's food, too. Burgers, hot dogs. Cooper's off hunting and gathering for me," she said with a beam. "I've had the weirdest cravings, right now it's chili and chocolate, together."

"I whipped up some spicy chocolate cake at the bakery," Summer added.

"It's actually kind of great," Brooke agreed.

"Try some, and tell me if it should go on the menu."

"That's my cue." Cal kissed her cheek. "I'll go fill some plates."

He strolled off towards the food. The moment he was out of earshot, Poppy grabbed Eliza's arm and bounced. "Is it true, did he really buy you a house as an apology?"

Eliza's jaw dropped. "How did you . . . ? Oh." She paused, realizing. "Aunt June." She winced, imagining the gossip that Cal's gesture must have inspired. "Is it all over town now? Cal will hate that."

"What, the fact everyone knows that he's wildly romantic and completely loaded?" Brooke laughed. "News flash, we kind of figured that out. Still, he's setting a pretty high bar for himself," she said, her eyes sparkling mischievously. "What's he going to do for your anniversary, splurge for a private island?"

"Guys!" Eliza protested, laughing. "Come on, you know I don't care about that stuff."

"Aww, we know." Poppy hugged her. "But it certainly doesn't hurt."

Eliza looked over to where Cal was chatting with Cooper and the guys. She exhaled, trying to calm herself, but it didn't work. She still had butterflies just seeing him there. She'd figured it would settle down, but instead, her feelings just grew stronger, every day. And knowing she would wake up again with him tomorrow to do it all over again?

It took her breath away.

"So, enough about Cal," Brooke said, pulling her attention back to the group. "What's this about a new job? Don't tell me the *Cape Cod Caller* is folding again."

"Not on my watch." Eliza shook her head, smiling. "I got an offer to join the editorial team on a new magazine, but I thought about it, and I decided to turn them down. I'm going to be freelancing for them instead," she explained. "So I can stay down here and work on the *Caller*, too. And any other articles that strike my interest."

"That's great!" Brooke exclaimed. "I mean, I'm biased. I want my maid of honor in the same zip code for all the wedding plans."

"Uh-oh," Eliza teased. "Babyzilla's here!"

Brooke laughed. "Seriously, I'm really glad you're staying."

"Me too." Eliza looked around. This town already felt like home, but she was excited to put down roots, after years of bouncing around. And to do it all with Cal . . . That was an adventure she couldn't wait to get started.

ELIZA CAUGHT UP WITH HER FRIENDS FOR A WHILE LONGER, THEN made her way over to where Cal was drinking with the guys. It was dark out now, and the party was kicking into gear—people dancing and celebrating, laughter echoing into the night.

"Feel like dancing?" Eliza slipped her arms around him from behind.

Cal turned. "Yes. But we'll spare the good folks of Sweetbriar Cove that particular horror story."

"You can't be that bad!"

Cal kissed her, smiling. "Your faith in me is sweet. Misplaced, but sweet. How are the girls?"

"Happy I'll be moving here." Eliza snuggled against him. "Did Marion say when she'd be kicking you out?"

"She emailed," Cal said. "She's actually taking a detour to India. Something about a meditation retreat. So, the Pink Palace is ours for a while longer."

"Good. I'm kind of attached to that place. Especially the bathroom," Eliza added.

Cal drew her closer. "That reminds me, I have a gift for you."

"Cal!" Eliza protested. "You don't have to get me things."

"This is for the both of us." His grin turned wicked. "I figured it was time we replaced that old shower head. The new one arrived today. Detachable. Five settings, extra pressure . . ." He leaned in, whispering in her ear. "Imagine the fun we can have with that."

Eliza shivered with delight. "OK, new rule. Joint gifts are allowed."

Cal looped his arms around her, and then they were swaying softly to the music. "I thought you said you didn't dance," Eliza said, smiling.

"Shh," Cal murmured, drawing her closer. "It's a secret."

They danced on in the shadows at the edge of the party. Eliza rested her head against Cal's shoulder and smiled, watching the flicker of the bonfire. Around them, her friends toasted and cheered, and the music of friendship spiraled up into the night's sky.

This was where she belonged.

In Cal's arms, she'd finally met her match. With a love that had only just begun.

THE END

(Well, almost…)

# EPILOGUE

Declan Nash could never resist a party—even if it was to celebrate his old wingman taking himself off the market for good.

"It's not too late to change your mind," he joked, slapping Riley on the back. "It's not over until someone says 'I do.' "

Riley chuckled. "Thanks, buddy, but the torch is all yours."

"Hey, I'll carry it proudly," Declan said. "But good luck to you, mate. Seriously, I'm happy for you both."

He went to get a beer, and he watched Riley wrap his arms around his bride-to-be. He wasn't the only one. Cal was slow-dancing across the way, looking at Eliza with an expression that said it wouldn't be long before he was heading down the aisle, too.

Damn. Were there any guys left resisting the call of commitment?

Still, that just meant there was less competition when it came to the rest of the women around. Like the hot blonde sitting over on the flatbed of a truck, sipping from a plastic cup as she watched the crowd.

Declan sauntered over. "Hey there," he said, flashing a smile. "How do you know the happy couple?"

"I don't, not really." The blonde's cheeks flushed. "I'm gate-crashing."

"I won't tell if you don't. I'm Declan," he introduced himself.

Recognition flooded the blonde's face. "Oh, you're the playboy chef."

Declan laughed. "I see my reputation precedes me." He held out his hand. "Pleased to meet you."

"Paige Bennett," she replied, shaking it.

"Ah, the sister."

Now it made sense. Eliza didn't sugarcoat things, that's for sure. But where his buddy's new love was all attitude and fire, this Bennett woman looked like butter wouldn't melt in her mouth. She was pretty, sure, with her blonde hair caught back from her face and the firelight reflecting in her eyes. Another man might have been polishing up his best lines right now, but Declan knew better. Up close, that sweet smile and demure blouse screamed "good girl" a mile away, and while Declan had earned every bit of his reputation, he still lived by a set of rules.

One, everything tasted better with butter.

Two, life was too short for cheap whiskey.

And three, good girls were off limits.

"So," Paige said, taking a sip of her drink. "Are you as bad as they say you are?"

"Sweetheart, I'm even better." Declan winked. OK, so maybe she was off limits, but it would be downright rude not to flirt a little.

But instead of giving him another pretty blush, Paige burst out laughing. "Sorry," she spluttered. "Ignore me. I'm sure that line works great for you."

"Most of the time," Declan said, a little thrown. "In fact, always. Girls love the accent. Maybe I should have done the hair thing." He ran one hand through his too-long locks and gave her his best smoldering look. "How about this time?"

"Better." Paige grinned. "If I were ten years younger and twice as dumb, I'd be all over it."

"Ouch." Declan clutched his chest. "And there I was, thinking you were the nice Bennett sister."

Immediately, Paige winced. "I'm sorry. You're right. I don't know what's gotten into me. I've had the weirdest day."

"What happened?" Declan hopped up on the back of the flatbed beside her, his legs swinging free. From here, he had a clear view of the party, and the brunette in the cute blue dress dancing over by the fire. He didn't see a boyfriend around, but hell, that had never stopped him before.

"I nearly died."

Declan's head snapped around. "Damn, really?"

"Yes. No. I don't know." Paige shook her head. "One minute I'm crossing the street, and the next, my shoe's stuck in a storm drain and there's a termite fumigation truck speeding towards me. Termites! I thought to myself, this is it. The part where your life flashes in front of your eyes, and everything gets clear. And you know what?"

"What?" Declan asked, fascinated.

"Nothing happened!" Paige exclaimed. "I couldn't picture one interesting thing I've ever done. All I could think about was the load of wet laundry sitting in the machine that nobody would come claim. Then my shoe got loose, and I was able to jump out of the way. Doesn't that say it all?" she sighed. "Even my near-death experience was as boring as they come."

"Hey, you're not dead yet," Declan pointed out. "There's plenty of time to add to that highlight reel."

"True." Paige glanced over. "So tell me, what would be on yours?"

"Hmm, good question." Declan thought back. "There's that

weekend in Cabo with the swimsuit model . . . Jumping out of a plane over Belize . . . The South of France was a blast, got to love those nude beaches," he said, smiling at the memory. "Oh, and then there's the time me and Cal got lost hitchhiking in the desert outside Morocco and wound up at a sheik's palace with— Wait, I probably shouldn't tell you that one." He flashed Paige a grin.

"Wow." She looked wistful. "You really get around." Then she blushed. "I didn't mean . . . You know."

"Yes, and yes." Declan gave her a mock-salute. "Hell, life's short, why not enjoy it?"

"But don't you worry about the future?" Paige asked, looking anxious. "Retirement accounts and health insurance and finding someone to settle down with. What if you wake up one day and find it's all too late, and you're the only one left without a chair when the music stops?"

"Then I'll find a friendly lap to go sit in." Declan grinned. "I'll figure it out, I always do. And hell, at least I'll have some damn good memories."

Paige didn't seem reassured, but then again, she seemed the kind of girl who was tucked in bed by ten every night with a mug of herbal tea and a good book. Declan was more likely to stumble home around dawn, with a killer hangover and lipstick smeared all over his good shirt. His travels had taken him a long way from his home in Sydney, Australia, and even though he'd set up shop now with his own restaurant here on the Cape, that didn't mean his adventuring days were over. It just meant he kept them limited to the tristate area, so he could be back in the kitchen cooking up a storm in time for the dinner service.

Sure enough, Paige stifled a yawn.

"Past your bedtime?" Declan teased.

"Getting there." She made to get down from the flatbed, but Declan had some manners left in him, after all this time.

"Let me." He hopped down and took her hand to help her, but when she was on solid ground, Paige didn't let go. She narrowed her eyes at him.

"What?" Declan asked, but whatever he was expecting, it definitely wasn't Paige suddenly going up on her tiptoes and kissing him, right there where he stood.

*Damn.*

Her mouth was hot and sweet, tasting like the bourbon she'd been sipping. Instinctively, Declan's arms came around her, pulling her closer, until her sinful curves were pressed right against him, and he could feel the heat of her body as she boldly teased his mouth open and stroked her tongue into his mouth.

Declan's senses roared to life. Dear God, who was this woman? He'd been wrong about her, that's for sure. Because demure was the last thing Paige seemed, kissing him deeper, setting his body on fire and his head scrambling, blank with lust.

He growled against her, tangling one hand in her silky hair as the other roamed over her incredible body. Paige shivered under his touch, so responsive it made him dream of ripping those clothes off and showing her exactly what he could do, skin to skin. He bit down softly on her lower lip, and Paige moaned into his mouth. His blood rushed south so fast he saw stars, and he held her tighter, lost to the rush of heat, and sweetness, and—

Paige stepped back.

"There," she said, looking thoughtful. Declan's blood was surging, and his body was already demanding more, but Paige smoothed down her blouse, as unruffled as if she'd just given him a peck on the cheek. "At least I've done one interesting thing. Thanks." She broke into a smile. "Enjoy the rest of your night!"

And then she walked away, leaving Declan panting there on the sand.

What the hell just happened?

He shook his head, still dazed, and watched her silhouette disappear into the shadows. Suddenly, taking that cute brunette home for the night and wowing her with his usual lines didn't seem to have the same appeal.

That proved it. He'd been right from the start.

Good girls were the most dangerous type of all.

TO BE CONTINUED . . .

Paige and Declan's story is just getting started. Discover their romance (and catch up with Eliza, Cal, and the rest of their friends in Sweetbriar Cove) in the next book in the series, WILDEST DREAMS - available to order now!

ALSO BY MELODY GRACE:

The Sweetbriar Cove Series:
1. Meant to Be
2. All for You
3. The Only One
4. I'm Yours
5. Holiday Kisses (A Christmas Story)
6. No Ordinary Love
7. Wildest Dreams
8. This Kiss

The Beachwood Bay Series:
1. Untouched
2. Unbroken
3. Untamed Hearts
4. Unafraid
5. Unwrapped
6. Unconditional
7. Unrequited
8. Uninhibited
9. Unstoppable
10. Unexpectedly Yours
11. Unwritten
12. Unmasked
13. Unforgettable

The Oak Harbor Series:
1. Heartbeats
2. Heartbreaker
3. Reckless Hearts

ALSO BY MELODY GRACE

The Dirty Dancing Series

The Promise

## ABOUT THE AUTHOR

Melody Grace grew up in a small town in the English countryside, and after spending her life reading, she decided it was time to write one for herself. She published her first book at twenty-two, and is now the New York Times bestselling author of the Beachwood Bay series, which has over three million downloads to date.

She lives in Los Angeles, writing books and screenplays full-time with the help of her two cats.

*Connect with me online:*
www.melodygracebooks.com
melody@melodygracebooks.com